THE PORCELAIN PROMISE

PRAISE FOR JORDAN REED
AND *THE WIZARD'S BREW*

"Jordan Reed knows how to spin an action-packed tale of intrigue and suspense that will keep you guessing until the very end."

Daniel K Miller, Texas Institute of Letters award-winner and author of Fire on the Firth and Loch and Key

"Hits the ground running and pulls you into a gas-lit world of magic and mystery. ... keeps you guessing right up to the end."

Ryan McSwain, author of Four Color Bleed

"The universe created by Reed is as rich as it is fascinating. ... The Wizard 's Brew is a stunning debut novel that fit right into the mystery subgenre of urban fantasy. "

Magdalena Nitchi, ImaginAtlas

THE PORCELAIN PROMISE

A ZANE VREXON MYSTERY

JORDAN REED

For information, address:
Blue Handle Publishing
2067 Wolflin Ave. #963
Amarillo, TX 79109

For information about bulk, educational, and other special discounts, please contact Blue Handle Publishing, www.BlueHandlePublishing.com.

To book Jordan Reed for any event, contact Blue Handle Publishing.

Cover and interior design: Blue Handle Publishing

Editing: Book Puma Author Services, BookPumaLive.com

ISBN: 978-1-955058-12-4

I would like to thank my family . . . especially my Joella and Meme, who always strived to see that this book was as good as it could be.

To my publishers, who gave me the chance to write this, and to my editors, who were gracious enough to put up with all my questions.

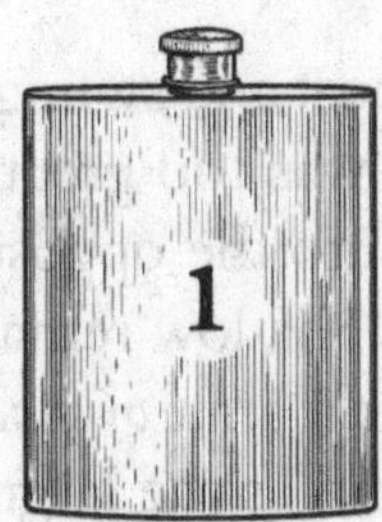

1

Pain rushed through Zane's right arm as the wooden post slammed into it. His legs had been too slow for him to dodge the surprise attack. In front of him stood a half-naked dockhand with long hair and a tan complexion. The dockhand's hair fell in waves around his face and foam flowed from his mouth. Zane leaned heavily against the wall. "Do you think we can talk about this?"

The dockhand reared back to hit him again, but Zane was prepared this time. Gritting his teeth through searing pain, Zane slammed his cane into the dockhand's inner thigh. The dockhand slammed into the wall face-first with a wet crunch as his leg gave way.

Zane's limbs felt as if they were filled with molten lead weighing him down. His breath came in ragged bursts, but his military training took control. The detective took stock of his surroundings. He was in an alleyway just past Dock Ten, two blocks short of the place where he had been caught unawares.

Zane couldn't see past either end of the alley through the thick fog that rolled in from the ocean. He hoped and prayed that Alyssa would find him soon. Two red eyes peered out from the dockhand's shadow, and a silky voice whispered in Zane's head. *She is two blocks over with guards in tow, but they are heading to your originally planned location.* Zane grunted in acknowledgment of Shadow's help.

The dockhand righted himself and turned to face Zane. Blood rushed down his nose and joined the foam from his mouth, like a river of blood meeting the sea. Zane saw something in the man's eyes that made him jealous. *He doesn't feel any pain.* The big man again lifted up his wood post and swung it hard at Zane.

The weight behind it was too great to parry or block. Zane lurched back, slamming into the opposite wall. The post passed just inches from his nose. Shadow remained calm. *Why don't you just run your sword through the brute or shoot him with your wand?* He didn't have time to respond as the large man reared back again. Zane lunged to the side, striking the man's bicep as he passed under his swing. The post went flying out into the smog of the night.

In a hushed voice, the detective answered Shadow's question. "I was asked to take him alive."

You need to stay alive first.

The dockhand charged Zane. He caught ahold of the detective's collar and pressed him into the wall. Zane couldn't break his grip as the dockhand grabbed his throat, choking him. The detective bashed his attacker with his cane, but the dockhand was unfazed.

The savage gripped his neck tighter as the sound of whistles and running drew close. Help was nearby, but the smog was thick. Zane tried to get their attention, but the air was trapped in his lungs.

Zane dropped his cane and pulled his wand from its brown leather holster. He pointed the wand at the dockhand for a moment, before jerking it away. He pulled the mental trigger and a blast of blue fire erupted from the tip of the wand. Each round slammed into the opposite wall, echoing in a loud thud. Zane fired again and again until all six shots were spent. He started to see black spots as his consciousness faded.

The dockhand slammed the detective into the wall, jarring him awake long enough to bring his legs up. Zane kicked the man hard in the face with all of his remaining strength, knocking him down. Coughing, the detective grabbed his cane and pulled the sword free from within.

Zane was ready to kill the dockhand as the man stood up. Before either moved, Alyssa's form cleared the smog. She knocked the dockhand off his feet with an eldritch word. From behind her, five imperial guards dressed in black uniforms with red trim and breastplates rushed forward. The guards pinned the dockhand down and arrested him.

Alyssa's raven-black hair clung in a sweaty clump over her face. Zane clicked his sword back into the cane as she rushed over. She dropped to the ground next to him. "I was so afraid I wasn't going to find you!"

Zane looked into her eyes. He despised being looked at with concern; it felt too close to pity. He ignored her attempt to help and forced himself to stand using his cane. The pain from his old, injured limbs seeped into his bones and through the rest of his body. He felt it even in his teeth. "What took you so long?"

The hurt on Alyssa's face was obvious as she turned away; Shadow mocked him. *That was rude, detective. She was only trying to help.*

Zane sighed, knowing Shadow was right. "I'll apologize later, after the pain has subsided," he whispered to his parasite.

Zane shook off his hat, taking a moment to rub the ashy mud away before returning it to his head. He leaned heavily on his cane as he fished out his flask and took a large gulp of the green sappy liquid. Warmth and strength poured into him, but it wasn't as effective as it once had been.

The imperial guard stepped into the street, a wisp of smog trailing behind him. He was young, and his clean-shaven face made him stand out from the other guards. The star on his breastplate shone brightly in the gas lamps.

"Mr. Vrexon, thank you for your assistance. I wasn't sure we were going to root out the seller."

The detective nodded. "It's why you hired us, Lieutenant Kellim, but you must know that this won't stop the spread of this stuff."

Kellim directed his men to take the small bag tied to the dockhand's waist. He opened it up and nodded; inside was a red, sugar-like substance. "Yes, but if an outsider tries to sell this Rush powder, we'll notice. The last thing we need is more Ragers out and about."

He pulled the bag's strings tight and tied it to his own belt. He looked the detective over before handing him several banknotes. "You are a brave man for risking your life to deal with a known Rager, especially after he had started to rage. But a little advice: You won't live long if you keep doing such things. I'll be by tomorrow to drop off the payment. Please accept this outside of our agreed amount."

Zane knew Kellim was right, but he didn't feel like letting him know. He pushed the notes into his pocket. Alyssa and Zane walked back toward their homes through the foggy night. As the sounds of the guards at work faded behind them, an awkward silence settled over the two like a fine morning dew.

2

Alyssa stomped through her apartment until after midnight. She had no plans to meet Zane at the office until late the next day. "How dare he be angry with me! It was his plan, not mine. All I did was follow it. It's his fault for fighting that man."

Her left hand held her side where she had been stabbed by the infamous Red Hood. The scar was faded, as if it had happened years ago, but it had only been a few months. Despite how quickly the healing potions knitted the wound back together, the muscles around the injury were still stiff with a dull ache.

As she passed by her table, she looked over the books and spell wick supplies that covered it. Alyssa snatched the nearest book and reeled back to throw it, but the title caught her eye. She stopped mid-throw and read it again: *Lean's Ten Principles of Eldritch Combat.*

Alyssa opened to the worn bookmark. "Anger, much like fear, clouds the mind. The differences lie in what is unclouded. Either anger or fear can lead to desperation and defeat."

Following the book's advice, she focused on the breathing exercises she'd recently learned to bring herself under control. Alyssa set the book down and looked at herself in the mirror. Heavy bags hung under her eyes. She was exhausted to her very bones. With a free hand, she traced her faded injury. She wondered whether Zane felt like this. The memory of him screaming in the night played again in her mind. She felt like she understood him a bit better than she did before.

Alyssa yawned, then closed the book and set it back on the table. Her robe and night clothes floated around her as she slipped into them before heading to the kitchen. She ignited the stove with an eldritch word and set the kettle to boil. Herbs lay on the counter next to her, ones meant to help her sleep. As she mixed them into the kettle, she wished for her nightmares to end.

She walked back to her living room and sunk down into a soft chair. During the last few cases, she had learned about Zane's flask—filled with Troll's Blood, one of the best types of healing potions—and how it helped with his old injuries.

Alyssa had seen some of his injuries when a knife tore his clothes and he was forced to change. Wicked scars covered his shoulder, leaving it looking like a raisin. *Those scars must hurt on nights like this.*

She released the little strength she had left from the long night with a long sigh. Despite her fatigue, she doubted she would sleep. Alyssa heard the kettle's whistle. She picked herself up and turned off the home's gas lamps on her way back to the kitchen. As she poured her tea and made sure the sleep aid was mixed in, she heard her mirror ripple with a ding. She shook her head in frustration. *Who would be calling me at this hour?*

With an eldritch phrase, Alyssa snapped the lamps back on. She stepped up to the black iron-framed mirror by her desk. With elegant movements, she traced the runes needed to answer the call. The mirror rippled faster and faster until an image of a young woman with glasses came into view.

"Frame? How did you get hold of my mirror?"

The young woman had large, heavy bags under her eyes. In the background, Alyssa could see Institute students working in labs. "Sorry to be calling so late . . . umm, early? I sometimes forget what time it is outside the Institute. Your grandfather was kind enough to give me the information for the mirror."

Alyssa was tired, but felt a small pulse of happiness at the call. "Well, Frame, how are you doing since the case?"

Alyssa looked past Frame at the students and their experiments. Frame glanced around before answering. "The brainwashing? I'm doing much better. Agwen's Fey magic was easy to get rid of once the archmages knew how it worked."

Alyssa was happy to hear that. Since she had taken leave from the Institute, she wondered about Agwen and his living victims. Alyssa remembered the funeral of some of the less fortunate, still grateful that Zane had come with her. The archmage had been committing fraud using the Institute's money. When Agwen feared he would be discovered, he hired an assassin to kill those connected to his endeavors. At the Institute, Agwen had used a hypnotic magic that gave him the power to alter people's memories and actions.

"Any side effects?"

Frame shook her head. "It seems that any were temporary, but the staff still likes to check on us every few weeks. My head hurt for a few days, but sleep seemed to help. . . . I think that the following night was my last decent sleep."

Alyssa laughed softly. "How is your research going?"

Frame smiled from ear to ear. "Splendid! I plan to write up a thesis for submission if I can ever get enough time off."

The conversation died suddenly, leaving an awkward silence. Alyssa guessed that there was more to this call than pleasantries, but Frame seemed reluctant. Alyssa broke the silence first. "What happened to Agwen? I never asked my grandfather, and he never said."

Frame brushed some hair from her face. The young woman brought her mirror in close and whispered. "I'm not supposed to talk about him, but the rumor is that they imprisoned him in the deepest rooms of the Institute, with an unlocked door, without a compass. They bring him food, water, and books for research, but if he leaves his room, he will get lost. Some people claimed to have found him wandering the halls late at night. Others said they found his starved corpse. I don't know how much is true, but those are the rumors. The Institute has politely suggested to everyone involved that we act like the events never happened."

From what Alyssa knew, such imprisonment weren't unheard of. It was the Institute's way of discipline without losing any of their scholars . . . or secrets. "Thank you for calling me, but I assume you called me for more than this."

Frame nodded, her face red in embarrassment. "Yes, my cousin Vine is asking for Zane Vrexon's office address. She'd like to hire him for a case. Is it true that you're working with him now?"

Alyssa gave an exhausted nod. After just completing one case, she was not ready for another. "Yes. It's an easy request. Do you have a pen? . . . Good." Alyssa gave the address and district.

Frame set her pen to the side. "Thank you again. I really do hope he's treating you all right. You were such a nice professor to give me the opportunity to make my mark."

"No need to thank me. You have yourself to thank for that. You recognized the value of what I had brought in and took action. I also had other things going on. I wish you the very best, Frame."

Frame waved goodbye and the mirror rippled until Alyssa was staring at herself. She finished her tea, turned the lamps off with an eldritch word, and finally let sleep wash over her.

3

The goblin dipped his hat down into the pool of blood, giving it a crimson hue. He had large muscles, like strands of rope laid over each other. The goblin looked over to Lash with his needle-tooth smile. "You're a lucky rat, hume."

Lash laid against a table just outside of the growing sea of blood. The goblin stood at the center of the mess, crouched on top of one of the dead like a carrion bird. The tune he hummed as he dyed his hood contrasted starkly with the surroundings and left Lash feeling uneasy.

I must be cursed. Of all the damn goblins, it had to be Red Hood.

Red Hood jumped from one body to another, landing with a wet thud. Lash wondered which body was which. *Was it Joan? No, she was by the door, so it must be Leak.* Lash wasn't sure, due to the brutality of the injuries. His mouth was filled with blood from when the goblin had struck him with his stone-like fist. His right arm was a ragged mess of deep gashes, with bone and tendon showing. With his good hand, he applied pressure at the biggest wound, hoping to slow down the bleeding. He spat out blood to clear his throat, not having the energy to make sure it didn't fall onto him. "Why?"

The goblin stopped for a moment to study Lash before turning his gaze back to his hood. "Your hume gang was butting into our business."

"Business? Red Tusk doesn't deal in Rush powder."

"We do now. Now shut your mouth, hume. You're ruining my mood."

The goblin rolled his hood one last time, admiring the hue. With one last grin, Red Hood looked at Lash. "You're lucky I don't need any more hume blood for this. But ya might want to tie off that arm before you bleed out."

Red Hood ripped a belt free from one of the bodies on the ground, then tossed it to him. The goblin laughed as Lash hesitated to touch his friend's bloody belt, but he knew the goblin was right. He cinched the belt as tight as he could at the shoulder, staunching the flow of blood.

Lash's head felt light from the blood loss. The goblin crept up the side of the wall and into the ceiling through an opening Lash hadn't seen before. *That's how he got the drop on us.* The clouds overhead reflected the orange glow of the street lamps. He tried to stand up, but passed out from the effort.

When he opened his eyes, the dull light from the windows and the hole in the ceiling told him that it was morning. He inspected his right arm, finding it covered in blood and flies. Even worse, he couldn't feel it. Before Lash could decide what to do next, he heard knocking at the door that echoed through the room. The door opened to reveal a rat-faced man with a broad black hat. He looked around the room, knocking the ash from his hat and coat. "Are you sure, Doc, that you wanted to come down here with me? My line of work is not very pretty."

"I would be shocked if it was." The jolly voice was out of place in this room of death. It came from an older bearded man with round-rimmed glasses. He stepped in behind the rat-faced man. "Doc" appeared unaffected as he looked over the corpses. "Of course, if we're going to be working together so closely, then it would only make sense that I need to know the quality of your work."

The rat-faced man shrugged and looked down at his own clothes. "But of course. It's your clothes that are at risk."

The doctor laughed, but stopped when he noticed Lash watching them. "Well, well, it seems Red Hood has left someone alive."

The rat-faced man smirked and shook his head. "Alive? Look at that arm, that man must be banging on Shade's realm. You can practically hear the knocks! Give him just a few minutes and he'll join the lot in my wagon."

The doctor ignored him and approached Lash with a soft smile. Lash would have thought he was being kind if it wasn't for his piercing eyes. They stared at him as if he was an object. "What is your name?"

Lash spat out some dried blood from his mouth. "Lash."

The doctor pointed to Lash's right arm. "What value is there in your ruined limb?"

"What—"

"What value do you see in a ruined arm?"

A deep anger burned inside him at the question. Lash felt adrenaline sear its way across his body. *My skill with this arm has enabled me to survive this long on the streets.* "Nothing! It has no use if I can't use it! The only thing I had going for me was how quick I was in a fight. Now that's gone, since I can't use my knife."

His breath came out in ragged spurts as he tried to stand up, using the table behind him for support. The doctor offered his left hand to help. "What would you give if I could return your arm to you?"

Lash stared into the doctor's face. His eyes had the look of someone ready to make a deal. Lash spoke in a weak voice. "Don't patronize me, old man. I've seen people lose limbs from less."

The rat-faced man was already directing his crew through the door to the dead on the ground, and directing them to drag them outside. "He ain't lying to you. Doc here is a genuine miracle worker. If he says he can give you back your arm, he will deliver."

Lash slipped, but the doctor caught him. The old doctor was stronger than he looked and easily helped Lash sit on top of the table. He pulled away slowly as the doctor spoke.

"Sorry for being short, but you don't have much time," Doc said. "So, I 'll get to the point. If I find you interesting, then I might help you live. If not . . . well, there's room in the cart. Understood?"

Lash thought it over for only a second. He wasn't ready. He had not made his peace, in any sense. If this doctor was a miracle worker like the rat-faced man said, then Lash needed his help. "Fine."

The doctor nodded his head with a twisted smile. "What was your role in this gang? What happened here?"

Lash pointed with his good hand to the knife discarded on the floor. The edge was red with the little blood he had drawn from Red Hood. "I was part of the 'muscle' for the crew. I know that I'm not the biggest, but I was damn good with my blade—"

The doctor cut him off. "Have you killed people before?"

Lash narrowed his eyes. "Yes. In fights, and I've even ambushed people when required."

The rat-face man yelled over. "I have a question: Why was Red Hood here? He's the best enforcer for the Red Tusk gang, but they don't usually operate in this area of town."

Next to Lash on the table lay a bag of red powder. "We were moving some Rush powder. This stuff was going to make us a fortune, but I guess the Red Tusk gang wanted us out of the way."

The rat-faced man nodded and called for someone outside. "I thought they were busy with their gang war with the goblin mob, but it seems they're trying to widen their business. I need to shake the tree and see if I can find more of these . . . 'aggressive business takeover' attempts." There was a smirk on the man's face that gnawed at Lash as if he was being mocked.

If only my arm worked, I would beat his face into something I could stand.

The doctor stepped between the two so Lash couldn't see him. "I can give you back your arm, but I want you to be 'muscle' for me. Is that a fine deal?"

Lash didn't need to think it over. "I'll do whatever you need. If you need someone gone, then you can count on me."

The doctor moved the good arm over his shoulder, then helped Lash cross the room and exit through the door. Blood ran freely, covering the doctor's nice clothes, but he didn't seem to notice.

"My personal carriage is just outside. Don't worry, I have healing potions inside. Once we get you to my workshop, I'll go to work on your arm."

Workshop? Lash thought about the word for a moment, then chose to ignore it, grateful to have some hope. "Are you gonna do some type of surgery on me?"

"Surgery, yes, but there will be no saving your arm. Instead, I'll give you one that is better. By the saints and the first knights, I will. Perhaps, if you are brave enough to try, you can even attempt the perfect procedure and have everything fixed."

The doctor laughed, sending a chill down Lash's spine. He hesitated for a moment, but gritted his teeth in resolve. *If this doctor had asked for my soul, I would have given it to him, if only to be able to keep from being worthless. What have I gotten myself into?*

4

Frame had been tired when her shift started, but now she was exhausted. The long hours at the lab had eroded her mind, leaving her thoughts a mess. At this point, all she desired was sleep.

Diana Cilean, her neighbor and best friend, stopped by her desk. Diana brushed back her curly black hair. "Frame, are you ready to head back?"

She nodded and stacked the last of her reports. A state mage was trying to make a new potion mixture, and Frame had taken notes as it brewed. "Yeah, I'm just finishing up. Anything interesting happen to you tonight?"

Diana shook her head. "Interesting? No. It was the same old, same old. Then again, not many people have the chance at groundbreaking research falling into their laps."

Frame smiled and remembered that she had the rights to a report about the proof of polymorphed hair. It was debated whether it could occur naturally and whether it could be created through the lab.

Frame had been lucky enough to be there when Alyssa had requested the test on what looked like a strand of unremarkable hair. Frame grumbled at the lack of the time to write a paper, one she hoped would help her toward her Institute goals.

Frame responded, her voice dry and tired. "Nor do we all have the luxury of being mind-controlled."

Diana looked confused and then hurt before trying to play it off. "Sometimes I think it wouldn't be that bad if it made the lab hours go by faster."

Frame sighed and shook her head. "Trust me, the headaches

that follow are very painful."

Diana looked embarrassed. "Well, umm, are you ready?"

Frame nodded, reaching for her bag. They followed a trickle of students making their way out of the labs. An olive-green door opened to a staircase, and both women pulled out their compasses, as did several other students. Diana mumbled under her breath. "Don't you ever wish we didn't need these stupid things?"

Frame nodded as she focused on the spin of the needle. At the bottom of the stairs, they exited into a long hall of multiple doors. Frame reached for the door that the needle pointed to, but at the last moment the needle flung off toward another door. "Yes! I've gotten lost so many times, even with these stupid things. It's still hard to believe that the only ones who can navigate the halls are those born inside the building."

Frame thought about that special gift of insight and the sheer number of people that could have been born inside the Institute. *That number can't be too high.* Although, with the changing halls and the magically condensed space, it was hard to tell how big the Institute actually was. According to the rumors, every few years they built a new wing as older ones slipped from memory and became harder and harder to find.

What memory or mind had to do with finding a place in the Institute was beyond her, but it was a subtle and dangerous part of this unstable magic.

They followed the compass through doors, windows, stairs, and hallways. Eventually, they came out into the morning light peeking above the rim of clouds that circled the Institute courtyard like a halo above the tower that created it.

Diana shoved her compass into her bag. "Thank the saints! I hate having to go down all those halls. I can't wait until I have a Transit Key. Then I won't need this compass ever again."

Frame rolled her eyes. Transit Keys were only given to archmages, a title that few ever reached. Most of the students, including herself, would work as a state mage for their house or some other noble, acting as advisors and delivering communication, while hoping to have the funds to conduct their own private research. "Keep dreaming, Diana. But while you do that, what should we get for breakfast?"

Diana shrugged. "What else? Let's go to the Magician's Café, like we always do."

Frame nodded, thinking about her future. Her concentration was so deep that Frame didn't notice the young man waving at her from across the courtyard. He was slightly taller than the people around him, with a sharp chin that fit his features.

Diana pointed to him. "Isn't that Felix? Didn't you go on a date with him?"

They had indeed gone on a few dates, but after a while he insisted on knowing what she was doing all the time. She once left her lab to find a stack of charmed letters pressing up against the door trying to get to her.

After breaking up with him, she had not seen him for over a month. When he did show up, however, he always insisted they should go on another date.

Her voice started strong before growing weaker. "Yeah, but it's over. He just won't stop trying to see me."

Diana raised her hand. "Oh, say no more. Follow me."

They slipped left into a crowd of people making their way to the Institute's large iron doors. As the wave of people crashed into them, Felix vanished from sight. Frame smiled, her shoulders relaxing. "Thank you," she called out to Diana.

Diana turned back with a grin. "Of course."

They cut through the crowd and snuck down a nearby connecting street. Already, Frame was thinking of cooking breakfast as a way to make up for missing their normal breakfast at the Magician's Café across the courtyard. As they stepped down the intersecting street and toward their apartment, a figure at the edge of the crowd caught her eye. He stood there for just a moment before moving. His scarred face and mismatched gloves was strange, but his gaze sent a shiver down her spine.

lyssa pulled on Atom's arm, but the large shopkeeper moved as if he was underwater. She pulled with all her might, but it was no use. A sudden vibration traveled through his arm, and she was forced to look up. Riding upon his shoulder was a goblin wearing a red hood. He was big for his type, and he wielded two large daggers.

One dagger was driven into Atom's shoulder. With evil determination, Red Hood used the dagger to keep his balance on the large man's shoulder. He held a second one loosely in his other hand, ready to be used. The goblin's eyes glowed in the dark room, and his teeth were a sickly yellow. His laugh echoed off the walls.

"Where are you going, hume?"

Her hands shook violently as she let go of Atom and leapt away toward the only door that she could see. The light spilling from it was blinding and all encompassing, swallowing everything beyond it. She felt the threshold within reach. She knew she shouldn't turn around, but she did. Just as she started to turn, her body froze with intense pain that threatened to rip her apart. Every fiber of body screamed at her not to finish turning around.

"Don't do it," Alyssa whispered to herself. "Don't do it."

She turned to face the evil laughter. As she faced the goblin, still mounted on Atom's shoulder, the pain in her side erupted. She looked down to see a knife, her blood turning the whole floor red as it spilled from under the hilt of the blade. The blood rose higher and higher until it reached her chin. With one last gulp of air, she slipped below the surface. The goblin's voice rang out clear in her ears as it laughed.

Alyssa jerked from her bed in a sweat, panting as if she had just finished running a race. The room's vast darkness was unbroken.

With eldritch words, Alyssa started her gas lamps. As the light bloomed into existence, her nerves calmed. It took a strong effort to force herself through the breathing exercises recommended in the books and the training she had been doing.

She was still a little shaky, but she refused to be controlled by a dream. Rising from her bed, she saw that it was still dark outside. Alyssa made a mental note to either adjust the strength of the sleep aid or find a better substitute. Moving past stacks of books, she made her way through her apartment to the table where two wands laid side by side.

One was a thin, wooden wand good for stunning or slightly injuring someone. Her grandfather had given it to her during the first case with Zane. The second wand was bigger and made of light metal with a dark sheen that gave it an ominous feel. Alyssa had bought it during their second case together. She'd needed a wand with a heavy whack to knock people off their feet, even though it held only three spell wicks.

The caps of the wands were unscrewed and lay nearby. Next to them was a cleaning brush to clean out any burnt spell wicks. Next to those were capsules with special paper and ink. Alyssa picked up the book on the top of the stack: *Beginner's Calligraphy for Spell Wicks.*

Alyssa opened the book to the marked page and started to go through the process of enchanting the spell wicks. These arcane words were simple in comparison to the ones taught at the Institute, but their practicality gave them a certain beauty. After two failed attempts, her hands ceased shaking, and she began to move with ease and calmness. With deep concentration, she completed a half-dozen spell wicks. By the end, she'd nearly forgotten her horrid dream.

Taking a deep breath, the former professor set the spell wicks to the side and moved on to her next project. The events of the previous night had reinforced a growing problem she'd been forced to deal with when working with Zane in the streets. They often ended up separated; Zane would end up in a dangerous situation and she'd be forced to find him. Searching for the necessary books, she began to research methods to make a tracking charm.

Reading through the instructions, she knew it was a two-part charm. One charm would indicate who or what was being tracked; the second charm, attached most often to a compass, would point toward the first charm. The charm itself was highly illegal without the permission of the person being tracked, but she doubted Zane would argue after last night. Alyssa put her pen to the side, tying the second charm paper to the compass needle.

The city bell rang out eight times, telling her it was time to get ready and meet Zane at his office. She set the spell wicks aside and finished dressing herself. Before she put on her coat and hat, she strapped two thin leather holsters across her chest, loaded the wands, and slipped them in. She put on her coat, adjusting it so she could reach her wands quickly through the slit built into it. Almost out the door, she stopped and went back for the tracking charm. With a glance in the mirror, she gave a satisfactory nod. She put on her hat and made her way out into the ash-covered city of Alviun.

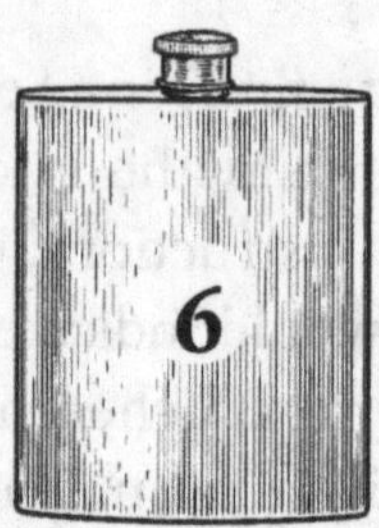

6

Detective Zane felt the ash sticking to his hat and his coat. The physical weight of it was almost nothing, but it weighed on his mind like a rock strapped to his back. It was a constant reminder that he needed to clean his clothes of all the filth of the city.

Even his boots were covered with a mixture of mud, ash, and whatever was in the gutter of Potion Lane. He leaned over to inspect the rainbow sheen left by poured-out potions that now covered his boots. *Will this even wash off?*

He sighed and shifted his focus to the shop in front of him. Above the door was a sign that once read The Wizard's Brew, but now read The Gnomen's Brew. The ash scattered on the threshold indicated a steady stream of customers.

Zane's throat was tight, and his old injuries felt knotted. With his free hand, he reached into the coat pocket opposite his brown wand holster to find his flask. He pulled it out and took a measured gulp. The tightness in his throat relaxed, but the knots didn't.

After a second swig, the knots released. He put the flask away and pushed it as deep as it would go into his pocket. Stepping into the store, he saw Fex, a gnome, standing on a stool and busily adding to the stack of potions on a center table.

Fex turned with a smile at the sight of him, waving the detective closer. "Zane! I wasn't expecting you today. Let me finish stacking these."

Zane nodded, pulling his gloves off and sliding them into a pocket. He took the moment as Fex finished up to look around. A human boy was busy sweeping away the dirt from their last customer. Following the path of the muck, Zane noticed a shelf lined with amber-colored bottles and neatly wrapped bags of balm containers. His eyes drifted to the many colorful potions, but nothing was as tempting as the swirling ones inside the bottles that lined the opposite wall.

The sight made his throat tighten anew. Zane tried to ignore it as Fex made his way over to the counter. "Have people started buying those shatterproof bottles again?"

Fex nodded excitedly. "Yes, I really thought they would never take off, but they've started to pick up. Now, we even just sell the bottles with nothing in them. People seem to like to be able to fill them with whatever they want, especially those who carry multiple types of potions on them."

Zane pulled a list and laid it on the counter. The detective looked down awkwardly at the gnome. Fex was using the crossbars of the stool as a ladder to reach the counter. Once seated, Fex read the note before rubbing his eyes. On the note were three lines: One for four bottles of a generic healing potion, one for two bottles of a mid-grade potion, and one for a bottle of the high-grade healing potion better known as Troll's Blood.

Fex shook his head. "I think I need to cut you off. You're going through this stuff so fast that I'm surprised you don't already have tumors the size of your fist! I gave you a crate—a small crate, mind you, but a crate with at least mid-grade stuff—just a few weeks ago. Now you tell me you need more?"

Zane blushed and looked away as the human child stocking the shelves caught his eye. The detective told the lie that he used to justify it to himself. "I-I work in a rough profession. Just the other day, I had to fight a Rager who was foaming at the mouth."

Fex narrowed his eyes at Zane, reading his expression. Fex pointed to the back area of the shop, just past a door. "Let's step into my workshop for a moment."

As he got off his stool, he told the boy to let him know if a customer came in. In the back was a gnome with longer hair than Fex, hard at work mixing and brewing potions. She looked nervous when she saw Zane, but Fex signaled that it was okay. With a deliberate nod, she went back to her work. Zane and Fex took a seat at the other end of the table. The small gnome ran his fingers through his hair. "So, how long have you been on this stuff?"

"What do you—"

"You know what I mean. The only people that go through stuff that fast are addicts. Even guards and doctors don't go through it that fast."

Zane sighed and laid the cane on the table. "Since the Ghoul War, so maybe five, no, six years now."

Fex's voice was sympathetic. "I've seen this before. The military doctors are usually liberal in their use of this stuff. But I thought Dennis was your doctor. I'd have thought he would've tried his hardest to keep you from getting addicted."

The detective was quiet for a moment as his eyes scanned the room for Shadow. The two piercing red eyes were nowhere to be seen. "It wasn't the military that gave me so much. During the war, I was captured by a Ghoul Lord. I was kept alive to be fed on. H-he used healing potion daily to make sure that I wouldn't die—"

Fex stopped him, nearly falling out of his seat. "Stop! You don't have to say any more! It's okay."

Zane hadn't realized it, but his voice had dropped into an al-most-whisper as he talked. The detective forced a cough and ad-justed his clothing, trying to smooth out wrinkles both real and imaginary. "Sorry, I try not to think back to those dark tunnels."

Fex shook his head in agreement. "Saints, I don't imagine that you do. Still, have you drunk that much usually? If you have, I am truly concerned about your health."

Zane shrugged nervously. "My drinking habit was more con-trolled before we met, before the case with Dennis. The stuff used to last longer and give me more strength. But now I feel like I need to take so much more for something even close to the same relief."

Fex gazed at Zane for a moment, his face abuzz with thoughts.

"I've noticed this a lot lately, especially those who were former customers of Atom."

The gnome adjusted his seat. "There has been a rumor that Atom had Ambrosia in his shop. That stuff is illegal for a reason. You didn't happen to find any of it, did you?"

Zane felt uncomfortable, his throat painfully tight at the thought of healing potions being made just next to him. A part of him wanted to drink it all until his pain was gone. With a slow nod, he answered. "I might have, but even if I did and even if I had taken some, why would it have such an effect? It's merely a stronger version of healing potion."

Fex shook his head. "That is where you're wrong. No one really knows how to make it, and the reason it's illegal isn't because of the stress it puts on the body. Well, on the body of humans. When you take it, it keeps you from changing."

Zane raised an eyebrow in confusion. "What do you mean change?"

Fex scratched his head as he looked for the right words. "It's vague, because the old Fey that made it wrote everything in verse, which I hear doesn't always translate well. But I have been around long enough to have heard talk about it and even read an old book about it once. Everything agrees that Ambrosia makes your body more whole; that's the reason it heals your body. Saints! It will even help healing potions by making their effects more 'complete.' But it also makes bodies harder to change. That is the reason why healing potions have less effect after taking too much of it."

Zane opened his mouth, then closed it; he didn't know what to say. He had done more damage to his body than any wound he could have received in a fight. "So now I just have to live with this . . . this hunger?"

Fex's eyes narrowed before he closed them in thought. "I think so. Let me ask around, but I can't promise anything."

Zane nodded his thanks, then stood up to leave.

Fex stopped him, passing the purchase request to his apprentice. "I didn't say I wouldn't accept your money. I will get you half the things on the list, but I don't feel comfortable giving you any more than that." He sighed. "At least now I know what's going on with some of my customers. Damn, if I'm not careful with their orders, they'll end up in the gutter with the other addicts."

Zane's mouth felt impossibly dry as the question rose in his throat. "Can I still get a bottle of Troll's Blood?"

Fex sighed weakly. "Aye, I will make you a bottle."

Shadow had been watching from a secluded corner of the workshop, purposefully avoiding the detective's gaze. With long invisible tendrils, he reached out to the detective. He tried to take over Zane's personality, his mind, and his body. Despite his best efforts, he could not seem to dislodge Zane. *Just a few months ago, I was able to take over for a little while.*

The plan had been so simple once Shadow had realized the detective's constant drinking allowed for greater ease in pushing him out. The monthly blackouts had been picking up, and Shadow had grown accustomed to being able to walk around once more. Ambrosia seemed like a blessing that would have sealed the situation. Yet, what the gnome had mentioned was news to him.

Shadow cursed himself for not being better read in life. Fear rolled through him that would have chilled him if he could still feel such things. It was a fear that he might have damned himself to fading away or, worse, merging with the detective.

Shadow brushed this feeling away. He had learned many things in his elongated life, much that would have driven a normal person mad. All of it was hard-learned, but he knew the greatest tool for those blessed with long lives is patience. All that he had to do was wait—opportunities were always around.

He watched as Zane left with the crate under his arm. The creature sighed, knowing the problem now was the healing potion. What good was an escape if he had to live in a tumor-ridden body on its way to the grave?

Zane moved through the streets with a grim determination, leaning heavily on his cane. Shadow winced at the sight. *I need to rethink my plan.*

7

The office door was unlocked when Zane arrived at his apartment. He pushed the door open with his foot and peeked inside. Alyssa was sitting behind her new desk. She looked up from her book and eyed the crate under his arm. He started to say something, to give some excuse, but stopped.

She returned to her book without a word. Head bowed, he took off his coat and hat in yet another awkward silence. He knocked the ash from his coat onto the floor before hanging them up. The gray pile bothered him, but the pain in his leg screamed louder.

Zane set the crate down by his desk. Already laying on his desk was the local paper. He sat down and spread the pages open across the surface, taking time to smooth out the wrinkles and folds. Shadow's silky voice spoke into his ear: *You should apologize.*

Zane looked up from his task to see the pair of red eyes that held residence in the shadows of the far corner of the room. He hated that he had to be reminded by Shadow, and wondered why he helped him with such a thing. He pushed the train of thought away and, with a cough, he started the conversation. "I-I'm sorry about last night. I was out of line."

She half-closed her book and looked over at him sympathetically. "Thank you for apologizing, but I do understand you were caught up in the moment."

Zane nodded, not wanting to dwell on the subject. "What time did the lieutenant say he would be by to drop off the payment?"

"Soon, I think. Within a half-hour to an hour."

Zane tried to turn his attention to the newspaper, but the

lonely island of ash and the thin trail made by his boots bothered him. The detective's eyes drifted to the crate. The potion was calling to him like a siren song.

The silky voice of Shadow spoke in his ear. *Is that a good idea? What would the professor think?*

Zane's eyes broke away from the crate to meet Shadow's. He hated that the parasite was right and that Shadow was trying to antagonize him. With a deep breath, the detective stood up, straightened out his clothes, and started to clean his office. Alyssa laid the book on her desk. "Do you need help?"

Zane shook his head. "I appreciate the offer, but I just need to clean this. Thank you, though."

She raised an eyebrow, but nodded and returned to reading. Zane limped to the window, opened it, and dumped the dustpan full of ash back into the dirty world it came from. His muscles still radiated pain, but his throat wasn't as tight. The siren call had passed.

He returned to his newspaper. The recent arrests they'd made were not mentioned at all. Instead, there were mentions of famous dancer Shelina the Fey Lily's legs getting crushed in a carriage accident, discussions over the politics of new ambassadors to the Eastern Territories, the gang war among the goblins, and various major events in nearby countries.

The article about the goblin gang war was the only one that concerned him. Many people called for the removal of the goblin district. The sheer hatred and racism written into the article made Zane surprised that the page wasn't penned in goblin blood.

As he looked through the pages, he found an isolated column. It was a speculative piece discussing a new type of prosthetic. It claimed they functioned much like that of a normal limb without any faults. Zane highly doubted that. Having been through war and medical school, he knew that even with the aid of magic, regaining full use of a ruined limb was not possible.

He folded the paper shut and stared again at the crate. Fex's warning hung in his mind. He shook his head, opened his newspaper, and started to read it again. Halfway through the second read, a knock on the door shattered the silence. "It's open. Come in," Zane called out in a rough voice.

The door swung open carefully. Standing in the doorway was the young officer, Kellim. He smiled with the fresh face of a person who never tires. He marched through the room with an air of superiority and control. His uniform jacket hung around his shoulders like a cloak, and a broad-brimmed hat covered his head in place of his plumed helmet.

On his belt was a red-dyed leather holster that held a military grade wand. Kellim's breastplate was polished to a shine, and Zane wondered how the lieutenant kept it so clean despite the city's constant ash fall.

Kellim smiled as he took a seat in front of Zane's desk. The lieutenant angled the chair so Alyssa was also a part of the conversation. "Some of my fellow officers think I should feel ashamed for asking for help outside of the guard with the recent Rush powder issue, yet the results speak for themselves. The both of you have helped us get into communities that wouldn't have trusted the guards."

Zane shrugged as he folded the newspaper and put it to the side. "Something I find helps is not threatening them the moment I meet them."

Kellim nodded vigorously. "Yes! That is something that I have brought up before. Many officers don't understand this novel idea. I had even requested to do street interviews without our uniforms, but that was always denied."

Alyssa joined in, her voice filled with curiosity. "Why *do* guards always wear their uniforms? Wouldn't it make things like this easier if they weren't always dressed like that?"

Kellim nodded. "I believe it would, but the Imperial Guard has stood at the watch since the founding of the empire. Some say since the city's founding, which stretches even further back into history. As such, we are rooted in tradition, and that tradition, for better or worse, defines who we are."

He sighed, his smile fading for a moment as his eyes seemed to focus on problems outside of the room. "This makes us slow to change. Adapting to an ever-evolving world has proven difficult. Even now, sword training is given more importance than wand or staff training, even though only a few guards actually wield a sword. Our uniforms have only been altered three times. Not to mention, we were not taught anything about how to actually 'solve' a crime. We seem to be little more than an old military unit that has not seen war in centuries."

Kellim perked up again as he focused on Zane and Alyssa. The detective wondered how much of his smile was a mask he wore. "That is why I find working with both of you to be such a refreshing breath of air. Here is your last payment."

He reached inside his coat to pull free some banknotes and laid them on the table. Zane was happy at the sight of the notes, but the word "last" hung in his mind. In the last month, they had worked for Kellim on several small cases. Zane wondered if he was being used to train the younger guards on how to handle things.

The detective organized the banknotes and put them in his top drawer. "From what I read this morning, there still is a major problem with this Rush powder."

Kellim's face was friendly but firm. He crossed his legs. "That is true, and it is a growing problem. We don't know who is supplying the drugs now. In fact, the major players we had our eyes on, like the Kane brothers and the Lumpin Gang, have started to show up dead."

Zane raised an eyebrow. "How?"

Kellim stood up. "We are not sure, but each scene looks the same. Slashed throats, legs with gashes from the thighs down, and some with stab marks around the shoulder. A few victims mentioned a goblin before dying of blood loss, but we haven't been able to prove anything."

Zane heard a small gasp and the sound of a book falling onto the floor. He turned to see Alyssa's face, pale from the description. Her breathing was ragged before she brought it under control. Her voice wavered. "If it's possible, may I take a look at those reports?"

Kellim thought about it for a moment before agreeing. "I could make it happen, but I won't be able to pay you for anything unless you find something concrete. The powers that be are trying to make this mess disappear before it gets any worse, so they're throwing more and more manpower at it."

The former professor thought for a moment, then looked to Zane for advice. He shrugged, trying to make it look casual. *I'm sorry, but I don't understand what you're doing.* She sighed and adjusted her hair. "That's fine. I have an idea, but I'm not completely sure. If I do find anything, I'll let you know."

Kellim nodded, then stopped himself. "I must thank you. Having someone else to give a look may help us see something that we might have missed. I am, as always, open to suggestions."

He adjusted how his belt and wand holster sat on his hip. "With that, business is concluded for the time. I look forward to working together again. Detective, Miss Benedictus."

Kellim pivoted on his heels and marched out. When the door closed behind him, Zane turned to Alyssa. "What are you looking for in those reports?"

She opened her mouth, but seemed lost for words. She tried again, but still nothing. Finally, she softly said, "I am not sure, but it sounded familiar."

Zane felt she wasn't being entirely truthful, but he didn't want to push her. He trusted her, and she would let him know if she needed help. Before he could return to his newspaper, she spoke again.

"Oh, a student named Frame from the Institute contacted me. Her cousin needs a detective. She may come to us with a job."

Tension that he didn't realize he was holding in his shoulders relaxed. *Another job would be welcome.* "That's good. I was a little afraid that we would be without one."

8

Frame crumpled the paper with Zane's address in her pocket. She rubbed her temple, annoyed with fetching things for her cousin. *I should have taken Diana up on her offer to come with me to see Vine.* She sighed, fighting off nervousness about the meeting. Her family had a business office in the city.

The waiting room of the family business had glass vases with crochet flowers in them, adding bright colors to the otherwise-cold room. Such fake flowers were a common sight among both the upper and lower classes. Frame knew that her cousin had the budget to afford real flowers, brought from outside the city, but Vine didn't like to spend the money on such things.

A tall man with horizontal scars across his face, wearing a black coat with matching gloves, stood like a statue by the door. Frame knew all the servants of her family estate, but she didn't recognize this man. She hadn't seen him move, not so much as blink, since she arrived. Her eyes traveled down his face to the saber on his hip.

The thick wooden doors to Vine's office were ornate, with silver painted handles and a white frame. Next to the scarred man was an aged silver bell that hung off the wall. The bell paired with another bell that shared its charm. When one rang, so would the other. Vine would use them to signal to open the door.

Frame attempted to stare out of the stained-glass window. She couldn't see anything through it, but even if it were a normal glass, Alviun was known for its filthy windows.

Vine had called on her with a charmed letter a week ago to find the name of the detective that uncovered professor Agwen's black market dealings. Frame believed the Institute would not have told her family, so she wondered how Vine knew.

A yellow cushioned chair sat in the hall by the door. It looked inviting and friendly, but Frame knew the trick to it. A needle lay under the cushion, and one of the legs was slightly shorter than the other. All things were set up to make any guest coming for business purposes distracted before their meeting.

The silver bells rang, and the tall servant broke posture to open the door with feline grace. Out stepped a clean-faced man wearing round-rimmed glasses and a tan suit—a strange choice for a city of endless filth. In his left hand, he held a packet of paper, but that wasn't what caught her eye. Each movement of his prosthetic right hand was followed by a subtle clack. The skeletal fingers captured the light of the lamps in a dull reflection.

Are those porcelain?

He stopped in front of her, and she blushed in embarrassment at being caught staring. "May I help you?"

Frame took a step back and bowed her head in apology. "Sorry about that, but your hand . . . It's very well made. Is that porcelain?"

The man smiled politely, setting the packet down, as he pulled his sleeve back to reveal his arm up to the elbow. As he worked each finger, the clacking sound could be heard. It moved with the elegance and grace of a real hand. "Yes. It's amazing, isn't it?"

Frame nodded, and the man slid his sleeve back down as he picked up his packet. He smiled widely, as if showing off his arm was a moment of pride. "I am Chiron Falto, a lawyer. Have a good day, ma'am."

Before Frame could give her name, Chiron stepped past her and continued down the hall. She stared as he left, thinking the hand looked too much like a skeleton's hand. From the office yelled a hard female voice. "Frame, get in here!"

Frame's head snapped to the open door as if it were the roaring maw of a large beast. The scarred man stood there with uncaring eyes, like an executioner. Frame could already feel tension building inside her as she stepped into the office. Her cousin sat in a large leather chair that almost enveloped her. The ends of her sleeves were unbuttoned, the fabric cascading around her arm as she reached for the long cigarette on her desk.

"I thought you would have been here faster. You know how long I've been waiting?"

Frame moved to sit, but stopped short, recognizing the tell-tale signs of the altered chairs. "I was busy with my studies. They had me up all night—"

Vine clicked her tongue and took a long drag. "Who do you think is paying for you to play scholar?"

Frame's cheeks turned bright red. "We both know that I don't *play*. I am—"

"—a second-rate scholar," Vine interjected. "Never forget that it is our great-grandmother's connections that got you into the Institute. Now sit down. We have family business to discuss."

Frame hesitated next to the chair. Vine stabbed the tray with her long cigarette. "Sit, now."

She sighed and sat down, causing the chair's legs to rock ever so slightly. Frame pushed forward the crumbled paper with the address.

"So, then, you've managed to get the address of this detective. Detective Vane Vrexon?"

"It's *Zane* Vrexon, and yes. His office is on Fourth and Traders Street, on the third floor in his flat."

Vine nodded and wrote the name down on her own notepad. She rested her eyes on Frame. "I heard that he solved the murder of a state mage and uncovered a professor dealing in black market goods?"

Frame raised her eyebrow, feeling the chair shift under her. "H-how did you hear about that?"

Vine grinned. "The Institute, for a government organization, is not very good at covering up rumors. It was the subject of some debate among my contacts."

"Debate? Over what?"

"Over whether they should reach out to the detective or

whether that would upset the Institute. Already, many circles of nobles have started talking about this detective. I wouldn't doubt that before long they will get over their hesitations, and many people will come to his door, if not for any other reason than to say they met him."

Frame's mouth hung open for a moment. She wondered how much her cousin really knew about what happened, including whether Vine knew that she had been controlled by Agwen. It shouldn't matter, but her cousin would twist it.

"Did you meet this detective during the case?"

Frame sat still for a moment, feeling the pressure of the needle under the cushion, before shaking her head. "No, I didn't."

Vine narrowed her eyes, giving Frame a hard stare. "Are you sure? I know you were one of the students put under spell by this criminal. The compensation letter even claimed that you were possessed against your will."

She tried to find a comfortable spot, but couldn't. *Compensation? What compensation did they give my family?* "Not *possessed*. Possession isn't really possible. I was under an arcane form of hypnosis. B-but I met with Alyssa Benedictus, a professor who was working with the detective."

Vine looked away, rubbing her chin before turning back. "Really? Then you were directly related to the scandal . . . I could play this up."

Frame's chair shifted with a thud, and she raised an eyebrow. "What do you mean?"

Vine placed her hand on her chest and acted hurt. "My dear cousin, you helped in catching an evil murderer. Tragically, you were assaulted by the deranged teacher and forced under his control. This scandal is sure to inspire sympathy from many of the naiver courtiers in the city. Several people know of someone that was affected by the archmage professor, but you actually played a small role in catching him."

Frame shook her head at the idea of using her situation for politicking. "Is there anything else?"

Vine looked absent-minded for a moment, with a mask pretending innocence. "No."

"Are you sure?"

Her cousin smiled. "Yes."

Frame hesitated, standing and slowly making her way to the door. Each step was slow, because Frame knew what was coming: The yanking of the chain. Before reaching the door, she stopped and turned back. "Is there anything else you need?"

Vine replied, "No, I am sure."

Frame narrowed her eyes as she opened the door.

"Oh, now that I think about it . . . there is something."

Frame closed her eyes and sighed in time with the door shutting. "What else can I do for you?"

"When I go to meet the detective, I would like you to join me. I would like you to act as my agent as the detective works my case."

"But I have classes to attend and labs to run."

"Don't worry. I have already contacted the Institute, and they are more than happy to give you the time off. I told them that due to the stress of a little incident, you were in need of some time off. They were quick to oblige after that."

Frame felt violated by Vine's actions. "Shouldn't I—"

The look on her cousin's face said it all: *Please question me on this.*

Frame sighed, giving in. "When will you be going over there?"

9

Zane sat behind his desk, his newspaper folded in his lap. He reached for a small brush to clean off his workspace. It was clean already, but he needed something to distract him from the healing potions. He glanced up at Alyssa, still reading calmly at her desk. The dull light penetrating the dirty window aided the wall lamps in lighting the room. With a sigh, he put the brush away and returned to the newspaper, rubbing out its wrinkles.

Alyssa sat her book down. She picked up a pen and scribbled something on a notepad before opening up another book that lay on her desk.

He just wanted to drink the potion calling him from the bottom drawer of his desk. *Why not just have a strong drink?* Alyssa hadn't said anything, but she gave him an unspoken look when he drank in the office. *I shouldn't care,* he thought, and started to slowly open the drawer.

Shadow's silky voice returned to his ear. *You shouldn't be drinking so early in the day. Fex was right to be concerned about tumors. Just imagine what Alyssa must think.*

Shadow was right, which always rubbed Zane the wrong way. Shadow's touch of concern bothered him, too. Zane rubbed his right shoulder and moved down the arm. He did the same to his left thigh. His limbs ached from the old Ghoul War injuries.

"Alyssa, about the other night. I am—"

A rap at the door interrupted his apology. A rough man's voice carried into the room. "Is the detective Zane Vrexon in?"

Shadow hummed to himself before speaking to Zane. *Two women and an armed man. Looks like a bodyguard of some sort.*

Alyssa closed her book and stood up. "It sounds like a customer. I hope it's the one we've been expecting."

She crossed the room and opened the door, greeting the three guests. A tall man dressed in a thick coat and gloves with a saber at his side entered first. Zane noticed the horizontal scars on his face and the way he walked as signs of a trained swordsman.

He recognized the woman in the back as Frame. She was the one that Alyssa had frozen during the Wizard's Brew case. He hadn't seen the woman in front before. She wore men's trousers capped off with riding boots. A coat draped like a cloak covered her white shirt.

Only someone of status would dare to wear such clothes . . . or someone who doesn't come into the city often. His eyes drifted from her clean shirt to his own vest. He noticed some small smudges of ash and cursed under his breath.

The scarred man shook his umbrella by the door before leaning it against the wall. The first woman walked around the room, taking it all in, judging everything as she crossed it. The man followed, keeping an even two-stride distance from her. He then pulled out the chair in front of Zane's desk so that the lady could sit.

Zane put his newspaper away and leaned back, trying to wipe away the smudges on his vest. "Welcome. I am detective Zane Vrexon, and this is Alyssa Benedictus, my assistant. How can we be of service?"

The woman smiled, but it did not look genuine. "I am Vine Lexone, and I have a special job for you. You might find it distasteful, but I understand that, as a detective, you are willing to spy on people."

Zane arched an eyebrow as he tried to read Vine. From the way she smiled to the way she crossed her arms, he could tell she was prideful and arrogant. "I prefer to call it an investigation, but yes. Spying is something that I have done before. Who do you want looked into?"

She grinned and leaned her head to one side, like a cat playing with its still-living food. Her eyes tested him. "What do you suspect?"

Zane shrugged. "Usually if a woman comes to me, it's to follow around her husband to see if he's cheating, drinking, or gambling their wealth away."

The detective glanced at her hands, but noticed she didn't wear a wedding ring. Then he looked to the hardened man standing like a statue. "But you don't strike me as someone who would need a detective to investigate that."

She laughed, deeply and haughtily. "Yes. If I was married, I would have my own people take care of him. Then, I would deal with him in my own time."

Zane stole a glance at Alyssa, who was whispering to Frame near the door. Frame was red in the face as she pointed in angry jerking movements. "That brings us back to your reason for being here."

Vine nodded, resting her head on her hand. "To the point, I like that. I have a great-grandmother, who is spending my—"

She stopped with a wince. "Her money. Right now, she has hired a doctor who I believe is swindling her."

"How so?"

"My great-grandmother is bedridden, due to fragile bones and joints. From what I understand, the doctor is working on a way to heal her of these problems."

Zane smiled politely. "Isn't that a good thing? How do you know that the doctor can't actually provide what he's selling?"

Vine gave him a frustrated glare with a hint of what Zane could only guess was disgust. "He can't; I know that for fact. It's something that no doctor can fix. She had me look into it multiple times. Trust me. It can't be done, even with arcane methods."

Zane shrugged his shoulders. "It's her money, yes? What am I supposed to do?"

Vine lifted her head in irritation. "Look, I need you to find evidence that he is a fraud, that he is selling her snake oil. I need some type of proof that he can't back up what he promised."

Zane nodded his head in surrender, pulling out his pen and notepad. He wrote down his rates and passed the pad. "I can't guarantee what I will find, but I will look into him. These are my rates. Are they acceptable?"

She looked it over for a moment, then nodded in agreement. She signed and pulled the paper free. Zane quickly made a copy on the notepad as Vine put the paper away. "Yes, this is more than acceptable. The name of the doctor is Franxen Aluxen."

Vine stood and slowly walked to the door. The scarred man followed close behind. Zane called after her. "Wait, where can I find this doctor?"

She shrugged her shoulders. "That is your job. I have my own business to handle today. Oh, before I forget: This is my cousin Frame. I do believe your assistant is already familiar with her. She is a student, and will be acting as my representative during this case."

The scarred man picked up his umbrella and checked the hall before letting Vine step out. The door closed with a click. Frame's jerky movements exploded into a violent storm of stomping, with her fists balled so tight that they turned white. She looked on the verge of tears.

Alyssa placed a hand on her shoulder softly. "Take a seat. Zane, can you set the kettle to boil? I think we need some tea."

Frame nodded, and Alyssa guided her to her desk chair. Zane stood up and leaned on his cane as he made his way into his room.

"I can do that," he called back.

His apartment office was two rooms with a single bathroom. The office took up most of the space with the rest given over to living space. The kitchen area was small and only a few feet from his bed.

As Zane turned on the stove and filled the teapot, Shadow's eyes reflected in a full-length mirror in the corner. *Something isn't right about that duelist.*

Zane watched the kettle. "How so?" he whispered.

Shadow was silent until the kettle began to whistle. *There was something about him that was similar to how things felt around the Well.* Zane looked toward Shadow, but he had already left his corner. It was the second time that Shadow had mentioned the Well. It was something he couldn't explain due to a curse, something that he had sought and found.

Zane put his cane under his armpit and carried out two cups. He placed both on Alyssa's desk. Frame's eyes were red and puffy, but she looked more composed than she did before. He laid his cane on the desk and grabbed his broom. The ash and muck that Vine brought in bothered him to no end.

Alyssa picked up the pen and notepad from his desk. "So, what's your plan? What do you normally do for cases like this?"

The detective kept cleaning. "Normally I just follow, watch, and record what they do. Then, I report it to the client. But, first, we need to find him."

She scribbled ideas on the notepad and underlined some of them. "Where do we start?"

"I have two ideas. We can talk to the local doctors and ask if they recognize the name Franxen Aluxen—the house doctors often talk to each other—and we could try going to the College of Surgeons. It acts as a type of guild and school for doctors."

She nodded and looked at him. "After that, we follow him?"

Zane picked up the dustpan after reaching the door. "Yes, but since there are two of us, we should make some sort of rotation, taking turns watching him. After collecting information, we report it. It's easy, really."

Frame's weak voice called out to them. "What about me?"

Zane walked to the window behind his desk with a full dustpan. "What did Vine ask you to do?"

Frame shrugged. "I am supposed to be the go-between person and send her letters on the progress of the investigation."

He tapped the pan, emptying it out the window. "Then that's what you'll do."

"Are you sure?"

Alyssa set the pen down and turned to Frame. "It sounds to

me like you were forced into this, so you don't have to help us. Just keep her up to date."

Frame sniffled. "Really?"

Alyssa nodded. "Yes; in fact, you could use your free time to write your paper."

Frame stood up. "If either of you need my help, just ask. I'll come by every day, or at least every other day."

Alyssa gave Zane a glance, pleading for help. Zane shook his head. "There won't be a need. We'll be in and out of the office for the duration of the case, so we can meet somewhere close to your home."

"Thank you."

Frame collected her things and headed out the door. After she had stepped out, Alyssa turned to Zane. "So, who do we go see first?"

10

Shadow watched from his favorite corner as Alyssa and Zane discussed their case. Such subtle movements made, each worth a thousand words. He watched, faintly jealous that he could not be there in flesh. *The warmth, the touch, and the sensation. Oh, how I miss it.*

Shadow reached out his invisible limb to touch the detective, but his hand faded through the resistance. The detective wobbled for a brief moment in his chair before steadying himself.

Almost! Just a little more! Shadow thought with excitement. Zane's descent into his world had slowed. It had been two months since the detective had a blackout. During the last session, Shadow took the opportunity to carve a beautiful rendition of a client on the wall. The detective now hid the work of art with new panels.

Zane fidgeted in his chair before reaching for his potion drawer. Shadow spoke in his silky voice. *Now, detective, do you really need a drink just to sit there in your chair?*

The detective glared at him and shook his head. Zane acted tough, but Shadow could see the subtle signs of pain. *Deal with that pain. Just don't destroy my body, my escape with your attempts.*

Shadow wondered when his next escape might reveal itself. As he watched, he felt a ripple from a nearby shadow. He focused his full mind on it. *That's strange.*

He dove back down into the realm he inhabited. As he did, he remembered the old conversations he had with his former comrade about the nature of shadows. Already at that time, he was looking for the Well, exploring every clue he found.

Jefarson had told him that every ancient document he could

find described shadows like water. Normal shadows were like puddles, the Well like a spring. Shadow had laughed at his friend's description and asked him if there was a sea as well, and his friend had nodded. Shadow found the name Sea of Stars, a description that he'd found overly poetic . . . until he saw it.

He dove until he reached this sea and turned his gaze up. Above him, in his dark void, were white lights, much like that of stars in the night sky. Each speck of light was tied to a shadow cast in the world above.

He swam through the silent void. The Sea always reminded Shadow of stagnant water. He followed the faint ripples in the dark water, eventually pulling himself out to see the duelist that had stood guard by Vine. With each movement of his right arm, the man sent out faint ripples through the shadows.

What are you? Where are you from? Shadow spoke the words, but none could hear them. The duelist ignored his invisible red eyes as he spoke to the driver of the carriage. "Take us back to the house."

"Not the office? I thought maybe the lady needed to finish some things up—"

The duelist gave a hard look at the man before cutting him off. "Did I ask for your opinion? No? Just drive."

The duelist stepped away and reached for the handle on the carriage door. Shadow reached out one of his invisible hands and tried to grab his right hand. That arm made little ripples in his world, so he followed. The man's arm hesitated for a moment as if frozen, and Shadow felt an icy heat. The man stared at his arm as Shadow's grip passed through it. The arm jerked forward, and he smacked the door with a loud thud.

From inside the carriage, Vine yelled out. "What was that? Is that you, Davidson?"

Davidson, who are you?

The duelist opened the door and stepped inside. "Sorry, ma'am. I was distracted for a moment. It will not happen again."

The door shut, and the carriage took off. Shadow watched it

leave down the street, through the ash and smog. He attempted to follow, but the tether that connected him to Zane restrained him. It felt like the detective was leaving his office. Already, the boundary of his range shifted. He fought it for as long as he could before giving in and letting the detective's movement pull him back down into the depths of the Sea of Stars.

11

Alyssa stood outside the College of Surgeons. Their dirty marble pillars were pitch black from ash on one side, like a tree covered with moss, while the other side was a dirty white. Alyssa pulled her coat tight against the chill of the wind. Carried on the breeze was the yelling of a priest in dirty purple robes, his bare chest exposed to the world. Across his body were several tattoos designating the saints he tried to emulate. His hair was greasy, matted to his face by clumps of ash.

"Do you people not find them horrid? Do you not know that the righteous fire of saints will fall down on these people who rip flesh from bone? As if man was a clock—"

Alyssa paused for a moment to study the tattoos. Most of them were common in the city: One for the empire, one for the capital, and one for humankind. The one that stood out, wrapping its way around his arm up to his shoulder, was an emerald snake with empty, black eye sockets. The symbol of Mouthtress, a saint called the "caretaker of the dead" and "opposer of ghouls." The former professor registered the man's intention.

The man continued to scream to any who would listen—and many who wouldn't. The attention given to Mouthtress priests had lacked political power ever since the end of the Ghoul War. Alyssa pushed her hat down to avoid his glare as she approached the large doors past the pillars. These metal doors were left ajar, just wide enough for a person to step through.

Heavy drapes inside the doors covered the gap, keeping the airborne ash out. She pushed them aside and stepped into the lobby. In the corners were brooms with piles of ash ready to be collected and taken out. Almost caked into the floor was a line of footsteps made of ash and mud.

The footprints led through a doorway off to the left. Alyssa followed it to find a smaller room with a closet and a counter. A clerk adjusted the papers at the counter and motioned for her. "Hello, I'm Alan. Is there something I can help you with?"

Alyssa nodded and stepped closer to the desk. "Yes, I'm Alyssa Benedictus. I work for detective Zane Vrexon. We're looking for information about a doctor named Franxen Aluxen."

The name seemed to shock Alan, who looked ready to leave. Alyssa smiled kindly. "We're not sure if he's even a doctor; our client is worried that this person is a con man."

The clerk furrowed his brow and looked to be debating himself. "Sorry, please wait one moment," he said, looking through a small booklet.

Alan nodded and looked up. "I think I can help with that. Please follow me."

He stepped away from the counter and left the room through a side door, leaving a small plaque on his desk that read, "Stepped away. Please ring the bell." Alyssa followed into a long hall. Alan gestured for her to be quiet, then nodded toward a large classroom at the end.

Alyssa could just barely make out a few words of the lecture about human anatomy. Before they reached the classroom, they turned down another hall and into a library. She admired the neatly arranged rows of books; while the space was not as large as the ones at the Institute, it was still impressive. In one corner, she noticed another small pile of ash by a broom. She looked down to her feet and realized she had tracked in the mud and ash from outside. "Oh! I am sorry. I didn't mean to dirty your floor."

Alan dismissed the concern with one hand. "Oh, that is no problem. We have staff to clean up the floor."

She had never thought of such a job existing. All the years of working at the Institute of Sorcery and Science had made her accustomed to the casual use of magic. In the shifting halls of the Institute, constant charms were applied to keep the halls clean.

Even the clothes they made there were designed to repel the filth of the city.

Alan politely held his hands behind his back. "Now, if you would follow me over to this room. We keep records of every member of our organization, for tax and membership purposes, of course."

They stepped through the door into a locked room filled with file cabinets. Alan stopped and turned to Alyssa, looking nervous and eying the door behind her. "We don't normally allow this. Membership is confidential, but the College of Surgeons is making strides to have a better reputation. We wish to become a government agency, like the Institute of Sorcery and Science. To do this, the ones in charge believe we need to do away with the snake-oil sellers and such."

Alyssa nodded her head. "That makes sense. If this Franxen Aluxen is—"

He smiled as he cut in. "Then we can dismiss him from the college and distance ourselves."

Alan started his search through the files. It was a minute or two before he gave a sigh of relief and turned to her. "I don't see this name anywhere in here. If this man, Franxen Aluxen, is a doctor, he is not associated with the college."

The clerk seemed more relaxed and even happy. He smiled as he guided Alyssa back out of the library and into the hall. As they walked, he spoke quietly. "I was concerned that a doctor of ours might have had shady dealings that would have reflected poorly on us. Now that I know that it has nothing to do with us, it's a big relief."

Alyssa remembered faculty members of the Institute being let go over similar things. Politics are everywhere. Out from the hall came a voice. "Be careful, boys. These bodies don't need any more damage."

Bodies? Alyssa stopped and refused to follow Alan as he tried to direct her away.

"Please come this way."

From a large doorway, she watched as men moved gurneys into the hall. It was the smell that she noticed first as the cadavers, covered by dark brown cloth, made their way past. The recognizable smell of death was not a pleasant one, though nothing in the building had smelled nice so far.

Through the door came a small, rat-faced man yelling orders. He stopped when he noticed Alyssa. He smiled and approached her. He gave an exaggerated bow, taking off his hat. "Hello, I'm Rufus. Sorry for disturbing ya, miss, but we needed to get these out of my wagon as soon as possible."

Alan's weak voice spoke up behind her. "Please take them around the corner to the elevator, and then come by the desk in—"

Rufus waved his hat at Alan. "Aye, aye. I know where to find my pay."

His eyes turned back to her. "Are you new here? I hope this will be the beginning of a great working relationship."

The man's direct attitude brought a slight color to her cheeks, but she shook her head. "No, I am here asking about information on a doctor." Her eyes followed one of the gurneys as it made its way down the hall. "But where did these unfortunate people come from?"

Rufus lifted his head and arched an eyebrow. "Ah, that is the work of the infamous little devil, Red Hood."

Red Hood—the words burned in her head. The memory of the fight and the echoing feeling of pain as his knife drove into her nearly overcame her. Sweat dripped from her brow and down her neck. The world seemed to fade into oblivion. Words came out of Rufus's mouth, but she didn't hear them.

He reached down as if to kiss her hand, trying to be courtly. Alyssa spoke an eldritch word in surprise. The air around her shimmered as static electricity followed, shocking the rat-faced man.

He squeaked and jerked his hand back, nearly tripping over his own feet. "Ouch! What the hell was that?"

Behind her, Alan slipped to the floor in surprise. "Magic! What are you doing using magic here? Don't you know you can get in trouble for performing magic? What if the Institute comes here?"

Alyssa could feel her cheeks glowing red in embarrassment. She turned quickly to help the clerk up. "I am a state-certified mage, so don't worry about the Institute. But I'm sorry. My mind wandered, and I—"

Rufus looked nervously at his hand. "Is my hand going to be okay? It's not going to become anything weird, is it?"

She smirked and shook her head. "No, that was a small spell designed for self-defense. It's largely based on eels and how they conduct electricity, but it was altered to make use of static and air as—"

The rat-faced man whipped his hand behind his back and bowed nervously. "That is great and interesting and all, but I think I should go before my team, uh, before they damage something."

He scurried off. Alyssa turned to Alan and apologized again. "I didn't mean for my slip of magic. When he touched me . . . I, well, reacted poorly."

Alan looked irritated for a moment before rubbing the back of his head. "Well, that is to be expected. That man . . . he can at times leave a bad taste in your mouth. If he wasn't so good at bringing so many bodies for us to work on, I wouldn't put up with him."

As he motioned for her to follow him, she got curious. "What exactly do you plan to do with them? If they had been attacked by Red Hood, then I doubt that they would make very good examples of anatomy."

Alan shrugged. "That may be, but they do make for great practice in learning how to stitch someone back up. That way, students can have experience in working on all sorts of horrible injuries before moving on to living patients."

That is a practical and reasonable use of the dead. They were nearly back to Alan's small office when he spoke again. "Even though that man is always bringing in victims of some sort, lately it has been victims of Red Hood. I don't know how he finds them, but it's like he knows where the little goblin is going to be."

She stopped as a sort of primal energy coursed through her. "Does he know where Red Hood is going to be?"

Alan nodded. "It does always seem that way, but there are other rumors, of course. I have heard he has another buyer for the bodies, which is fine of course. I mean, I assume he goes through all the paperwork and channels in order to legally obtain the bodies—"

Alyssa glanced behind her. "I-I left something back in the library. I remember the way to it. I'll be right back."

She took off, tracing her steps back the way she came. In the hall, she noticed Rufus's hat. *He must have dropped it when I shocked him.* Alyssa reached into her pocket and found the tracking charm she had made for Zane. She placed a small piece of paper from the charm inside the hat, hoping it wouldn't move.

Rufus's voice carried from just outside the door that his team had used. She followed it. The door handle moved, so she pushed it open. From the doorway, she watched as the rat-faced man directed his crew and readied to move out his wagon. Alyssa waved his hat. "Mr. Rufus, you forgot this."

Rufus jerked as he turned to see her, and coughed as he walked over. "Well, thank ya, Miss . . . ah, I don't think I caught your name."

"Alyssa Benedictus."

"Right. Well, thank ya."

Rufus went back to his wagon and climbed up the side. "Let's get to it. If we're lucky, I bet we get one more haul for the day."

Alyssa pulled the door closed behind her as she slipped back into the college. Her hands shook with just a slight twitch as she pulled out the compass. She brought it to her mouth and whispered into it. The inked runes that covered the paper on it glowed, and the needle swung around until it faced the door. She breathed a sigh of relief and made her way to the clerk's office. From the door leading to Alan, she could see that the priest was inside and was yelling at him. Two guards were politely escorting the man out.

Alan grumbled under his breath as she approached. Before she could ask him anything, the clerk cut her off with a harsh gesture. He looked tired and irritated. "Sorry to be blunt, ma'am, but you have your information, yes? Then please leave."

Alyssa followed the trail of muck leading out onto the cold, filthy streets. The ash dancing on the wind met her. The priest was back on his corner, his body black from a mixture of ash and sweat. The guards that had escorted him back out stood nearby as he yelled at the crowd. "They dishonor the saints! They violate the dead. There is blood on their hands."

Alyssa shuddered from the chill and pulled her coat tight. The voice of the priest faded into the distance. But that smell, the smell of the bodies, followed her through the streets. She reached into her pocket and pulled the compass out. The needle didn't spin freely or point north but followed its partnered charm.

Alyssa gripped it tightly in one hand. "What in the world am I doing?" she whispered.

12

Zane leaned heavily on his cane, his old injuries feeling as though burned by an evil flame. The pain could only be lessened with large gulps from his flask. It felt like a millstone in his hand. He tried to ignore it, but relented.

Shadow's eyes reflected in the nearby shop window as he walked. *Perhaps you shouldn't start drinking so early in the day. How much of that have you gone through already? How much do you think you'll need for this day?*

Zane glared at the window and mumbled to Shadow. "Whose fault is that?"

Shadow gave a shrug, which irritated Zane. The parasitic entity had become more and more active since Zane had learned that he wasn't a figment of his imagination. Part of Zane still wished Shadow was a part of his mind. The truth haunted him far more. Shadow was the one who tortured him during the Ghoul War. The injuries, both physically and mentally, had come from him.

The detective spat on the ground as he tried to pick up speed. "You carved me up like some lamb to be slaughtered for your dinner! Of course my need is your fault."

Shadow's voice chuckled in what sounded like a strange sense of agreement. Zane pressed on, stopping every once in a while to catch his breath. With firm determination, he made his way to an apartment and knocked. A thin man with a receding hairline opened the door with a smile. "Detective Zane, what a surprise. Please come in."

Zane shook his hand politely. "Thank you, Jaxen, but I'm just stopping by to see if you have heard of a doctor named Franxen Aluxen."

Jaxen looked away in thought. After a few moments, he turned back to Zane. "Sorry, but I don't think I have. If I do, I will make sure to come by and let you know."

The detective smiled at Jaxen. "Thank you. It's much appreciated. Now, if you'll excuse me, I need to get over to the next district doctor—"

"Wait, are you going district to district, searching for this doctor?"

"Yes, it is the only way I can think of to find him."

"Have you checked the surgeon college? They might have information on him."

Zane shook his head. "That's only true if he's above-board."

In each district, he approached a local and asked where to find their doctor. The cycle continued, with some districts not having doctors and others being absent. As the day waned, Zane had walked many miles on his quest, with each doctor having nothing helpful to say.

The blanket of clouds overhead began to take on an orange hue as the sun made its way toward the horizon. His limbs ached more now than ever, and he was forced to drink from his flask again.

After finishing off the potion in his flask, he decided to make one last stop before turning back. One last doctor, he told himself, then he would go home. He looked down at his clothes and found that the ash had invaded his jacket, smearing his shirt and vest. His temper rose at the sight of the filth that covered him. His throat tightened as his mind went over what he needed to do to clean it.

Zane was relieved that the last doctor lived on the ground level. The door was nice and well taken care of for being in the weather. *Impressive.* The detective knocked using its ornate knocker, and in a few seconds it opened. The last doctor was hunched, with long eyebrows that hung down the sides of his face.

The man was so happy to have a guest that he brought Zane inside. The detective was happy to be out of the constant ash and off his feet. The doctor sat in a small apartment eating dinner. "So, Mr. Zane, you're looking for Franxen Aluxen? Are you sure you want to find him?"

The detective was distracted by the dirty dishes in the sink. "Well, that's all right. I didn't—wait, you know this man?"

The old doctor nodded as he sipped his soup. "Oh yeah, he's famous in these parts. At first, he was a blessing, but . . ."

The old man paused and looked into his bowl. Zane's throat felt like dry leather, and the image of the dishes captured his eyes. He sighed as walked over to the sink, rolling up his sleeves. "So he was a blessing?" Zane asked. "How?"

The old doctor looked quizzically at the man cleaning his dishes, but did nothing to stop him. "Dr. Aluxen's results were nothing short of miracles. I have seen men lose legs from accidents, but he would give them a chance to walk again."

Zane washed, rinsed, and dried the dishes before setting them to the side. He turned to face the doctor with raised eyebrows. "You mean that he was able to heal their legs? Is he a wizard or an alchemist of—"

The doctor cut Zane off. "No, not heal. I meant it when I said lose. I helped to amputate the legs of some of those people myself. There was no saving them—a carriage had fallen on one of them. Crushed the bones beyond healing. But then Aluxen took them on, and they came back with prosthetic limbs."

Prosthetic? Zane remembered an iron-fisted soldier from the war whose hand could do nothing more than hold a sword. "So what? Prosthetic limbs can be found all across the city, if you have the money."

The doctor spoke with a small measure of reverence. "These are different. They moved perfectly like a normal limb. Beyond perfect, actually. I had thought one of those people had regrown their whole leg. A-and some of the patients even claim to feel things with them. Saints, it's no wonder that they worship him."

"Worship?"

He nodded. "Yes, that's part of the problem. A large group of the patients have gathered together in a small section of town not far from here to form a community around Aluxen. The locals call them clankers or clackers, due to the sound the limbs make when moving. It strikes me as something close to a cult, and the doctor is their living saint."

Hero worship? Zane had heard of extreme cases, but had never seen it. "Can you point me to the section of town they live in?"

Zane turned away and finished the last of the dishes and dried his hands. The old doctor's voice was hesitant. "I don't know. They're almost fanatical about him. Are you sure you would want to go there?"

Zane grinned despite the pain that fired up and down his limbs. "I'm sure."

The old man sighed and gave him directions. Zane collected his coat and headed out. That corner of the city was not far. It was a long, narrow street of shops with apartments above, ending in a cul-de-sac. Despite being small, it was packed with people. The air was filled with clicking and clacking. It seemed to come from everywhere. The sound from one person was subtle, but together they made a loud cacophony.

From his periphery, a young woman stepped forward to hand him a flower made from wire. Her sleeve slipped back to reveal a prosthetic limb. Covered in a painted flower design, it was beautiful—except the fingers. They were bony, like that of the dead. She smiled gently. "Welcome! Have you come seeking the doctor?"

Zane looked from the lady to the flower and back. Her eyes were bright, and her concern seemed genuine. "Yes, but how did you know?"

Her smile was disarming as she stepped closer to him. He stiffened as she pushed the end of the flower into his jacket pocket. The color and style of the flower clashed with his outfit, but he didn't try to remove it.

"My name is Laure."

Laure looked from his cane to his leg. Zane could feel her studying him. She gently grabbed Zane's free hand. "You have come to the right place. The good doctor can help you."

She pulled him through the crowd. The people cleared a path. He watched them as they watched him. Their eyes were sympathetic to his limp and exhausted stride. Laure looked Zane in the face.

"Many like you have come to see our doctor. He is unlike any other."

Laure pulled too fast for Zane to keep up, and his bad leg slipped in muck. He caught himself with a heavy thud, his cane stabbing into the street. With a jerk, he pulled his arm away to adjust himself.

Laure turned back to him with pity and embarrassment. "I'm sorry. I forget that each injury is different."

Her gaze focused on his leg. The intensity of her look made Zane move his bad arm behind him so it would be harder to see. He felt as if he was trying to hide a part of his soul.

Laure slowly stepped closer and tentatively reached toward him with a tender hand. "But the doctor can help you with it."

She motioned him forward, and with a heavy sigh, he followed. Shadow's red eyes reflected off of the local shop windows as they passed. *She seems nice enough, but she has a devoted feeling, like the caretakers of the temples of Zon.*

Zane didn't understand what Shadow meant by the temple, but he figured that it was like Church Madain, which cared for the palaces and priests. He shook his head and filed the information away for later.

Zane didn't like how the people watched him. The job was supposed to be him spying on the doctor, not meeting him. He couldn't miss the opportunity, though, so he continued to follow. This misunderstanding was as good a way as any to get an up-close view.

Laure stopped outside of a large building with a long window display. It was the biggest building on the block. Zane noticed several men stationed around it. Each gave him a suspicious look. The detective took a step back and looked over the building in more detail.

Laure remained next to him. "Are you not going inside?" he asked.

She shook her head. "The first meeting is always the most personal, so we like to give each person a chance to meet with the doctor alone. You are lucky to come at this time, because he is both in and with no other patient."

He looked at the office from across the street. The windows were amazingly clear. Zane looked at the roof overhang to keep the people who stood under it clean.

"You need to go over there."

"I'm not sure yet."

Laure gave a small nod, as if that answered everything. A broom leaned against the nearest corner of the building. One of the men would occasionally pick it up and sweep away all the ash that blew over.

On the overhang was a large mural, ash stuck to it in a patchy mess. Zane squinted to study it. There were thirteen figures, one in the middle dressed in what appeared to be gold, and six on each side. Six figures were dressed in white, while the opposite figures were dressed in gray, except for one in white that destroyed the symmetry of it.

Laure's voice interrupted his thought. "It's the mural of the first emperor and his twelve knights, from the founding of the empire."

Strange. Half the knights had died in the founding, so they are symbolized in white. The survivors are in gray, but why is one of the survivors in white? Zane pointed it out to her. "One of the survivors looks like one of the dead."

"That is how Dr. Aluxen wanted it. He says that is the correct 'truth' of the knights. We don't know what he means by it, but then again, does it matter?"

Showcasing the knights, even altered, was something usually reserved for government buildings or old grave sites. "Is he patriotic?"

Laure thought about it for a moment before shrugging. "He has never come across as such. I have never heard him or anyone else mention him talking about the empire."

"Then was it here before he took over? Left from the previous owner?"

She shook her head. "No, I saw when it was being installed. He looked very proud to see it hanging up there."

Zane's eyes shifted from the first king and his knights to the store name that hung above the door. Even from across the street, he could make out the name: The Body Shop. Something about the name left an unpleasant taste in his mouth, as if it was a bad joke.

Laure gently pulled on his sleeve. "You should really go over there. A new life is just through those doors."

His plan was only to scope out the surroundings, but he didn't want to seem suspicious. *Damn, I'm sticking out too much. Maybe I can play this off.* "What if something goes wrong and I lose the use of my leg? It hurts, but at least it works."

Zane leaned heavily on his cane, waiting to hear some response. Laure was soft-spoken at first, but her voice rose in calmness. "I was a small child, and I was playing in the streets. A carriage driver lost control of their horses. I-I tried to run, but I slipped. The carriage toppled over and fell on me. For better or worse, it landed on my leg and crushed it."

Laure pulled on the right side of her dress to reveal the ivory shine of another prosthetic, clean against the backdrop of the street. It reached from her shoe up past her knee. Zane flinched at the sight. Laure let the dress drop back down and brushed it flat. "I was more fortunate than a lot of the people here. My father taught me how to make these flowers to sell, so I wasn't just abandoned like so many others, but—"

Her voice brightened as she pointed to the shop across the street. "But the good doctor did the impossible. He gave me a new leg and arm. The ability to walk again. I can go anywhere and no one would look at me like I was a person to be pitied. I can imagine that you have gotten those looks, too."

Zane looked down to his leg. He had seen the look, of course, but what was he to do about it? He still had a leg to stand on, and he wasn't about to lose that. Zane pointed to the people that stood outside the store. "The doctor has a lot of guards for a man that heals people."

Laure's face grew grim, and she nodded. "It wasn't always like this. We had no need to guard the doctor. But recently we had a break-in and . . . it was rumored to be an attack on his life."

The guards had not looked away from Zane. They stared at him as if he might jump up and charge them. The detective forced a smile to Laure and nodded. "Thank you. I think I will head home for the day."

Laure tried to stop him. "But you came all this way. Why turn back now?"

He shrugged, trying to think of something. "It's been a long day, and this is a major decision. Lots to consider. I would like some time to decide. Thank you for being my guide."

"You will be back?"

Zane nodded. "I will be back," he said as he turned away.

The detective made his slow, tired way back home. A chill wind blew through the streets. His mind focused only on how clean Laure's prosthetic limbs were, as if the filth of the world could not touch them.

13

Shadow wondered how fish felt when it rained. Ripples, much like he'd felt with Vine's guard, radiated off the people of the district. He made a list in his mind of the things that could affect the Sea of Stars—it was short.

Something's not right. Only things connected to the damn Well should be able to do things on this scale.

Who knows about the Well? Another list, this one even shorter. He dipped his head out of the sea and watched from the comfort of the detective's shadow. Spying on those he passed, he noticed the majority had a prosthetic limb.

Damn, I should have listened better when Jefarson gave me an explanation about the working of shadows. Shadow had not talked to Jefarson in nearly fifty years, and then another thirty before that. The man was always busy with his many projects. Suspicion gnawed at the void that was his heart.

He dipped deep into the Sea and pulled as far as he could on his tether to Zane, testing the distance of the ripples he felt. He allowed himself into Zane's mind and listened through him to the conversation with Laure.

The disturbance of the Sea of Stars was all focused on the cul-de-sac they stood in. Fear slowly tightened on him. *Could this be a test zone for Jefarson? A cult? I have known a few, but would Jefarson use one for a cover?* The answers eluded him. It had been so long that he couldn't remember whether Jefarson preferred to use his family as caretakers of his experiments or whether he used guilds.

"It's the mural of the first emperor and his twelve knights from the founding of the empire."

Shadow stopped in his search and dove toward Zane. He

emerged and looked out across the street toward the mural. He listened, and fear took hold.

He had thought himself numb, and was shocked to feel, well, anything. *Damn it, one of them is involved.* He studied the mural's image and its strange change. The single white knight on the wrong side was something only he and a few others would have understood, that one of the six was now dead. He descended into almost-insane laughter, but stopped just short. *They think me dead!*

So close and far from freedom he felt. The detective's proximity to a hornets' nest put him on edge, but Shadow reminded himself that he could make it.

14

Alyssa walked among the endless halls made of shelves. Countless objects lay on them, but she couldn't make out any of them. All she could tell was each item was old and priceless. The rows continued to reach up into a yawning void of darkness that hung overhead.

With each step, she progressed toward a place that had left a scar in her heart. Around a bend, she found a glass orb, large enough to fit a person inside, resting on a metal base in the shape of a flower. Sweat dripped down the back of her neck as fear gripped her spine. She could hear faint breathing from behind her. She turned to see a familiar form. The clothes and hood were the same, but his body didn't look right.

"Agwen? What are—"

His eyes seemed to glow from the dark space of his hood. "We didn't need him in our department."

Confused and hurt, she responded to the specter. "What? No, Dennis had as much of a right as any of us. No, it's you and your secrets—"

Alyssa's voice was drowned out by a rough bark, like the laugh of a goblin. On a shelf above them stood Red Hood. His features were crueler than any living thing should be, and the color of his eyes matched the color of his hood. He smiled with his needle teeth. Agwen yelled at Alyssa, fighting Red Hood for her attention. Her eyes darted between the two as her heart beat faster and faster in her chest. Agwen cursed and charged her as the goblin dropped from his perch with blades in hand.

Agwen shoved Alyssa with all his might into the glassy surface of the memory sphere. Her body hit the form as the space faded from view. "I am sorry," Agwen called out. "I never meant to hurt you."

Alyssa flopped and rolled in bed, her sheets covered in a cold sweet. She pushed herself up and rested her face in her shaky hands. *What was that? That didn't feel like a normal dream.* Alyssa looked over to her nightstand at the soporific tea. "M-must've been a bad batch," she decided, getting out of bed. It was still early, before sunrise. She sighed. *It's still at least a couple of hours 'til I meet Zane and Frame.*

The compass following Rufus, the body collector, sat on the table by her books. She was shocked to see he was on the move already. She worried that she might not be able to find him efficiently.

Why do I need to find him? The bell rang out through the city, and she pushed that worry away for later.

She rubbed her tired eyes, deciding what she should do next. *I can wait, or I can go to Gruala's class.* With a resigned sigh, she dressed, collected her things, and stepped out into the hazy streets. She felt truly alone in the dim light of the street lamps, as if she was the last person in the world.

The dream of Agwen bothered her. *Blaming me for his decisions, but it was my dream of him. Am I blaming myself for his actions?* It was the hiring of Dennis that had pushed Agwen toward murder, which caused Zane to become involved. Agwen's actions just piled up from there as he worked to keep his misdeeds quiet.

Alyssa felt a wave of relief when she arrived at the edge of the Institute district. She made her way past a general store and around to a staircase that hung off the side, leading up to a second-floor room. It was just a few blocks away from the Magician's Café where she was going to meet Zane and Frame. Alyssa opened the door and was welcomed by the light and sounds of The Classroom.

The Classroom, as the instructor Gruala called it, was an open space that had once been used for storage. The floor had since been padded to help break students' falls. Gruala was a tall woman whose shoulders were as broad as any man Alyssa had met. Crisscrossing scars from a life she claimed to have left behind covered her forearms. Her face might have once been pretty, but it was now rough and worn like a statue that had seen too many hard seasons.

Alyssa had sought the place after Zane closed the case of The Wizard's Brew. Alyssa had felt powerless against all that happened to her, starting when Agwen pushed her into the old Fey device, just as she'd dreamed that morning. She had magic, but was it was only good if one had time to speak it.

Gruala noticed her deep thinking. "Ms. Benedictus? I didn't expect to see you here at this hour. You normally are one for the evening classes. . . . Are you doing all right this morning?"

The instructor was wearing the same clothes as the students, a soft long-sleeve shirt that crossed over the middle and tied closed on the far side. It was a garb from across the sea that she claimed was used for training.

Alyssa nodded. "Yes; just some dreams keeping me up. I have a meeting later this morning close to here, so I thought I would drop by."

Gruala nodded her head in sympathy. "I understand. Go get changed. We will help you through the morning, at least."

Without another word, Alyssa went to a private room and changed into the garb. The other women who had been within range to hear what Gruala said did not react to the comments. Gruala had made it her job to know their private lives and their past problems. She was always ready to help those who had been hurt, abused, and otherwise left to violence. They were all victims and survivors. Very few had stories as exciting as Alyssa's, but each had sought the same help. They wanted a way to defend themselves.

Alyssa stepped out onto the padded floor and found a partner. The two warmed up by practicing hand and wrist locks before moving onto larger joints. Once they had run through the list of possible moves they knew, Gruala started the core practice. They held their hands at the ready in front of them, each one trying to get a firm hold on the other. Their feet shuffled under them as they fought over positioning.

Alyssa was the first to miss the mark. She was taken by surprise when her partner snatched her outstretched arm. She flipped Alyssa over her back and down to the floor. Alyssa let out a gasp of air and slapped the floor as she had been taught to break the momentum of the fall. With that, she was fully warmed up, and the two continued.

An hour flew by before she knew it. She thanked Gruala and her partner. When Alyssa changed and walked back outside, the light from the clear sky over the Institute's plaza shined down. The dreams of the night were behind her, and she was ready for the day.

15

F rame wasn't sure when she noticed it, but once she did, she couldn't unsee it. The way Zane and Alyssa acted around each other was different from how they acted with others. Their arms were always almost touching, but never quite. Both had room to spare, but like two magnets, they pulled as close as they would allow. And yet, this never registered on either of their faces.

The clink of Zane's cup brought Frame's attention back to the conversation. "I'm going to go into The Body Shop and talk to the doctor," Zane said with a curled lip of disgust.

Alyssa looked up from her drink in concern. "Wait. I thought you were only going to watch them. Now you're going to go into that place?"

He gave a tired nod. "Yes, I've already been mistaken as a customer looking to have my leg replaced, so I am going to go with it, see if I can make contact, and investigate the place up close."

Frame took a note about the day's plan, and then looked to Alyssa. "Do you have anything to follow up on from the College of Surgeons?"

She shook her head, her gaze distant. "No, they said that Dr. Franxen Aluxen is not listed among their members."

"He could be using a false name."

"He could be, but we still don't have much to go on. I think I'm going to start looking into the Rush powder cases that we discussed with Lieutenant Kellim."

The detective rubbed his bad leg. "That's fine with me. If I need an extra hand, will you still be available?"

"Oh, yes. If you need anything, just let me know. Until then,

I'm going to check into some case files. I need some advice, though."

"Sure."

Alyssa shifted in her seat uncomfortably. "Well, from Kellim's description, I have a hunch. Mind you, only a hunch, but it may be . . . goblin-related."

Zane stopped and looked at her, concerned. "Goblin or Red—"

She cut him off. "I don't know, but do you have any idea of how to check?"

He was quiet for a moment before shaking his head. "No, I don't. I think you would have to ask a goblin about goblin things. I could go ask the mob, but I'd rather not."

She sighed in frustration before smiling in realization. "I don't need to go to the mob. I can send a charmed letter to Neb, the art dealer. He might be able to help."

"He might. Give it a try."

Frame had finished her notes for their case. "Anything else we need to cover?"

They shook their heads and stood to leave. Frame bowed slightly in appreciation. "Thank you both for meeting me here, outside of the office."

Zane and Alyssa smiled and made their way out into the cold city. The ash looked like snow to Frame as she stared out the café's window. She watched as a young boy with a rag tied to a pole stepped up to the window and wiped it clean.

Frame turned to the blank paper in front of her, trying to decide what to report to her cousin. She dearly wished that the letter was charmed so she could go straight home once she was finished, but it was just a regular letter. Frame would have to go to a postmaster to send it to her cousin.

With a sigh, she picked up her pen and started.

Dear cousin Vine,

My first act as the family's agent is going well so far. The trust placed in the combined work of Alyssa and Zane is well deserved. In the last week, the two have scoured the city searching for information about Dr. Franxen Aluxen. Alyssa found that he is not listed among the ranks of the College of Surgeons.

Zane found a lead by asking around the city's house doctors for information. From there, he found a house doctor who had worked with Dr. Aluxen in the past. He was directed to a small, hidden part of the city in the Racker district. Being somewhat isolated from the rest of the city, Dr. Aluxen works as the beating heart of sorts for the local community. All the people who work there have benefited from his prosthetic limbs. Zane stated that the prosthetics there are the best he has ever seen. On that fact alone, he doesn't believe the doctor to be a fraud.

He clarified, though, that the doctor's actions might not be legal. I am not sure what the arrangement is between our grandmother and the doctor, yet we should monitor it lest we become involved in something illicit. As you are aware, she has a habit of trifling in things that most would not dare try. This could be another one of her "self-care" projects.

I shall keep you informed as soon as possible.

Frame set the pen aside and closed the inkwell. To send Vine a charmed letter would be a simple thing to do, but Vine refused to receive charmed letters when she couldn't return them. Frame silently cursed her cousin for refusing to hire a state mage for the job, or instead waiting for her to graduate. The family's last one had passed with the rest of her family. *I am the wizard replacement,* she reminded herself. It was a sad thought that her days at the Institute would end one day.

Looking at her half-full cup, she laughed. She had gotten more sleep in the last week than she had in the previous two semesters. Perhaps it wouldn't be all bad.

"Frame! I-I think you have been avoiding me."

Frame looked up to find her ex-boyfriend, Felix, with a charming smile, but she wanted nothing more than to disappear. "I don't want to talk to you."

Felix pulled out the chair Alyssa had sat in, moving the cups and small plates to the side. "Let me pay for your breakfast here. Waiter—"

"It's been paid for already."

She folded her letter, placed it in the envelope, and sealed it. "Was it the couple that was sitting here? They seemed nice. Are they relatives of yours?"

Frame looked up at him, aggravated. Felix's smile seemed genuine, but she realized he was fishing for more information about her. She gently laid the letter down. "Please understand: We're over. You don't need to feel jealous."

"Jealous? Nothing to be jealous of. You were having breakfast and talking about your family."

How long had he been sitting there listening, watching me? What is he thinking?

Felix called out to the owner. "Is it possible to get the heat turned up?"

The owner smiled with a nod before turning to a group of students sitting around the stove. "Time to earn your pay, boys."

One of the boys sighed, but stood up and started to work the arcane stove. Frame shook her head. Being a part of the Institute gave them the privilege of wearing rune-laced clothes. Their clothes held several features, including repelling ash and dirt. "There is no reason for that! You know that these are our Institute clothes. They have runes to warm themselves."

He brushed off her words with a wave of his hand. "Bah, those runes have hurt people. I know a guy named Dave, and let me tell you he burnt his butt with those runes. Turned them on and *boom*! The rune overheated."

Frame rolled her eyes, as it was not the first time she had heard the story. Dave was an idiot who altered the rune to be constantly on and caused it to overheat. She fished out a stamp and pressed it to the envelope. "Look, I need to go mail this. It was great seeing you, Felix."

His face became downcast, but he tried to shrug it off. "What? But we could have a drink or some food—"

Frame ignored him and continued out the door. As she stepped out into the street, she could hear him calling out. "Sure, sure, we will catch up some time."

She reached inside her clothes and found the rune. The coat began to warm itself against her body. She smiled to herself, being careful not to turn the temperature up too much.

The air was gaining a chill that flew through the wind like invisible razor blades, cutting everyone to the bone. The streets here were cleaner than most in the city due to their proximity to the Institute's plaza. The famous tower, designed and built by the Institute, kept the plaza clear of clouds, smog, and even fog. It was the only sunny spot in the city.

Frame walked along The Learned Avenue, one of several streets that surrounded the Institute. Here, all sorts of rare goods could be acquired, along with many things that were completely useless. Exotic goods poured in for research and study.

Frame made her way to the post office and sent the letter off. Outside the postmaster's office, she noticed a man standing across the street. A burnt cigarette hung loosely in his mouth. A hood hung over his face, but she noticed a patch covering his left eye. He reached for the cigarette with his right hand, knocking the end off with clumsy movements. Before turning away, the man worked his fingers back and forth.

He walked back from the direction she had come, except on the opposite side of the street. It was strange—it felt like the man had been watching her. Her muscles tensed, and she pulled her warm coat closer. "Creep," she mumbled under her breath as she turned on her heel and made her way to her apartment, following the flow of other students heading back.

16

Zane's whole body ached as he found his way back to the small corner of the city where Dr. Aluxen's shop was. The healing brew had helped take the edge off at first, but had since worn off. The knots from his leg and shoulder ached with each step. He could feel the ash clinging to his coat, dirtying him. His mind went to what he'd had to do to clean his shirt last night.

He rubbed his forehead at the futility of cleanliness, even as the growing filth assaulted him. The cul-de-sac was abuzz with people moving goods and shopping. The air hummed with the noise of people and the clicking of their prosthetic limbs. It was almost annoying. Zane wondered how the people could even think.

Near the edge of the district, Zane saw Laure selling her crafted flowers. She smiled at his approach. "Oh, I am so glad you decided to return today!"

He tried to shrug, but his stiff shoulders didn't move easily. "I said that I would be back."

She smiled and waited for Zane to make his way, then followed beside him. "Have you put any thought into how the doctor can help you?"

Zane had not put any extra thought into that. He was here for a case. "Yes, it might be beneficial for me—"

She finished the thought. "To be free of this cane."

Laure's smile was bright and infectious. Zane caught himself with a cough and corrected any changes to his face. "I don't know about that. There are some benefits to a cane, such as being able to rest on it or use it to protect myself."

"I had not thought of that, but if your leg was not injured, then you wouldn't need to rest on the cane."

He nodded in agreement as they strolled through the growing crowd of people until they stood in front of The Body Shop. Even after a night of rest, the name still felt distasteful to Zane. The men standing outside the day prior were still there under the mural, protecting themselves from the ash.

Zane turned to Laure and gave a slight bow. "Thank you for showing me the way. I hope you have a good day."

She nodded. "I hope by the saints and the first knights that you find what you're looking for."

He eyed the motif above the eave. "By the first knights?"

Laure smiled brightly, then pointed him to the door. "Dr. Franxen Aluxen."

She turned away, making her way back through the crowd. He shook his head and turned his attention to The Body Shop. The men stared at him with a mixture of suspicion and understanding. He took a deep breath, then walked past the guards to the door. A bell above the door rang out to announce his presence as the door swung closed with a loud slam. He waited a few seconds before moving around the shop.

Zane was disturbed by the dozens of prosthetic limbs hanging from the ceiling. He poked the limbs of different sizes and shades of bone white and yellow with his cane and watched them swing back and forth from their hook. Zane's stomach turned at the sight, and he turned his face down to the floor. The place felt like a twisted butcher shop.

Sitting on a nearby table were more complicated devices. One of them caught Zane's attention. He picked the machine up and looked it over, being cautious with each movement. Nearby attachments showed it was a model of a lung. A thin leather bag acted as the lung itself, with tubing to mimic the rest.

It was a simple design that replicated the movement of the lungs, but Zane knew it wouldn't work. Zane remembered a medical class featuring a similar design. It was a grim lesson about the evidence of it being placed in a person and how it never worked quite like a real lung would. The next item was even more ridiculous, but more finely crafted: A three-chamber heart pump.

The right chamber of the heart was set aside from the rest. Small pipes acted as the veins, and small internal pumps acted as the muscle. It was so well-made that it might have been able to replicate the motions of the organ. As he looked through the parts, though, he couldn't find the one that could actually do the pumping.

The sound of a door closing snapped Zane's attention away from the heart. The man who entered wore a leather apron lined with carving tools. "Hello, stranger. I am Dr. Franxen Aluxen."

Zane set the artificial heart down on the table. "I am Zane Vrexon. I was admiring your work."

"Are you a doctor of sorts?"

The detective shook his head. "No, but I was studying to be one before I joined the war effort. Where did you get your training?"

"I was never really an academic sort. I was trained in the field as an Army surgeon, though I would dare say my skills are better than that of a normal doctor."

Zane knew several Army surgeons. Some were very impressive, while others left him afraid to be their patient. "What made you start your own practice? Surely you didn't leave the Army just to be pestered by the College of Surgeons one day."

Dr. Aluxen looked at the window as one of the bodyguards stood just outside it, cleaning the glass. "In my last campaign, I learned something. Something extraordinary, and I knew that I needed to share it with the world. Can you find fault with that?"

Zane followed his gaze. "If you mean those people out there, and the help you have given them, then I can't."

Dr. Aluxen cleared his throat and picked up a roll of measuring tape. "What do you do for a living?"

Zane smirked. "Does it matter?"

"I get all sorts. Some come here looking for ways to save their crafts, and others just for the simple power to walk."

Zane turned his face away while his free hand fingered the outline of his flask. Aluxen looked kind, with a smile and beard that reminded Zane of his grandfather.

"So, what can I do to be of help?" The doctor's eyes slowly lowered and followed the cane to the floor.

Zane avoided the question. "I may have heard of your skill in the newspaper, and now seeing it in person, I am shocked."

The doctor raised an eyebrow. "Shocked how?"

"How accurate the newspapers were."

The doctor smiled and gestured toward Zane's leg. "So then would you like to have one of your own?"

Zane followed the stare to his leg. He tapped the floor with his cane. "I know what this cane cost me, and I know that I can get another. But what do your limbs cost me?"

"Are we bargaining now?"

Zane shook his head. "The war I served in was the Ghoul War. Between it and medical school, I know that a good prosthetic costs a lot. A magically enhanced one is something that only the very elite can afford, usually nobles. But your limbs are different. I would say they're better."

The doctor turned around and pulled a limb off a nearby hook. He ran one hand up and down the thigh's length. "How so?"

Zane smiled and shuffled his weight from his cane to leaning against a table. "It's the range of motion. I've never seen a prosthetic do what you have made them do. The grace and precision are unthinkable for someone not using magic. But you're not a wizard of any sort."

The doctor laid a leg next to Zane and pulled out a tape measure. With it, he motioned for Zane to show his leg. With a tired sigh, the detective obliged. "How do you know I don't employ magic? How can you be so sure?"

The detective pointed to the front. "You don't have a sign of magic authorization in your window. The Institute is strict about such things."

Aluxen took more measurements of Zane's leg. The length of his thigh, shin, foot, then the width of each. "A keen eye, sir. Most don't care for such things so long as they can get what they need. But I assure you that my prosthetics are not something that the Institute needs to worry about."

"Because they are not magical?"

Aluxen looked up with a polite smile. "Because they are little miracles. Just like everyone out there will say, saints and the first knights as witness."

Aluxen stood up and brushed off his knee. "Now, Mr. Vrexon, I have a question for you. What is the worth of a limb?"

Zane looked at his leg, and then glanced at his right arm. The worth of my leg, my arm . . . what a strange question. What are my limbs worth? He shook his head. "That's a silly question. How can you judge something like that?"

Aluxen's attention returned to the leg on the table, gesturing to it with his hand. "Everyone answers that question differently. It is interesting to hear how people respond to it. Some say it's worth their life, others say it's a matter of convenience, and others still say it is a matter of the respect they are given—"

The doctor stopped and stared at Zane with a hard glare for a moment before smiling again. "This is the next step in the medical field. These are easy to make and give the best range of motion out of all prosthetics ever. With them, people won't need to deal with shame, pain, or despair. Just think about it: You can walk the streets without a cane, without worry of your leg giving way. No longer would you be limited by a defect of your body."

The confidence in Aluxen's face sparked emotion in the detective. A wave of emotions that he was not expecting washed over him at the word "defect." Anger, confusion, grief, and pride.

He wished he didn't live in pain, but he also felt anger at his leg being called a *defect*. His arm and leg were scarred, weakened, but they were his, a price he had paid in full to survive. He turned away from the doctor.

The doctor seemed to notice how he felt and slowly set the leg back on the hook. "Sometimes worth is a personal thing."

Zane frowned and shook his head. "It's a stupid question. What is the worth of anything?"

"Nothing, until we give it worth, and even then, does it hold the same value if it can be replaced?"

The detective turned to face Aluxen. The wrinkles added to the kindness of his face, but there was a greed about him. "Perhaps the cost for this would be too great for me to afford."

Aluxen chuckled with a nod. "Give it some thought and come back later. No reason to make a decision today."

"Are you sure?"

"Yes. For most, this is their only option. But your limb is still, for the most part, usable. All the same, an injured patient is always welcome."

Zane bowed politely. "Thank you."

The detective left as quickly as his stiff leg would let him. The people standing around the shop watched him with suspicion. He pretended not to notice. The crowds parted as he walked away from The Body Shop. He was a block away when a man bumped into him.

"Hey, watch it!"

Zane changed the grip on his cane, ready to swing it, when the man grabbed and pulled him close. "Meet me at Laze Pot. The password is *False Eye*."

"What?"

The man shoved Zane away. "You better keep walking!"

The man walked away quickly. Confused, Zane looked around until he spotted a pub with a dirty sign above the door: *Laze Pot*. Zane turned back around to look for the man, but couldn't find him. Zane shook his head. "I should have gone home earlier." With a grunt, he pushed off toward the door.

17

lyssa stood in the central hall of the Imperial Guard Bureau. The clerk in front of her was taking his time. "Are you sure you want to see these reports? I mean, they're filled with murder and stuff. It ain't something a woman should be dealing with."

She nodded. "For the seventh time, yes. I am sure Lieutenant Kellim told me that I could pick up these reports, and I am here at his request."

The clerk sighed and slid a waiver across to her. "Then I need you to sign this. It states that you'll be responsible for bringing them back in one piece. These are private and confidential, so you are not to leak any of this to the newspaper. Them damn idiot reporters like to write about anything they can get their hands on, even if they don't know nothing about what they're writing."

The clerk went on complaining about the newspaper, from the writers themselves to the quality of the paper. Alyssa ignored him, moving as fast she could to fill out the document. After the last signature, she picked up the stack of paper and made her way out the door.

She returned to her apartment, worried that she'd be late for her meeting. She was a day late in getting the reports because the bureau had been busy preparing copies. She had planned to spend the previous evening reading and going over the files herself first.

She reached into her pocket and pulled out her compass. Its needle pointed east and was moving south. Alyssa was glad to know that her charm was still working, but was worried it might fail before she had a chance to prepare for . . .

What am *I preparing for?*

The bell rang out six times across the city, marking the hour, just as she got to the ground floor of her apartment building. She cursed to herself and rushed up the stairs, holding the leather bundle tightly in both arms. She expected to see her guest, but no one stood outside her door.

She breathed a sigh of relief, thinking she had beaten them there. As she got ready to unlock her door, however, she found it ajar.

Alyssa was about to call into the room, but a passage in one of her books halted her: "If you feel in danger, then you are, and surprise is only good once." She moved the bundle under one arm, and quietly pulled her thin wand from the hidden slit in her clothes. She took a deep breath and prepared a charm to block wand fire in case she was being ambushed.

She slowly pushed the door open and stepped into her home. She eased down the hallway, stopping just before turning into the rest of the apartment. She had steadied herself and was ready to move into action when a voice came from around the corner.

"Miss Benedictus, is that you?"

"Neb?"

Alyssa relaxed and stepped around the corner. Two goblins sat at her kitchen table. The one who had spoken was dressed in a tailored suit and hat, while the other was wearing the patched, dirty clothing of a factory worker. Neb's smile was apologetic. "Sorry about the inconvenience. We noticed that you were running a little late, but my associate did not like the idea of waiting in the hall or outside. In fact, he refused and said it was too dangerous."

Alyssa put her wand up and smiled. "That's all right. I was worried that someone had broken into my apartment."

The factory-dressed goblin spoke in his native language, pointing at Alyssa's wand pocket. Neb nodded to him before turning to Alyssa. "He says you weren't worried enough because you were only using a low-grade wand, meant for stunning."

She noticed the factory goblin watching her with interest. "Give me just a moment. I'm going to shut my door."

Alyssa shut the front door and joined them at the table, setting down the leather bundle. Neb stood up on his chair to lean closer. "Are these the files that you spoke about in your letter?"

She nodded. "Yes, I have a gut feeling, I think is what Zane would call it. I believe that these cases may be connected with the goblin known as Red Hood."

She glanced at the factory goblin, who was brushing ash from his body onto the floor. "Is he the specialist you spoke of?"

Neb nodded. "Oh, yes. As I deal in fine arts, my friend here is also someone of a specific skill set and certain insight."

The goblin nodded and spoke, still in Goblin, which sounded like sharp barks.

"What did he say?"

"That his name is Zeub and that he used to be a soldier for the Northern Union Clans before the empire absorbed them. Claims to have seen just about every form of goblin combat."

Alyssa nodded and extended her hand to Zeub. The goblin looked it over for a moment before shaking it.

"Pleasure to meet you. I am Alyssa Benedictus."

The former professor unwrapped the bundle and passed the first document out. She was trying to hand Zeub a copy when he said something.

Neb coughed politely. "He said that he can't read Hume."

"Oh, sorry. Then if it's all right, I'll read them out loud."

She opened the file and started to read through it. Neb stopped her at different points, asking for clarity. Line by line, they went over the scene, then the autopsy. By the end, Zeub was nodding his head, and after a moment he began talking.

Neb translated. "He says that these do sound like standard goblin ambush strategies for humans. He says that they follow the pattern. Drop onto the shoulder and ride them, making allies hesitate to strike or hit their friend. Use the shoulder mount, then drop to the ground and go for the thighs near the groin to bleed them dry. Then exit out the same way through some ceiling exit."

Alyssa spoke to herself, almost under her breath. "But does

that mean that it's Red Hood?"

Zeub shrugged his shoulders and said some more.

"He says it could be. Says he trained several toward the end of the war."

She could feel a lump in her throat and her face paling. "Please go into more detail. I-I would like to document it."

I understand now . . . "certain insights." Alyssa felt like she had a stroke of luck at having Red Hood's mentor here to answer her questions. In an empty journal, she wrote down answers to every question that would form in her head, from Red Hood's involvement in the war to what he was trained to do and more. Zeub answered some of them and politely refused others.

The day waned into night and she did all she could to familiarize herself with the tactics of goblin ambushes. They then went back to the cases. As the hour grew late, Zeub stopped her reading.

"He asks what you are doing."

"What? I'm collecting information, so that I can—"

"Can what? Are you thinking about chasing Red Hood?"

Her hand mindlessly dropped down to her old wound. A slight dread quickly spiraled into fear. "I am not chasing!"

Zeub narrowed his eyes before dropping them to where her wand hung under her clothes. He nodded and spoke in a broken accent. "Monsters make monsters."

What?

Zeub got off his chair and stretched his back. He barked at Neb before making his way to the door. Neb turned to her. "He says he is done for the day."

Neb collected his things, but stopped before turning toward the doorway. "Miss Benedictus, please be careful."

Neb slipped out with Zeub into the darkness. She brewed a cup of tea and pored over the files. She thought for a moment about whether she was chasing Red Hood. Holding her side, she shook her head and went back to studying.

18

Frame stepped around the etchers who worked on the door frame of her apartment. They were busy reconstructing the old security runes. Inside the lobby, an Institute inspector was speaking to another resident. "So the man had several scars on his face and different-colored gloves. Anything else you can think of?"

The woman shook her head, her hand clinging to her chest. "N-no. I told him he was not supposed to be here and that he needed to leave. He grabbed my arm when I was about to call for help."

The inspector was writing it all down as she spoke. "What did you do next?"

"What did you think I did? I screamed!"

The woman had tears in her eyes. The inspector's gaze was distant, but his voice was tinged with concern. He placed a gentle hand on her shoulder. "It's okay. You did everything right. I will pass this information around and see what we can find."

The story of a stranger getting into the apartment building disturbed Frame. *The inspector will take care of everything.* Even as she reassured herself, she looked over her shoulder in fear of someone being behind her. As she fished out the keys for her apartment door, her neighbor Diana came out of her apartment.

"Frame! You weren't at the lab last night. Are you doing okay?"

She forced a smile. "Yeah, but it's complicated. I-I guess I'm on school leave. I have a family situation."

Diana frowned. "Did something happen?"

Frame shook her head and then motioned Diana into her apartment. "No, but let's not talk about this in the hall."

They stepped inside. Frame lit the gas lamps and light flooded the room. Frame set the kettle to boil as they got comfortable. "So what's going on?"

"My cousin Vine—yes, that one—pulled me out of the Institute to help with a . . . job."

Diana raised an eyebrow. "What type of job could she need your help with?"

The kettle whistled, and Frame poured them each a cup of tea. "Well, my great-grandmother, have I told you about her?"

Diana nodded as she took the cup. "Besides your cousin, she's your only living relative and she pays for your Institute fees. She owns a merchant business, right?"

Frame bit her lip, feeling weird talking about her family. She had kept quiet about the details because she felt like she didn't really match them, not like how they matched each other. "Yes and no. My grandmother is Clelia Lexone, the matriarch of the Lexone family. We own one of the biggest shipping companies in the empire."

Diana's eyes went wide and she nearly spilled her tea. Frame was not surprised by her shock.

"A Lexone! Wait, does that mean you're a noble?"

"I guess, technically. My great-grandfather had bought a title, though I think it currently belongs to my great-grandmother."

"Still, anyone who has worked in a store knows the name. Why didn't you say so?"

Frame stared down at the steam from her teacup, remembering the smoke from the fires of her childhood. "I was a member of a minor branch, not part of the main family, b-but there was a disease outbreak that wiped out most of my relatives. We had to burn their bodies. We weren't even allowed to bury them."

Diana was deep in thought, reflecting some internal embarrassment. "I never knew. I always assumed that you were of a noble station just because you seemed to know everyone, but I never would have thought . . ."

Frame picked up her cup and rubbed the rim before taking

a drink. *There was no way that you would have known.* She had deliberately not told people about her family connections. "It's all right."

"But what does this have to do with this job?"

Frame frowned. "Well Clelia has always sought to keep looking young. She has spent more money in her life than anyone can imagine. Mostly potions, medical baths, and herbs. However, from time to time, especially as she got older, she's been taken advantage of."

Diana took a gulp of the tea and rested the cup in her hands. "So you're checking to make sure that your great-grandmother hasn't been, or isn't about to be, scammed. That seems like a lot to ask a student. I don't want to sound like I'm questioning your ability, but—"

Frame cut her friend off to stop the awkward rambling. "No, no. I really don't think I have the skill to be able to handle this. She hired a detective named Zane Vrexon and the former professor Alyssa Benedictus. They're doing the work, but I am to report their findings to Vine."

Confusion spread across Diana's face as she set her cup down. "But why you? Surely that is something someone else could have done. Or no one. Couldn't the detective report to your cousin himself?"

Frame thought it over. "I don't know, but this is part of the reason I'm here at the Institute. Things like this will be part of my family duty once I graduate. Though knowing my cousin, she has something else in mind, some other angle. She's like that, trying to outplay everyone. On the bright side, I'll get some free time to work on my thesis. I also plan to buy plenty of stuff and charge it to her."

Her friend raised her cup with a smile. "Now *that* is a way to keep positive!"

A bell rang as Zane entered the pub. The small tables were close together, illuminated by candles. He noticed the people at the tables were wearing clothes typical of their own trades. Behind the counter were rows of bottles of various sizes, shapes, and colors. Zane wondered how many were reused bottles with generic watered-down drinks. A man with a mustache that curled at the ends waved for Zane to come over. With a grunt, the detective limped toward the open counter space.

"What can I get ya?"

Zane hesitated for a moment. "Do you have a drink called . . . False Eye?"

The bartender raised an eyebrow and nodded. "Ah, yes. That's a special brew that I keep in the back. Please follow me."

He stepped from behind the counter and opened a door leading to a small hallway. The bartender stopped in front of a black door that had a strange, oily shine to it. From his pocket, he pulled a key that looked to be made of granite. Zane noticed the hesitation and the concern he showed in handling the key, as if the bartender feared the key might hurt him. The door unlocked with a loud thud and a faint ripple. Magic!

Zane's suspicions were further confirmed when he noticed the hinges were on the wrong side. The bartender motioned for Zane to step inside. "False eye. Just go through this door, sir."

The bartender watched Zane with caution as he stepped past him into the dimly lit room. The room was old and plain, but the bare walls seemed to be flickering, hurting his head. The flickering disappeared after the door clicked shut behind him.

Zane shook his head, trying to rid himself of the sensation of vertigo caused by the shift. He tried to focus on the room around him to fight the feeling. In the corner were posts that touched the ceiling and walls. Runes danced across them, glowing and changing color. Two men looked over maps and drawings on a table lit by an arcane lamp built into the center. The younger of the two looked up at Zane. "The detective is here."

The other man nodded and waved for Zane to come closer. He limped forward. The bald man put out his cigar in an overflowing ashtray. "Detective Vrexon, we finally meet. I am Special Agent Will, from the Institute of Sorcery and Science. This is Crome."

Will crossed his arms and half-turned away from Zane, back to the maps on the table. Zane felt a tension in the air as the two agents shared a look. The silence in the room was eerie. Shadow whispered in his ear. *This place isn't natural, and it's not safe. If these men want to meet with you, let's get on with it.*

Not safe? Not safe for me or for you? The pain in the detective's head was growing slowly, and he winced. Now was not the time for those questions. Zane marched over to the table, his cane reverberating on the floor. To his surprise, it sounded like there was empty space below. "So, what's this meeting about?"

The two men looked at each other. Crome sighed and gave a defeated shrug. Will slid a paper over to Zane. The detective raised an eyebrow at the drawing of Dr. Franxen Aluxen.

Will pointed at the picture. "We want to know what you are doing around this man. We saw you come by yesterday and go into his shop today."

Zane's blood began to boil as he put the drawing down. *Of course my case is being looked into by the Institute.* He absentmindedly fingered the empty flask as he felt his throat tighten. "He is the subject of a case that I am looking into."

"What is the nature of your case?"

Zane shrugged. "Not much. A client asked me to look into the doctor to make sure he wasn't a con man."

Will's face looked grim. "What do you think after meeting

him?"

"I have only met him once, and that wasn't my original plan," Zane said. "I just wanted to observe him, but the locals mistook me as a future patient."

"That doesn't answer the question." Crome grumbled.

"The people living in that neighborhood are proof that he has some type of skill. After looking at those prosthetics up close, I know that they have to be made with some type of magic."

This time, Will raised an eyebrow. "Why do you say that?"

Zane smoothed out his vest. "I have seen my share of prosthetic limbs, and none of them came even close to moving like those. But I assume there's a lot more going on if you two are here."

Will nodded his head.

"You can say that," Crome said. "We agree with you. Nothing from the science departments can match the movements of those limbs. In fact, some of them look downright impossible. He has no permit for magic here, so we think he is using something that we are not aware of. That's the sort of thing the Institute dislikes—things it doesn't understand."

"Can't you just take it? I thought any illicit magic could be taken by the Institute."

Will laughed and shook his head. "Yeah, we can take anything that we can prove is magical. The prosthetics don't show any of the normal signs of magic, though. No runes, no activations, and no spell wicks of any sort. We have no damn clue as to what is powering them. We have used every method we can think of to study them from afar."

Zane could already feel that this case had turned personal to them. "Since you can't prove it's magic, why are you still here?"

Crome glared at Zane. "Because we know it has to be magic. Until we can prove it, we are here."

Zane looked down to the table with its three distinct maps of the district. He noticed the different dates on them and that each one had a different floor plan where Aluxen's Body Shop stood now. "Then why stop me? I just met the man."

Will rubbed his head and pulled out a new cigar, lighting it with an eldritch word. "You made a name for yourself when you pulled the Institute's pants down by discovering that black market dealing. Unofficially, we are to avoid you like the plague, but I will take any help, no matter where I can get it."

Zane felt irritated as Will's cigar ash fell onto the table and maps. The detective held back the desire to clean the mess. "But why me? Don't you have your own agents to send?"

The two looked at each other, and the tension grew. "We did, but something . . . happened."

Zane didn't like their look. It must be personal to them. "What happened?"

Will seemed nervous. "That is classified, and we don't even know if it is related."

Crome slammed his fist on the table. "That's bull, and you know it! We both know it's related."

Will glared at Crome until he backed away from the table, then turned to Zane. "Whatever you find out, we would like you to pass it on. Likewise, anything we can find out related to your case, we will pass on to you."

Zane thought about it for a moment before extending a hand. "That is fine with me. How do we communicate?"

Will quickly shook his hand before turning to his work. Crome returned to the table, his face less red than before. "We are here most days. Just give the password to the bartender. If we aren't here, he will take a message for us."

As Zane moved from the table and started back to the door, his temples pulsed. The door shook as he opened it to the hall. He noticed right away now that this space didn't feel like it was moving, and the pressure from his head was gone. He sighed and shook his head. *Why is there never a simple case?*

Shadow answered: *Because you would get bored.*

20

Back at the office, Shadow marveled from his corner at the former professor's surprise. "What do you mean that agents of the Institute are spying?"

Zane repeated to Alyssa who he had met. Shadow could almost feel the exhaustion in Zane's voice. "Why are you shocked that there are agents from the Institute watching? Everyone knows that the Institute is part of the empire."

"Yes, I guess I wasn't expecting this case to take a turn like that. Agents are usually a sign of illicit magic use, which can be dangerous. Those that practice outside of the Institute don't always have the safety measures that they should."

"Such as?"

Alyssa looked for the right words. "The more power behind magic, the more likely it is to rampage when let loose. That is the reason safety runes are used, or special materials. Gaining that knowledge and acquiring those materials is difficult without the Institute's resources."

Zane pulled out a bottle of Troll's Blood. As he poured it into his flask, Shadow whispered in his ear. *Should you really be drinking that much? Your body is completely fine.*

Zane eyed him with disgust before turning back to his partner. "So can we trust them?"

Frame sat quietly across from Alyssa. The former professor thought for a moment before answering. "I believe so, since they did come to you. But what if the doctor really is a miracle worker?"

Shadow had met living saints before, real miracle workers. This doctor had none of their qualities. He even laughed to himself at how the saints he had met were always hated, while the doctor was so loved. *Saints are never loved while alive.*

The image of the knights above the shop unnerved Shadow, the sign of his old comrades and their organization. Aluxen was working for them, but how closely? *They think me dead. Perhaps it's better to keep it that way.*

He whispered to the detective, unsure how much he should tell him. *I would think twice before getting too involved in this case.*

The detective gave Shadow a questioning glance before looking back at the women. "So we have established that Dr. Franxen, while not a fraud, might be a criminal, but we're still not sure. I suppose this all rests on whether he's using magic."

Alyssa spoke up first. "Then what does this leave us to do?"

Zane rubbed his eyes as one hand reached down for the bottle. Shadow cut him off. *It's still early to drink that.*

The detective glared and pulled his hand back. He straightened his clothes as he stood up. Picking up a broom and pan, he went about cleaning. Shadow relaxed, knowing that despite Zane's pain and hatred for him, the detective knew his drinking habit was bad.

"I have something I'm going to look into tomorrow night."

"What's that?"

Zane swept the floor as he explained. "The agents had some old maps, and it looked like different floor plans. I'm guessing the building's been burned or torn down at least twice. It reminded me of a case I worked on some time ago."

"What case?"

"I was looking into some stolen goods, but the thief led me to an abandoned building. I searched that place over but couldn't find anything. I waited, and sure enough, I caught him coming out of the floor. The place had once been burned down and built on top of. I took a look inside the floor space. It looked like smugglers had come through some time ago and made a hold for themselves."

Frame raised a hand. "What should we do?"

Zane shrugged. "Whatever you want, but you could give an update to your cousin. No reason to keep a client in the dark."

Shadow shook his head at the comment. *If only you knew how much in the dark all of you are . . . then you would know the dangerous game you are so close to.*

21

lyssa pulled her compass from her pocket. The paper-wrapped needle glowed dimly, moving as she moved. It was the first time she had created a tracking charm, and she didn't know how long it would last.

She patted the wands hidden under her clothes. Her jacket was made in the style recommended by the book *Wand Dueling: A Comprehensive Guide*. She hoped that what the book said about it being able to resist edged weapons was true, though she didn't plan to test it any time soon. Having some form of protection from a knife would be nice. Her hand absentmindedly touched the spot where she had been stabbed.

The needle led her deeper into parts of town that a sane woman wouldn't normally dare to go alone. She forced herself to walk with confidence, letting the compass guide her. People called out to her from covered spots that hid them from the majority of the ash. She ignored them and kept moving.

The hourly bells had rung twice since she had marched off in search of the rat-faced man. *What am I doing following a corpse collector?*

The needle turned sharply, pointing her down an alley. Alyssa could see a group of people sipping on bottles of various shapes and sizes. A rainbow shine reflected on their lips.

With a touch of hesitation, she stepped into the alley. "Do you have any money, ma'am? Can you help us? Do you have any brews?"

Each one of them wanted something from her, with some more direct than others. One older lady with a large tumor on her neck held a bottle of green sludge. Alyssa's stomach felt sick at the sight of the brown flakes floating atop the sludge, so she ignored everything and moved forward. At its far end, the alley opened into another street. Across the street was an apartment building with another group of people surrounding the entrance.

A wagon was parked in the middle of the crowd. Ash stuck to the wheels and its white side. When she approached the edge of the crowd, she could hear people talking to each other. There was crying all around her.

"Why did this happen? Were they dealing illegal goods?"

"Yeah, but even the guards don't care about people like us unless they want to try to look good in front of someone."

A man with a dirty mustache yelled to the guard looking over the bodies as they were pulled out of the building and laid out on the ground. "Who did this?"

The guard looked tired. "It's the work of some thugs," he said.

It's not just thugs, but goblins. Maybe even Red Hood! This was what she was looking for. Alyssa squeezed her way through the crowd, forcing her way closer to the dead. Sheets had been thrown over the body without care, leaving many of their injuries in view of the crowd. She could see the shoulders of a couple of the bodies, they were bloody from what looked like knife wounds. The injuries reminded her of several drawings she had seen in the reports.

She stepped closer to inspect the bodies, but a guard intercepted her. "Ma'am, you can't come here."

"I can help. I've studied the recent string of attacks."

The guard shook his head. "Attacks, what? This really isn't any place for a woman. Go home."

Alyssa pulled her state badge from her clothes and showed it. The guard's face twisted in confusion. He turned and yelled for his boss. Kellim trotted over, armed with a smile that overflowed with confidence. "Alyssa Benedictus, I was not expecting to see you. Are you here with the detective?"

She didn't expect to see him either. "No, I'm here on my own."

The guard pointed to the bodies. "She was trying to get close to the bodies."

Kellim turned back with a raised eyebrow. "Oh, is that so? What were you planning to do?"

"I've read several of the reports that you were able to get copied for me. I thought I saw a pattern. I thought it was similar to how Red Hood attacked. I was able to get in touch with a goblin-fighting expert and went over the reports with them."

Kellim looked impressed. "I had never thought about doing that. Please enlighten us."

Alyssa stepped forward and pulled the sheet off the first body lying on the dirty street. She felt her stomach crawl and flip at the sight. Muscle, tendon, and bone could be seen in the deep gouges around its shoulder and chest.

"Breath is the start and end of a battle of will," according to the book *Controlling the Mind*. Alyssa focused on her breathing and looked over the cuts. She kneeled down, gauging where the edge of the blade had been facing. Sheet by sheet, she went through all the bodies. When she finished the last, she wiped her forehead with a handkerchief from her pocket.

Alyssa looked to the guards. "Was there an opening in the ceiling? An open space of some sort?"

They looked at each other with shrugs and uncertain faces. Kellim sighed and shook his head. "Go up there and check, now."

A couple of men stormed off toward the apartment. Rufus came over and tipped his hat to Alyssa, but took a step back. "Ah, didn't expect to see you again . . . ma'am."

She tried to smile politely. "I have worked some for Lieutenant Kellim here."

The man nodded and leaned against his cart with his men. A few minutes later, the guards returned. One of them nodded his head. "We hadn't noticed it before, but part of the ceiling has been moved. We looked up there and could see what we thought was a new hole in the roof."

The lieutenant raised an eyebrow. "So what does that mean?"

She motioned to the first body, the one with a deep cut in the shoulder. "He died first."

"How do you figure that?"

"The expert I talked to said that goblin ambushes start from high points and drop onto shoulders. They use sharp short blades to mount the shoulder, and use the victim as cover while causing chaos."

Kellim's face changed to one of interest. "That's a good example, but what about the others? It could be just a coincidence."

She shook her head. "It could be, but there are too many similarities. For example, the others were struck down below the waist, knees, groin, and only a few of those had injuries to the chest. These are also signs of a goblin ambush. They like to make use of their short stature."

Rufus raised a hand. "Why the legs though?"

She motioned with her hand. "Goblins are about so high, and so the legs are easier for them to strike. It's also convenient because there are several arteries within range for them to sever."

The lieutenant smiled and extended his hand to Alyssa. "Sorry about any earlier disrespect, Ms. Benedictus. Your findings match up with the last few calls of this sort I have investigated. But now we are back to the original question: What are you doing here?"

Her mouth felt dry, like it had been filled with sand. "I-I was looking into those cases, those about gang violence."

He raised an eyebrow and shrugged. "Gang violence . . . Anything else you can point out?"

Alyssa pointed to the men lying on the ground. "Zane told me that gangs usually have territories, or specialties, that they watch over. What did these men deal with?"

Kellim stared at her for a moment before answering. "They dealt in Rush powder—"

Rufus spoke up. "Yes that's right, I've seen that stuff at most of these sites."

Kellim stared at Rufus for a moment. "Is that so?"

"Perhaps they're moving into the Rush trade," Alyssa added.

The lieutenant looked impressed. "Thank you for coming by.

This does help shorten the list of people I need to go talk to. If you have anything else, let me know."

Alyssa gave a polite bow. After Kellim and Rufus went back to work, she pulled out a small notebook and wrote down the building's address. *My first confirmed point!*

As she left the scene, she passed the corpse cart. While everyone was still busy, she pulled out another tracking charm and attached it to the cart. This charm was bigger and better than the one in the hat. As she walked, a shaky smile spread across her face.

22

Zane kept watch from an alley as ash collected on him in heavy heaps. As the day went on, his joints and old injuries ached from the growing cold. With a gloved hand, he drank from his flask. The last hour had felt long. The warmth of his bottle only seemed to aggravate his aching.

The porcelain shop across the street shared a wall with the doctor's office. Shadow's red eyes were tracking him. *How much longer are you going to stand here and watch?*

Zane kept his eyes on the shop, giving a dry response under his breath. "Until I'm sure."

Shadow sounded bored. *Sure of what?*

"Sure that this isn't part of the doctor's office."

What if I offer you help? Will it get you to leave faster?

Zane eyed Shadow with suspicion. "What kind of help?"

The red eyes sank into the darkness of the wall and emerged across the street on a building. Shadow's voice echoed in his head: *If you get closer, I can take a look around the shop.*

"What do you want from me?"

Do you want to stand in the cold?

Zane limped hard as he approached the window with his cane. Inside were rows of tables with cups, bowls, and plates. He moved toward the door, but was stopped by a young boy armed with a broom. "Look, we ain't a charity. If you want to stay somewhere, then go to the local temple. Or go ask someone else, but the saints know my boss will beat me if I let you in."

Zane stared down at the boy, confused, before catching himself in a window. The ash had not only covered him like some strangling moss, but it was also smeared across his face in streaks of sweat. *The boy thinks I am homeless.*

Shadow could sense his embarrassment. *It's fine, you're close enough. Just stall.* Zane hunched over and let his sore muscles control his posture. "But I don't need a place to stay. I just need a few coins."

"Coins?! We are not a charity! Go! Go get out of here before I call the guards."

Zane lingered, noting the tension in the boy's eyes. The broom shook in his hands. A bigger man stepped out a door in the back. "Hey, what's going on?"

I got a look.

Zane pulled back from the doorway and limped quickly down the street. Once out of sight of the shop, Zane leaned against a nearby wall and pulled out his flask. He drank all he dared to drink, and the tightness of his throat relented. He brushed the piles of ash from his shoulders.

Shadow's eyes penetrated the darkness farther down the alley.

"So what did you see?"

Shadow was silent for a bit before answering. *I want a favor.*

"What? Why negotiate now?"

Because you have little choice.

The detective wanted nothing more than to throw the cane at his parasite, but damaging his cane wasn't worth it. He sighed deeply, but coughed as he attempted to control himself. "What do you want?"

The red eyes studied Zane and then the street before answering in a meek voice. *A favor for later, with no questions asked.*

"That's it? I don't like the 'no questions asked' part, though."

Shadow's eyes bounced up and down in a nod. *What other options do you have?*

"Fine, deal. What did you find?"

In the back room, there are pottery wheels and farther in, a kiln, but the wall next to it has been modified.

Zane raised an eyebrow. "How?"

There is an extra exhaust shaft connected to the chimney. There must be another furnace, except that's the last room. So my guess is that there is a hidden door that leads down to a basement.

Zane rubbed his chin. "My hunch was right: The different buildings had leftover structures, maybe even old smuggling holds. But why a chimney?"

The detective looked to the ground and then to Shadow, debating his next question. "Why couldn't you look down in the basement? Do you need to know it's there or do you need to know how to get to it?"

Shadow's eyes darted back and forth. His words were slow and careful. *Nothing so grand. There is simply no light to cast shadows there.*

Zane stared hard at him for a moment. He checked the amount of healing brew in his flask, then decided to head to the apartment. Zane made a mental note about how Shadow worked, but he wondered whether he might be an exception. The detective was tired and filthy, but he had just enough time for a nap before heading out again.

23

The last bell had long since rung, and now the night was quiet except for a distant carriage on a cobblestone street. The air was filled with fog, and the ash clung to everything in a thick paste. With heavy feet, Zane slushed through streets and alleys until he came out across from the porcelain shop. The lights were out, and the store window reflected the light of the gas lamps outside.

Shadow's eyes seemed more piercing than normal. *How do you plan to sneak in? There's no back door.*

With his gloved hand, Zane reached down and picked up a handful of muck. He marched across the street, and with a swift throw, the ball of muck hit the post. The street light went out, plunging the storefront into darkness. He looked up and down the cold, dark street. There was no movement.

He wedged his cane between the wall and the lock. With a quick movement, he snapped off the lock. The resounding clang echoed out in all directions. Sweat poured down his back. He stepped inside the shop quickly, and pushed the door closed as far as he could.

Shadow's eyes barely reflected off the glass. In a hushed whisper, Zane spoke to him. "Now where is the furnace?"

The red eyes flashed as they moved across the surface of the room like a bubble on a puddle, up to and through a door behind the counter. Zane stepped lightly, being careful to avoid touching the tables. Once at the door, he reversed the grip on his cane, ready to use it to defend himself.

The door led into a large room with pottery wheels and a giant gas-powered kiln. He checked to make sure the gas was off before opening the kiln and ducking inside. On either side of him were racks for pottery.

The back wall was different. He couldn't see it well in the dim light from the lamps in the back room, but it was enough. Newer bricks had been placed in the middle in a section about the width of the chimney.

Zane walked back out, leaving the door to the kiln open. He inspected the walls next to it, looking for clues. He found a section that looked to be made from the same bricks as inside the kiln.

He ran his fingers over that section of wall, feeling and looking for anything out of place, until he found a loose brick. Pulling it out he found a hollow space behind it, with an iron handle inside. With a twist, he pulled and opened the heavy door hidden by a brick facade.

A draft carried the smell of fire and burnt debris from below. Zane pulled his flask out and took a long gulp before descending the stairs. He kept one hand on the wall to steady himself, with the other holding his cane out in front. The basement was dark, and he moved slowly along the edge until he found a wall lamp. He pulled out a box of matches and lit it, parting the darkness.

Along the lamp wall was a large oven. The size of it disturbed him; it was big enough to hold a grown man. Opening it up, he stuck his hand in. The side was clean, too clean to have been sitting abandoned. *It's being used and emptied often.*

Across from the oven was another thick metal door, its handle worn from use, that likely led into the space under The Body Shop.

Shadow whispered in his ear. *There are people coming.*

Zane rushed up the stairs, but he could already hear the voices from the front room. "The lock's been busted. You two go in there and check it out."

He didn't recognize the voice, but that didn't matter. He pushed the secret door shut and placed the brick back into place with shaky hands. Heavy footsteps caused the floor to creak. Zane rushed over to the kiln. He dove in and pulled the door closed just before two pairs of footsteps entered the room.

He imagined them holding clubs, ready to smash the first thing that moved. Zane was breathing hard. He covered his mouth with one hand, trying not to think about the dirt and filth that covered his face.

The feet stomped around before one of them yelled up to the front. "There's no one here, boss."

Much lighter footsteps moved through the shop. "Damn thief must have gotten nervous."

"But that's a good thing, right?"

The smaller voice yelled back angrily. "No! Now they know this is an easy mark. I will need to talk to the doctor and see what we can do to up the security."

Doctor! Zane smiled at the word. It was vague, but the connection was there. The smaller voice continued, now sounding calmer. "It is what it is. Now go to the cart and get the bodies downstairs."

"Aye, boss."

Bodies? Zane wondered what they meant, but then the cold realization came over him. He could feel shivers going down his spine. He prayed to the saints that the people were dead already. Zane sat there for what felt like the whole night. The darkness in the kiln was suffocating, leaving memories of the Ghoul War playing out in his head. Sweat poured down his neck, both from the nerves and from the heat of the room.

His head felt light, but he didn't dare move. The men stomped back and forth until there was finally silence. After a few minutes, Zane began to feel heat rising up through the wall on the back of the kiln. Shadow's eyes flashed in the darkness in front of Zane.

Zane pushed his body back against the opposite wall, and muffled a scream. For a moment, he was back in the Ghoul War when he was first attacked by Shadow. The silky voice in his head pulled him out of that.

All of them are downstairs throwing bags into the furnace.

Zane took some deep breaths. He opened the kiln and stepped quietly out into the room, glancing to the secret door before running through the shop toward freedom. He fled out into the darkness and down the street with a wisp of fog trailing him. About a block away, his bad leg slipped, and he collapsed onto the brick street.

With strained muscles and his cane, he struggled back up before limping the rest of the way home. He pulled his flask free and brought it to his lips. The red eyes glared at him, but Zane cut Shadow off before he could speak. "Don't even think about it!"

He drank the rest of the flask in sweet silence.

24

Frame sat in the Magician's Café near her apartment. The ash seemed thinner today and the air colder, but it was comfortable inside. Several students were helping, taking turns in keeping the place warm with spells. The license on the window permitted the students to work such magic.

From farther back in the café, she could hear yelling as a student was forced to stand up for his turn. "Why do I have to do it? Can't we set it up to run by itself, like the weather tower?"

Another student agreed. From behind his counter, the store owner shook his head. "Look, I'm not even a licensed mage, and I know the answer to that."

The young man spoke an eldritch word as the heater tube spun back up to max speed. "Well, what is it?"

The owner smirked and pointed to the runes on the tube. "How many runes are inscribed in there?"

The young man shrugged. "One, so what? We could add one to set the temperature, and then we could set one to control the spin to make it even."

"Sure, but how long should it spin and how do we control the temperature? Or how will it know the room is getting too hot and turn off?"

The young students listening thought about it for a moment, and then started to argue amongst themselves how they could arrange such an array of runes. But with each pass of the conversation, the device they described got bigger.

Not that long ago, I went through the same conversation with my friends. Listening to their argument, Frame whispered the answer. "One of the ten rules of runic spell work: Complication is equal to size. The more than one wants to do, the more details that must be accounted for."

She sighed and pulled a letter from her coat. Vine's letter had arrived faster than she thought it would. With a slight hesitation, she tried to have the letter unseal itself using eldritch words. The paper quivered before the seal creaked, and she smiled. Frame pulled the letter free and read it. The first few lines set her blood to boil.

Dearest cousin,

I have found your last letter to be lacking in the formality required. As being such, dearest cousin, I would like you to try to keep your letter less personal and more professional as one of our family status. Cousin, with that out of the way, let us return to the letter contents as a whole.

The bell above the café door announced a new arrival. The man wore a long jacket that reached his knees, and his right hand was wrapped as if he had been injured. On his head was a deep hood, a piece that was mostly out of fashion. The hood cast a large shadow across his face, but as rays of light from the gas lamp fell on him, she could see deep scars and a missing eye.

When their eyes met, she broke her gaze. The man did not look like a scholar, and he didn't seem to care about the looks he got. He found a seat in a corner and paid the waitress for something or another. Frame forced herself away from the situation and back to the letter.

A you had stated earlier, our grandmother has a taste for rare and specialized magical goods that are often too expensive. The limbs described, while mostly unknown, do sound like a product that we all might be hearing about in the next few years. The detective was worried that there is a possibility that the prosthetics might be related to some source of illicit magic, though. If this is the case, then I expect you to spearhead this discovery and keep our family's name from being soiled anymore.

From your dearest cousin,
Vine Lexone, Acting President of Lexone Shipping

As Frame crumpled the note in her hands, her face turned beet red. She slammed the wad down on her table, rattling her cup. *How dare she say that to me! She's the one who pulled me out of college to do this work for her. She asks me to be professional, but then acts casual.*

Frame paid her bill and went for the door. The sky showed the first signs of evening as the distant sun's light danced around the horizon. The falling ash slipped off her clothes.

An older student passed her on the opposite side of the street, lighting the lamp posts with precise eldritch words. Frame stopped and watched. From the corner of her eye, she noticed the one-eyed man from the cafe was now about fifty yards behind her. The man noticed her looking, then paused and leaned on the wall.

Something about him triggered her memory. Some detail there was important, but she couldn't remember what. Her nerves went taut, and she walked a little faster, glancing back behind her at each lamp post. He kept the same distance from her, never straying too far.

Sweat beaded her face as the worry about the man grew stronger. *He's missing an eye.* She remembered the other day, when she overheard about a man getting into the ground floor of her apartment building.

With a burst of adrenaline, Frame rushed into the student housing. Glad that the runes on the doorway had been freshly applied, she didn't look back as she rushed upstairs and into her apartment. She locked the door behind her, then sealed the door in place with eldritch words from her textbook.

With shaky hands, she hastily wrote a charmed letter asking Alyssa and Zane to meet her at her apartment for the next meeting. She hoped as the ink dried that they wouldn't find her request silly.

25

Alyssa didn't care about Frame moving the meeting, and she doubted Zane would mind, either. She quickly wrote a reply, but noted it would be another day before meeting because Zane was recovering from his stakeout.

With the letter sent, Alyssa returned to the open books in front of a map of the city. The map was filled with needles stuck in different districts, each with a ribbon and a date. She brushed loose hair from her face as she turned to watch the compass following the body collector.

Over the last few days, she had chased Rufus across the city, checking to see if there were more goblin ambushes. A larger pattern was starting to emerge, but she was being worn thin.

I need something more efficient. I can't keep running around like this. Alyssa stood, stretching her back, and stepped into the kitchen to put the kettle to boil. As she waited, she glanced over the towers of books, hoping something would jump out at her with a solution to her problems.

One book stood out to her from among her piles: The Elven Empire in Broad Strokes. She pulled the book out and thumbed through it until she eyed a map of the assumed shape of the Elven Empire. Below the picture was a theory about the map's main purpose.

It was believed that the large map was used to track the movement of important ships and military units by means of an advanced array of arcane towers across the kingdom. When something moved, watchers would update the map. It has been suggested that the towers could only keep track of the direction of the object, but they could cross-locate a target by using at least three.

Intersecting lines? Maybe I could create that. She looked at the map and the different districts.

Suddenly it hit her. "The Bell Towers!"

There was one in at least every other district, all built to keep everyone on the same time. *If I could place a compass in each one, with a charm to not only follow but to bind it with another, then I could set up the receiver charms here and get a mirror image.* She went over all the complexities that would need to happen to get it to work, if it could work.

As if already done, she could see the interconnecting lines showing her where the man's wagon went at any time. She would still need to double-check events with the guards, but she wouldn't need to follow Rufus.

Alyssa made a list of all the things she needed, including the addresses of the bell towers. It would take two or three days, but it would be well worth the time. The once-large city felt a little smaller than it had a minute ago.

26

Zane was tired, but he always felt that way lately. His head pulsed and swam, but he stayed focused on the diagram in front of him. On it, he sketched what he had found in the porcelain shop.

The two agents examined his work. Will threw the map across the table and rubbed his temples. "How did we miss this?"

Crome looked at the sketch again before dropping it back on the table, pushing his chair away from the desk. "Damn it! We were so focused on the doctor's shop that we didn't see it. Is he working with the shop next door?

Will nodded. "But what is he using it for?"

They both turned to Zane. "How did you notice this?"

Zane showed the multiple floor plans and pointed to the different schematics. "When I last spoke to both of you, I noticed these. I thought of an old case and the war."

Crome raised an eyebrow. "Which war? The Winter Front, the Pirate War, or—"

"The Ghoul War."

Will flinched and looked away.

Zane watched him with twisted interest. *What does an Institute agent know about the Ghoul War to make a face like that?* He filed the thought away and turned back to the table. "A few times throughout the war, tunnels would be altered or changed, either by us or them. We needed to keep a record of every tunnel. No tunnel would ever be written off, even if it had been sealed."

"Why?" Will asked. "Once the tunnel was sealed off, why should you worry about it?"

"The ghouls could dig tunnels at inhuman speeds using their

undead. We had to be very careful not to be outflanked by them branching from a closed tunnel to an open one. We lost good men before we picked up on that."

Crome looked at the floor plans. "But none of these blueprints include a basement. How did you suspect that?"

Zane shrugged, feeling a pulse of pain in his head. The wavering walls reminded him of a soap bubble sitting on top of water. *I hope this place can't pop like a bubble.* "Former case. Buildings getting built on top of each other can sometimes lead to unintentional basements. Smugglers and thieves like to use these. They're sometimes called smuggler holds."

Crome smiled. "This is our path in. We could sneak in and see what magic he is using."

Will shook his head. "No, the detective said they noticed him getting in. They will be watching. Instead, we should set up some remote viewing charms and watch what they do. If he is dealing with a rogue wizard, we can use that as justification to tear both shops apart."

"That will take too long! We need the evidence now. We need to do this for Jake—"

Crome stopped and looked at Zane.

The Institute treats its secrets with pride, Shadow whispered.

Will snapped his fingers and turned back to the table. "Let's have the detective steal a limb."

"What?!" Zane was shocked at the proposal. He had already broken into one store, but being asked to steal was different. "Why would I do that?"

Will rubbed his chin and looked hard at the younger agent. "We will give you immunity from the crime itself, along with the break-in. No charges will be brought against you. We will also talk to our bosses and see about giving you a contract with the Institute."

"I had one before, of some small measure."

"We know, but it wasn't with an agent," Will said. "With this agreement, you will be allowed to work independently, so long as you keep us in the loop on anything you find."

Zane smirked. "That is, if you don't figure things out from the limb."

"Doesn't matter. You will be paid."

The detective started to decline, but Shadow protested. *Didn't you say you needed to pay Alyssa for her services? You can't keep taking advantage of her help.* Alyssa had done much for him, and he hadn't even come close to thanking her for such service.

"Fine. I'll agree to it, but I want it in ink before I do."

"You don't believe us?" Crome asked with an edge of anger.

"Being careful is what you do if you hope to grow old one day."

Will nodded and started to write. Once finished, he spoke eldritch words into the paper, and let it fly up into a vent, vanishing from sight. Zane wondered whether the pipe connected to the real world or if it flew off to some other bubble.

Agent Will pulled out a cigarette as Zane pulled his flask out for a sip. The pain didn't subside, but the burning calmed some.

Within a few minutes, two letters arrived. Will looked over each, then Crome sighed. "We are in trouble, aren't we?"

Will nodded. He tore open the letter and Zane could hear him curse under his breath. "What did he expect us to do when some help fell into our lap?"

Will passed the letter to Zane. "Here is the contract. The fee isn't much, but you're getting paid to do a job that you're already doing. We can make sure you're not arrested so long as you're acting in the interest of our shared investigation."

Zane took his time to read it over. He couldn't turn down the protection or money, but he didn't want to sell himself into something he wasn't prepared for. The contract was short—one page—and seemingly prewritten. He wondered how often the institute used outsiders and how many of them were actually given their benefits when the job was done.

Zane didn't like the idea of stealing. *We signed on for mutual aid, not to be used like fodder.* Shadow whispered back: *You have sto-*

len before, but let's not make a habit of stealing. Let the fools hire a thief like they should have done.

His cheeks burned with anger and shame as he remembered stealing from Atom's store after it was destroyed. A deep breath brought him back under control.

Zane set the thought aside and smiled as an idea formed. It was something so simple that he felt stupid for not thinking of it earlier. *Fools and prideful men are two sides of a coin.* He signed the paper, suppressing a grin. "Give me two . . . no, three days to get it to you."

The two agents looked at each other and nodded. "That is fine. When, or if, the law gets involved, we will step in."

Zane passed the signed contract back and headed to the door. The men called out to him. "Where are you going?"

"To keep my part of the contract."

The smell of alcohol and food hit him in the face as he opened the door. He hobbled off, leaning heavily on his cane. From the window, he could see Shadow's red eyes watching him.

27

“So he was naked in the lab?” Frame cackled.

Diana was bent over, bursting with laughter. “Yes! I was just happy that I wasn't the one stuck with that request. None of us thought that liquid would stink that bad.”

“Bad enough to strip down?”

Diana nodded her head, recalling her day in the lab. “Oh, for sure. I smelled it from across the lab, so I can only imagine having that stuff spill on me.”

Frame reached for the teacup on her living room table. Next to it was a stack of signed document copies and a stack of papers. She looked down at the top paper with a sigh and marked out another line.

“What are you working on?” Diana asked. “Is it something to do with the job your cousin gave you?”

Frame's jaw clenched at the mention of her cousin. “No, she . . . this is for my thesis on the polymorphed hair.”

“Oh, the infamous hair. There is actually a betting pool in the lab about whether the hair actually exists.”

Frame raised her eyebrow. “Why would I lie about it?”

Diana's face turned bright red as she back-pedaled. “No, I didn't mean that you would lie, but, well, no one has ever actually shown evidence of polymorphed hair, or any polymorphed thing, for that matter.”

Frame pulled out a document, and Diana moved closer. “Yes, but look here. See, we have over five dozen books dating back to the old Fey kingdom periods that are described as what was later classified ‘polymorphed at will’ people.”

Diana shook her head. “Even first-year students know that

they can't compare anything about their bodies or magic to us. They were different in every way."

Frame nodded, then pulled out another document. "Yes, but we all know that the existing Fey are their descendants, and they're generally more mixed than their ancestors were back then, according to our records. But what if very specialized clans of Fey mixed with local humans?"

Diana thought about it for a moment. "I guess it could be possible that the descendants could have kept some of their traits. But there would be no guarantee that even one generation would even show—"

A sudden, violent knock at the door caused them both to jump. "Frame! Please open the door," Felix yelled.

"Felix? W-what are you doing here at this hour?"

"Please! It's an emergency."

He rushed in as soon as Frame open the door, nearly knocking her over. His face was a mess, but his clothes were spotless. He headed toward the sink and cleaned his face and hands vigorously.

"What's going on?" Diana whispered. "And why does he stink?"

Felix turned back to them, his face and hands raw. His eyes showed a mixture of anger and fear. "Frame, you need to leave now! Collect your things. I have a sister you can stay with—"

He reached out to grab Frame's wrist, but Diana cut him off with her body. "Stop! You aren't telling us anything. Leave? Leave for what?"

Desperation overrode his fear, making him look like a cornered animal. "No time! I can't explain right now, but you need to come with me."

The look in his eyes sent a chill down Frame's spine. Diana kept herself firmly between them, but her hands shook too. "That isn't good enough! You don't have any right to storm in here and demand she leave with you."

"But what if her life is in danger? Isn't that good enough?"

Diana didn't budge. "Right now, you look like the danger."

Could Felix be violent? Frame couldn't say for sure, which made her feel even worse. She knew he was controlling, but she didn't know how far he would go to keep control. "Felix," she said just above a whisper, "you need to leave."

"Frame—"

Diana grabbed a pen from the table and held it in front of her like a knife. Ink dripped from the tip like blood. "Frame said leave, Felix."

Frame was scared, seeing his body wound tight like a spring. *Is he going to charge?*

Instead, he deflated like a sad balloon, dread pouring out of him. "You have to understand that I care for you, Frame. I just couldn't stand by and see you hurt again. When I heard what had happened to you . . . When that professor took control of you, well, I had asked some friends in the district to keep an eye on you when you passed through. To make sure you're safe."

"You asked people to spy on me?"

Shame blossomed across his face. "Not spying! Well, not exactly. Most of the time, they had nothing to say, not until just recently. Look, you need to believe me. You're being followed. He is a creepy-looking guy missing an eye who keeps a hood up at all times."

She thought back to the lady reporting a strange man in the lobby hitting her. *Maybe I am being followed.*

"That is the reason you need to come with me," Felix said. "I can keep you safe."

Diana pushed Frame farther back. "No! The only one following her is you. You even said it—your friends are watching." She jabbed with the pen and with her words. "Move now, or I will cut you! Frame, get ready to yell for help."

"But—"

The strength of Diana's scream surprised Frame and caused Felix to jump back. Slowly and deliberately, Felix moved to the door with Diana and Frame following. From the hall, he gave one last pleading look. Diana slammed the door shut and locked it tight without hesitation. Frame almost didn't notice, but Diana had finally dropped the pen. Her friend's hands shook like leaves in the wind.

"I see why you left him."

28

Alyssa sweated under her cloak, but she would not leave without it. She pushed herself up the stairs of the third clock tower that day. Her legs protested until she relented and sat for a moment. She took out three compasses; two showed steady, constant movement, but the third was still.

She made a mental checklist of the charms she needed to make the setup work. It had taken several hours of reading and testing in her neighborhood to figure out. Pushing the compasses back into her pockets, she resumed the march up.

At the top, she took in the city air. It was dirty, but it felt good. Looking north, she saw the white stone palace, the heart of the empire. It was beautiful—white and clean, in contrast to the black columns of smoke that covered the landscape. Its spires and pillars were still studied by the Institute, as their construction had never been replicated.

This tower's bell looked the same as the last two: Taller than three men and at least two wide. Hanging by thick ropes, it was blackened by what she imagined was years of the city's ash. A rough script could barely be seen across it, obscured by a thick paste. Alyssa moved along the edge of the room, stopping at one of the corners. She stuck the charm to the stone wall with a thick, pasty glue, then covered it with a layer of leather for better protection from the weather. *It's just temporary and doesn't need to last long.*

Back on the ground floor, she passed by the guard. He nodded a greeting. "Everything all right there?"

"Yes, it is. Thank you again for letting me go up there."

He shrugged. "Why wouldn't I? A state mage comes here every month to check up on things. You're just a little earlier than normal."

Alyssa stopped mid-step and turned to face the guard. "Every month?"

He looked surprised. "Yeah, they come here for the bell, just like clockwork. They do it for every bell tower, really. Are you not here for that?"

The other guards hadn't spoken after she flashed her badge. *That explains that.* "I'm working on a project. Thank you for your time."

The guard waved goodbye. Alyssa stepped out into the street, covering the distance as quickly as she could, and waved for a carriage. The next stop was at the edge of the city.

"What's taking you to the wall today, ma'am?" the driver called from up front.

"I am preparing f-for a chase." The rest of the ride was silent.

It was hours later when she made it back to her apartment after the last stop. It was late and the sun had already set. Alyssa made herself dinner and ate at her map. The runes she drew on its edges matched those she dropped off earlier.

She laid her compasses down on top of the drawn representations of bell towers that matched them and offered a small prayer to any saints that would answer her. The three needles spun freely for a moment before they all pointed to the same location. Using string, she found the spot where the three overlapped.

Alyssa placed a pin and noted the time and date. She smiled at her success and let out a laugh. *Go wherever you want. I will follow you.*

29

Zane opened the door of the doctor's shop. The limbs hanging from the ceiling filled him with renewed disgust. He laid his cane on the edge of a table and lifted a porcelain leg off a hook. He examined it, moving it at the joints, working the knee back and forth. He listened as it clicked with each move. The joints moved with such easy, fluid motions that Zane couldn't believe the leg could support someone's weight without magic.

He had seen several prosthetics during and after the Ghoul War that were little more than a wooden pole to replace a leg, yet these limbs worked in a way that seemed to redefine what was physically possible. Zane glanced to the front door. All that kept people out was a simple bolt lock. Outside, a man was adding bars to the windows.

As the detective put the leg down, the door in the back opened. The doctor stepped in, cleaning his hands with a dirty cloth. "Ah, you're back. Sorry, but please remind me of your name."

Zane picked up his cane from the table. "Zane Vrexon. I had some thoughts on what you said."

The doctor smiled and joined the detective at the table. Aluxen looked down at Zane's leg. "What have you decided?"

"That I'm interested."

"Interested? Now that is an odd answer. Most say yes or no. Are you an indecisive man, Mr. Vrexon?"

Zane shrugged, trying to look cynical. "Skeptical. I have been taken advantage of too many times by those claiming to have cures. While yours are a bit more noticeable, with so many people walking up and down the streets, I would like to be without doubt—for my own sake."

Aluxen nodded his head and ran his hand through his beard. "I can see that, but what can I do to ease your worry?"

Zane pointed to the leg on the table. "I would like to take this leg with me. I have some friends who would inspect it for me. I need to make sure what it is I am buying into and if it is worth giving up what I have."

The doctor frowned and narrowed his eyes. Sweat dripped down the detective's back, and his heart beat loud in his chest.

"That would be difficult, you see. While these are masterfully made, they lack . . . a certain element."

"Element?"

Aluxen nodded, and drew the detective's attention to the ankle. "You see, a normal prosthetic limb could not function with such a limp joint. I have a secret that makes them useful. If you don't believe me, then go ask to look at anyone's leg out there in the streets."

Zane looked down to his own leg. "That may be, but I still want to be sure. I trust my friend to give me good advice."

"Who is your friend?"

The detective kicked himself for forcing a lie, but thought quickly. "A friend from the war . . . He has some personal experience with prosthetic limbs."

"Which war?"

His mouth felt dry. "The Ghoul War."

Aluxen looked confused for a moment, as if searching for a lost memory. "No kidding, I was there too, field medic and surgeon. One of many out there on that blasted mountain slope."

"Small world, then."

"Aye. I can tell you that your friend will say that it is useless as a limb, but I can allow it if you are set. I would expect you to bring that leg back."

Zane reached out to pick up the leg, but was stopped when the doctor spoke again.

"Of course, I would like something in return," he said, eyeing

Zane's cane.

The detective sighed, and laid the leg down. "Could I pay you some money instead?"

His voice was final. "Leave the cane. I will accept nothing else."

"Fine. I'll leave it here, but I get it back when I return the leg. Deal?"

The doctor smiled and extended his hand to take the cane. Zane hesitated, but finally let it go. With a painful limp, the detective left with the prosthetic leg under one arm. He didn't realize how bad his leg had been lately without his cane. Outside the shop, he took one large gulp from his flask and marched down the street with regained strength. The Laze Pot came into view, and he passed it without a glance.

I thought you were going to take the leg to the agents, Shadow whispered.

"I need to be sure of what I'm getting into. Alyssa is better than either of those two men. She'll give me some idea of how this thing works."

A lyssa sat on Frame's couch, leaning over the coffee table. Laid out across it was the leg Zane had brought back. The student watched as Alyssa took the leg apart, making notes on how it went together. Zane sat next to her, making comments about how it compared to normal prosthetics he had seen.

Knuckle by knuckle, Alyssa pulled the toes apart to find stiff, locking joints. Zane watched and mumbled to himself about the source of the clacking sound. "Any idea why they're so stiff?" Alyssa asked him.

He shook his head. "If enough force isn't used, then the joints would get stuck. Honestly, I think they would make these harder to use, not easier."

Alyssa made notes of each joint, even drawing small sketches of them and how they locked together. She moved to the thigh, running her hand over it until she found a thin lip. She wedged a piece off with a knife and looked inside. Clear tubes ran the length of the leg. Alyssa tried to pull the cover, but stopped when it didn't come free.

The former professor handed the leg over. "What do you think?"

"I have no idea," Zane said with growing irritation. "This thing does everything a normal prosthetic couldn't do."

The whiteness of the leg reminded Frame of Chiron Falto, the lawyer she had met in passing at her family's office. This leg and his hand both had that skeletal quality to them. The other thing that caught her attention was how close the two investigators sat next to each other, and how comfortable they were.

Frame couldn't help but smile at them.

Alyssa's hands were smudged with ink. She paused in her note-taking and looked up. "Are you okay with us working here?"

Frame nodded and picked up a book from the edge of her table. "Yes, of course. And thank you again for bringing me this book."

"Your thesis is going to need some reference material, and polymorphed bodies only really appear in documents copied from Fey accounts."

Deep bags hung from Alyssa's eyes. Zane offered to make tea, taking the break to step away from the confounding leg. After setting Frame's kettle to boil, he fished out a broom and turned his attention to the floor.

Frame thought the room was clean, especially since her clothes didn't collect the ash and muck from outside, yet the pile he collected grew with surprising speed. Alyssa didn't say anything, but watched him with the faintest of smiles. Frame shook her head. *I've been listening to Diana too much about those romance novels she reads.*

The kettle whistled just as the detective was pouring the dirt out the window and back out into the world. He looked down from the apartment window, watching as ash fell like snow, until the whistling brought him back. "Frame, do you need a cup too?"

Before she had a chance to answer, a steady stream of knocks came from her door and didn't stop. Alyssa looked at Frame, confused. "Were you expecting a guest?"

Frame shook her head, suddenly very glad that Zane and Alyssa were there. *Is it Felix again?* She had bolted and chained the door every day since Felix had showed up. The knock grew more aggressive as she unbolted the lock. The door flew open 'til the chain caught it.

Two well-dressed men were on the other side, both looking annoyed. The older man spoke first, showing his badge. "I am Agent Will, a state mage with the Institute, and an acting agent. Is there a Zane Vrexon here?"

Frame hesitated for a moment, but she remembered the name from their last meeting. She nodded. "Agent Will. I guess that must be Crome, correct?"

The younger man nodded. "Ma'am, is Zane Vrexon here?"

There was an angry edge to his question. "Yes. Please give me a moment to unlock the door."

She closed it, undid the chain, and let the two men in. They moved past her into the living room. Will looked down at the table covered in prosthetic parts. Crome confronted Zane. "I thought we had a deal. Are you double-crossing us?"

Zane kept a straight face as he passed Alyssa her cup of tea. "I told you both that I would have it to you in a couple of days. I haven't done anything that I said I wouldn't do."

Crome balled his fists. "Listen, you fool—"

Will barred his way and gave him a hard look until Crome relaxed. The older agent knelt down next to the table and looked up to Alyssa. "Are you taking notes?"

She nodded and passed her notebook to him. Will handed it to Crome, who snatched it and stepped away. "Why didn't you bring the leg to us?"

Zane found his jacket on the coat rack and pulled out his flask. "Last I checked, I still had some time."

Will smirked. "You know we're going to take it, right?"

Zane took a deep drink. Ignoring Will, Zane looked at Alyssa. "What did you figure out?"

The two agents turned to her, and she blushed at the sudden attention. "Well, I—"

Agent Crome looked up from the notes he had been reading. "Are you Alyssa? Benedictus's granddaughter?"

Frame was surprised that Crome didn't use the archmage's title, which was so common among those who worked in the Institute.

Will nodded. "Yes, she is Benedictus-Lasome's granddaughter."

The edge in his voice was sharp. Crome huffed and turned

backed to the notes.

"Sorry about that," Will said. "Please continue."

The former professor pointed to the leg. "This leg can be broken down into three sections: Foot, calf, and thigh. The foot is broken down further with the toes. Each can be taken apart into two pieces. They interlock and click as they move through their positions. We think the fingers work the same way, along with any major joint. That is where the noise comes from."

Will nodded. "So that's the clicking we hear in the district."

Zane sipped on his flask, slowly placing himself between Crome and Alyssa.

Frame stayed back in the entry hall, out of the way. Remembering Chiron's hand, she whispered to herself. "The clacking."

Alyssa moved to the next section. "The ankle is a loose ball joint. We don't know how it balances a person's weight. The same locking mechanisms as the toes can be found in the knee."

Crome eyed Zane as he handed the notes back to Will. The older agent took them and motioned for Alyssa to go on. "At the top of the thigh is a metal rod. We are not sure what it does, but Zane thinks that it might be connected to the bone—"

Zane jumped into the conversation. "It's a guess. There is a good possibility that the infection or the pain would kill them. They could use healing potions to help, but I can't imagine it working. At least not with the success rate we see in his patients."

Crome scoffed. "How did you come to that conclusion?"

"I attended medical school for a while. Seen some things and read some things, but this is only a guess."

Will cast an angry look at Crome before turning to the detective. "I also have a little bit of a medical background, and I see what you mean."

Frame had realized that she was basically a fly on the wall. No one in the room paid her any mind. It annoyed her, this being her apartment and all, but she dared not make any disturbance.

Alyssa went on. "The strangest thing we have found is the glass tubes in the calf leading up to some type of piping that goes to the thigh." She reached for the thigh section and picked up the knife.

Crome nearly jumped across the room. "What are you doing?"

Alyssa flinched away. Will snapped. "Agent Crome! Relax."

Will picked up the knife Alyssa had dropped and handed it back. "Please go on."

It took a few moments, but she found the seam in the thigh again. Inside the compartment, the flexible tubes led into a box suspended by thin metal poles.

Crome smiled like a maniac while jabbing his finger in the air. "See? That is the 'magician box.'"

Frame and Zane looked puzzled, but Agent Will seemed to catch on. "It's what we call the hiding place of illicit magical goods. Most of the time, it's a charm they are using for their business. You see it used a lot with con artists."

Frame had never heard this description before, but she could imagine such a thing. Will turned back to Alyssa. "I didn't see anything in your notes about it, but what are we looking at? Some type of runes system, a prolonged charm, perhaps a custom spell wick?"

She shook her head. "A charm, as you two know, wouldn't last this long—at least not without some major upkeep. The complicated movements of a limb, I think, would take several hundred charms. If they aren't doing constant upkeep, they would need runes to make it permanent. I see none, nor do I see a spot for burning a spell wick."

Alyssa looked closely at the box. "It's an empty box with small holes."

The two agents looked at each other, each firing off ideas. Zane was deep in thought before looking over his shoulder to a corner. He sneered and moved his hand dismissively before turning back to them. "What happens if we pour water into it?"

Everyone stared at him. "What?"

Alyssa looked down at the leg. "I'm not sure, but we can test it and see."

Before Alyssa could stand, Frame headed to the kitchen. "Let me get the water."

She came back with the kettle; the water was still hot. Alyssa spoke an eldritch word that cooled it. Frame poured the water into the box, but Alyssa stopped her from filling it all the way. She put the lid back on and gently rocked the leg back and forth. The sound of water could be heard moving through the pipes, down to the tubes. They all looked to Zane, who glanced again over his shoulder.

"Well, what is that supposed to be, detective?"

Zane turned to them. "I don't know, but I guess—" His eyes flicked back. "It is acting like veins. Something is placed in the water that gives its power, its motion."

Crome shook his head. "That doesn't make sense. Even if you put spell wicks into the water, it wouldn't do anything. Maybe it's some type of potion that is poured into the box."

Alyssa narrowed her eyes. "I doubt it. Every test I have read about involving water-based charms says that it fades at twice the normal rate. Even rune-encrusted items have a large reduction in ability. Water does help spread the power out, though."

"A rune-carved object would have to be huge for it to be able to do everything that a normal limb could do," Frame added. "The fluid motion that Zane has described would be hard to replicate. And there's still the question of how normal people without training can operate it."

Will turned to Zane. "What do you think?"

"Why ask me? You all are the experts in this field."

"Because you suggested we pour water into it. That is oddly specific. Do you have any idea what this could be?"

Zane looked down at the leg. "No, I don't."

Will studied him for a moment before nodding and standing up. "This has all been very interesting, but we still need to take the leg into our custody. Crome, help Ms. Benedictus with reassembling it."

Crome nodded. Frame watched as he and Alyssa put the leg back together, only stopping to review her notes on the assembly. As the men packed everything up, they turned to Zane. "How did you get the doctor to let you have the leg?"

"I told Aluxen that I was interested in the surgery, but I wanted a friend to look it over. He made me leave my cane until I brought it back. I need my cane, so if I could have the leg back when you're done . . ."

"We will try to get it back as soon as possible," Will promised. "Even with the help of Ms. Benedictus, we still would like to have our people examine it. You can keep her notes for your investigation."

The agents left with the leg, the door gently closing behind them. Zane stood staring at the corner long after they had left. Frame wondered what he was thinking about.

With a nod, he turned back. "They're gone. Alyssa, did they leave any type of spying device?"

She seemed caught off-guard by the question, but quickly recovered. She picked up her glasses and scanned the room.

"Why would they spy on us?" Frame asked. "Aren't you working together?"

Zane smiled. "Yes, but this case has taken a more . . . personal turn for them."

Alyssa turned to Zane. "We should let her know."

"Are you sure? Doesn't she have a reason to tell her family what is going on?"

Alyssa shook her head. "How the limbs work isn't really important, is it? At least, at the heart of the case."

Frame stood up. "You can trust me. My cousin forced this on me, and Alyssa has done a lot for me. If she trusts you, then I do."

Zane sighed and waited for Alyssa to finish her check.

"The room is clear," she told him. "Now what did Shadow say?"

lick, click, click, click, click. Shadow had always had the habit of clicking his tongue, and that didn't stop now that he didn't have one.

The detective looked grim as he walked beside Alyssa just outside Frame's apartment building, the ash falling around them. "Look, I'm sorry for bringing up Shadow in front of Frame."

"No, I shouldn't have stormed out like I did. It's just . . . I don't want people to know about him."

"But if more people knew, then maybe we could find help for you."

Zane shook his head. "No, I am afraid that they'd lock me up for being crazy—or worse—if there isn't any solution. The ash is really coming down tonight. We should get you home."

Alyssa nodded and they started off. Shadow watched as they traversed the city. He was glad Zane was hesitant to talk about him. He feared too much attention would bring the eyes of people he didn't want to see again.

The silence between the two seemed heavy. The weight of it broke Zane first. "Did you ever look into Shadow?"

Alyssa gave a grim nod. "After hearing about it, I did a little research. A few experiments had been attempted, but nothing succeeded, and usually it ended in both participants dying. That's why it has been outlawed by the Institute. The few experiments I read over were horrific. I don't know what this Shadow did, but he was a powerful mage."

"If he knows so much, then why is he cursed?"

As much as he liked being admired, Shadow was honest with himself. The first rule: Know thy limits. He thought himself equal to or perhaps less of a mage than Alyssa, but he was skilled in hunting down the tools and resources he needed. What he didn't know, he knew how to find.

"I don't know." Alyssa shrugged her shoulders. "One thought that worries me is that there are mages even greater than him out there. The Institute is supposed to be the best in the world, but that gives me doubt."

She stopped him under a passing street lamp. "What are you afraid of?"

He didn't look up at her, his voice almost a whisper. "That I'm losing me. That I'm becoming him, or he's becoming me."

She squinted. "What do you mean?"

Zane stared up into the light. "I think I can best explain it by comparing it to the dream sphere from when I first meet you. Do you remember?"

Alyssa shuddered. "I try not to think about it. But what do you mean?"

"You said it wasn't meant for two people. That if we stayed there too long, our memories would merge."

Realization crossed her face. "You two share a body, and so your minds are merging."

The detective continued walking, his limp painful to watch. Alyssa grabbed the edge of his jacket. "Zane, I-I can't say that I understand, but I just want you to know that we will figure this out together."

Shadow felt touched by the scene, a feeling that he thought was long dead. He wondered whether he felt that way because it involved him or because the detective's emotions were washing over him. He dove down into the Sea of Stars, getting away from the two and into the safety of the darkness.

32

Zane breathed hard, walking against the wind, as ash floated around and stuck to his clothes. The muscles in his leg ached and his throat was dry. He had only so much brew to help with his pain, and he had decided to save it until he really needed it.

The walk to the Laze Pot had taken more out of him than he had expected. The pub was busy with people moving back and forth, coming and going. Zane worked his way to the counter. As he moved through the crowd, he heard the familiar clacking. The detective's head snapped around, looking for the source, but the sea of people was too thick.

Zane looked at people's arms and legs, but could not find the source of the sound. Whoever was in the crowd was indistinguishable from the rest. A tinge of envy seeped into him, his right hand touching the scars that crisscrossed his thigh.

He was still scanning the room when Crome tapped him on the shoulder. "Detective, right on time. Is there something wrong?"

Zane looked, but the sound was lost among the crowd. "No. Are we meeting in the same room?"

"Yes, please follow me."

Crome led him to the same door and opened it with the same key that the bartender had used. The key had a strange glossy coat that unnerved the detective. The door quivered ever so slightly, and Zane took a deep breath in anticipation of the headache.

His skin crawled as he moved through the room, and his mind pulsed. Agent Will stood by the table with the prosthetic leg laid out in front of him. He passed a packet of papers to Zane. "Here is what our team found when they went through it. Alyssa Benedictus's notes pretty much revealed everything, though our team made some more finds. The oddest thing we found was the composition of the porcelain."

Zane picked through the papers, resting on his good leg. "Human bone mixed with animal." He looked up to both agents. "Is this serious? How much . . . that much!"

Crome looked disgusted. "We know that there are some uses of bone for porcelain, but that much is . . ."

Will nodded. "This leg was pulled at random, so I can't imagine we just happened to grab the one leg that just so happened to be made of human bone."

Zane felt a cold chill in spite of the temperature of the room. "What would the doctor gain from it being made of human bone?"

The two agents stared at each other for a moment. Zane noticed their reaction. They had discussed this before, and something held them back.

"Any information you have might help. Didn't we agree that we would be sharing everything we found?"

Will sighed and gave the go-ahead with a nod to Crome. "Human bone could be used in what we generally refer to as 'black magic.' "

"Black magic? Isn't that evil magic?"

The agent's face twisted in trying to explain. "As the Institute says, there is no evil when it comes to magic. Just evil ends. Black magic is old magic, making use of less-humane practices. This is a very broad description that the Institute uses. What is important is that sorcery like this is highly illegal. Depending on what the 'means' are, it could end with execution."

Zane smirked. "Illegal for those outside the Institute to partake in?"

Crome's face was red with frustration, but the older agent responded. "It has happened. Extremely rare, but it takes a lot of permission and is highly regulated. I have seen the research in such things, and the paperwork alone is enough to make someone think twice."

Zane shut his eyes and rubbed his temples. "Are you suggesting that it is possible to use some old or lost magic that makes use of something human? Like necromancy? Am I getting this right?"

"That is a possibility, but we can't find anything that registers as magic, or how he would find that type of magic."

Zane thought for a moment. "He mentioned to me that he was a surgeon in the Ghoul War."

The two men looked surprised. Will pulled a cigarette from his pocket and lit it. "If he did learn black magic, that would have been the place. But that isn't enough. We have a lot of authority, but we also have some strict rules."

"So where does this leave us? Can the Institute move against Aluxen?"

Will took a long drag on his cigarette. "We have enough evidence for the Institute to keep us on the case, but we will need to start working this from another angle."

Crome slammed down his fist. "We can't bribe our way into Aluxen's inner circle, and we tried the surge—"

"Crome, shut up! That is classified information. . . . Let's just say it ended in a death."

That explains why he's so angry. The detective picked up the leg. With his other hand, he fished out his flask for a heavy drink. "Fine. If I can get an angle, I'll let you both know."

Zane was headed to the door when one of them called out to him. With his head pounding, he couldn't make out which one. "Where are you going?"

"To get my cane."

33

Frame felt on edge, her foot tap, tap, tapping the floor. The tea she ordered had gone cold, but she couldn't stop herself from staring at the unopened letter from her cousin. With a heavy sigh, she leaned forward and quickly broke the seal on the letter. It was one page, with very little on it.

Dear Frame,

I am not looking for excuses, but results. Our dear grandmother is planning something big—and expensive. Too expensive. While I can't deny her spending, it is connected to this Dr. Aluxen. Prove he is a danger or a fraud. I don't care how.

It took less than a minute to read the letter, the pent-up stress leading up to it a complete waste. Frame flung the letter back down on the table. *It was never about our grandmother, but about her money.* She should have realized earlier: Vine never changes.

Frame paid her bill, stuffed the letter into her pocket, and headed out into the cold. Standing there in front of the tea shop window, she caught a glimpse of herself. "Why wasn't I the one next in line? Then I wouldn't be getting pushed around."

Ash fell around her as she watched daylight escaping through the courtyard of the Institute of Sorcery and Science. She smiled at the sunlight. "Time with friends sounds good."

The walk to her apartment was just a little over two blocks, then two blocks more to the courtyard. People on foot and in carriages moved up and down the streets. Suddenly, a voice cut through her placid thoughts, followed by a hand grabbing her tightly by the shoulder. It sounded urgent—and harsh. "Help! My friend, he's injured! Oh, please help!"

With his strong grip, the man pulled Frame into a nearby alleyway. She tried to make out his face, but couldn't see past his hood. When she looked past him to the fallen figure on the ground, the blood in her veins went cold. The man's voice didn't register in her head, but it should have.

"Ma'am, please help me."

She couldn't speak. The air was trapped in her lungs. Felix lay against the wall of the alley, blood soaking his clothes, as if he had spilled a bottle of wine. One of his hands was tight to his body, clenching the hole that drained him. Frame's voice cracked as she broke free of the man's grip and raced to Felix's side.

"It's going to be a-all right," Frame said. "We'll get help."

Warm memories of their good dates drifted through her mind. "Please don't die, not like this," she pleaded.

The gloved hand of the hooded man gripped her shoulder again, holding her in place. Frame didn't notice, as all her attention was on her friend.

Felix opened one eye weakly and flashed a brief smile. He looked past her, filling with anger. With the last burst of his strength, he spat out an arcane word. Blood sprayed from his mouth as he did, covering Frame's face.

Light exploded behind her, and the grip on her shoulder came free with a scream. She spun around to the clattering of metal on the bricks of the alley and the stranger gripping his face. On the ground in front of him was a bloody knife.

"Saints!" The hooded man shouted. "I thought you were dead already!"

One of his hands was covered in blood, and all the pieces came together in Frame's mind. He pulled his hands away from his face, giving a clear view of his features. Red hair and a missing left eye. The good eye blinked a few times before focusing on her.

She scrambled from the ground, sprinting toward freedom. The man cursed and swiped his right arm through the air. A blade extended from his fist with a snap. After an unsteady lunge, he chased her.

Frame stuttered through an eldritch word. The wall of invisible force was weak, but still brushed her assailant to the side.

Her breath came in heavy pants, her temples pulsing. She attempted to speak another charm, but bit her tongue. When it failed, she yelled out to the people walking down the street.

A hand gripped the corner of her coat, stopping her escape. Frame's feet dug into the ground. She pulled with all her strength, and lunged forward as her coat ripped.

Frame screamed again, but the words came faster than she could think them through. A few people rushed past her to Felix's body. Others stopped to make sure she was okay, but their voices didn't register. She looked down the empty alley to where Felix's killer had once stood.

34

lyssa smiled at her city maps. They weren't pretty, but she was proud. It had taken a lot of work to construct the web, and in the last two days Alyssa even had to go repair a couple of her charms. The system followed Rufus and his wagon across the map on the table. A similar map on the wall held pins with all sorts of ribbons tied to them. Red was for those she believed were goblin ambushes. Blue was for when she was unsure. Yellow was for those she didn't find relevant—places the wagon went, but that didn't line up with guard reports.

Already patterns had started to form. A line of crimes showed a clear, straightforward progression. She pulled out a ruler and made some marks and notes. Alyssa had a theory on where the next crime scene would be.

She smiled at her creation. "Am I right?"

Just as she was about to race to the location, a knock on the window drew her attention. Stuck to the window was a letter.

A charmed message? Is someone from the Institute looking for me?

She opened the window and snatched the letter from the air as it slipped past. Runes ran across its surface, smudged and smeared. She was surprised it had even been able to reach her. She opened it and read the short message that started with large, nearly bleeding words. *PLEASE HELP!*

It was clearly written in a rush and smeared by Frame's tears. Alyssa hesitated at her door for a moment, looking at the map and its moving needles. She sighed and put away her notes.

The blanket of clouds in the sky thinned as she rushed toward the Institute District. As she got close, she noticed a large crowd gathered around an alley. Something pulled her toward it, and she forced her way to the front. Near the edge, Frame was holding her shoulders and rocking. Her hands, face, and clothes were speckled with blood. An imperial guard stood in front of her with his notepad and pen.

Alyssa weaved through the alley until she was stopped by a guard holding a staff with glowing arcane symbols. "Step back! We don't need people mucking around here."

She reached into one of her pockets and pulled out her state mage badge. The guard took it with a nervous hand, looking it over for a moment to check its authenticity. The guard groaned as he passed it back. "What do you need, ma'am?"

Alyssa pointed to Frame, who hadn't even noticed her yet. "That student over there sent me a charmed letter, claiming she was attacked."

He looked in Frame's direction, confused. "Student? What—"

The guard's face went pale as he connected the dots. He motioned for Alyssa to follow. His captain glared at Alyssa. "Who is she? I told you to keep everyone back. I am in the middle of an interrogation!"

Alyssa was shocked at the word and moved forward half a step. "Interrogation! Saints, man, look at her!"

The captain's face gave off an angry heat. "I ought to arrest you for disrupting my case—"

"Boss!"

He snapped at his subordinate. "What?"

"She's a state mage, and she is claiming that your suspect is a student . . . of the Institute."

The captain's face paled. He cursed under his breath as two more subordinates approached. "Many of the people we interviewed claimed they saw a second person run away."

The captain cursed again, turning to Frame. "You are going to be released to this state mage, understood?"

He turned to the other guards. "Let's get out of here before *he* shows up. We did our part." The men turned off their staves, the runes fading, before taking off.

Alyssa took Frame into her arms and guided her home. It was only when they reached the stairs that she noticed Frame's blank stare. It was almost painful to watch the student fumble with her keys.

"Alyssa, thank you—"

"No, you don't need to thank me."

Frame nodded and opened the door. She stood there confused for a moment, unsure whether Alyssa was staying.

The former professor noticed Frame's clothes flickering. The tear in her coat had broken some of the runes. Alyssa reached down and turned them off before placing a hand on Frame's shoulder. "Let's make you some tea."

Alyssa stepped through the doorway and guided Frame to a chair. At the stove, Alyssa started a flame with an eldritch word, and placed a kettle on. "Now, what happened?"

Frame looked like she was about to sob, but she pulled herself together. "I was on my way home when a hooded man stopped me. He said his friend was injured and then pulled me down the alley. It was Felix—"

"He was dead, or almost dead . . . He's dead now. There was so much blood. Felix looked at me before casting a light spell. I don't know how he did it with all that blood in his mouth. It blinded the hooded man."

Frame's hands shook as tears flowed from her face. "He dropped a knife . . . I can only imagine what he was about to do. But then a different knife came out of his fist—out of his fist! How is that even possible? Oh saints, Felix."

"How did you know Felix?" Alyssa asked.

"I met him in a class, Introduction to Charm Work. I first noticed him smiling at me, and the next day he invited me to go grab some food. It was nice at first, but then he got too controlling. Always asking where I had been and what I was doing, so I broke up with him."

Frame wiped her tears away, and Alyssa placed a teacup in Frame's hands and motioned for her to drink. With a weak nod, she warmed her hands with the tea before continuing. "But he didn't deserve to die like that. No one does—"

A knock at the door distracted both of them, and a male voice called out. "Hello? Is Frame Lexone in? It's Inspector Lucos here. I have a report of an attack."

Alyssa knew the name, but couldn't place it. Frame tried to stand, but the former professor motioned for her to sit before opening the door herself.

Standing outside was a tall, wiry man with short hair. Two sharp eyes looked through his round-rimmed glasses. "Ms. Benedictus, I didn't expect to see you here."

He pulled a well-worn notepad from his suit jacket. "This is the residence for Frame Lexone, correct?"

Alyssa nodded and welcomed him inside. "Yes. Inspector, I don't think I've seen you since we graduated."

"Yes, our work seems to have put us in very different circles, though I wish we could have reconnected under different circumstances."

"You must be Ms. Lexone." Inspector Lucos kneeled next to Frame's chair. "Now tell me what happened," he said with a surprisingly gentle voice.

Frame nodded, and started from the beginning. He took notes and was careful to ask each question twice, giving her time to think before she answered.

He nodded and tapped his notepad with his pen. "Have you seen this man before?"

Frame looked anxious, then fearful. "I think I have, and also overheard a student giving a description of him in the building."

Her eyes went wider. "And the last time I saw Felix, he forced himself into my apartment. He told me that I needed to go with him for my protection. He must have heard about the man somehow."

"How would Felix know about this man?"

She blushed and gave an uncomfortable shrug. "He has friends all over the district, and he told me that they keep an eye on me for him."

Lucos nodded his head. "Do you have any enemies, Ms. Lexone?"

Frame shook her head. Alyssa couldn't imagine anyone wanting to kill the young student.

"What about your family?"

"Maybe, but I don't even use my family name around the Institute. How did you know my family name was Lexone?"

"I work for the Institute, so I have access to that sort of information. Now this might be a targeted attack, but we don't have a motive for it yet. Until we know for sure, my recommendation is that you find a different place to stay."

"Where should I go?"

"That is for you to decide. Here is a card. It has the address to send me charmed letters if you need to contact me. Please let me know where you decide."

Lucos stood up, his eyes filled with a mix of sympathy, rage, and sadness. "We will find this man and get justice for Felix."

With that, he said his goodbyes and left.

"What should I do? How do I know if I'll be attacked again? This neighborhood is supposed to be safe." Frame stared down at the table, overwhelmed.

Alyssa sat down next to her, trying to find the right words. "When I was attacked in the Institute, I found that being away from my apartment helped. Perhaps you can stay at the Institute?"

Frame shook her head. "No, I don't qualify. They reserve those apartments for students who come from farther away or who are poor. The Lexone family pays for my apartment and tuition here."

"What about friends?"

Frame thought about it for a moment. Her eyes narrowed in focus. "I could—

Her eyes widened with fear. "But I would still need to pass through this neighborhood to go to your office."

"You don't have to help."

Frame shook her head. "No, I do. It's complicated, but I have to help."

Alyssa sipped her tea, which was now cold. *Was this how I was after I was attacked?*

"You can come stay with me. It's a short distance between the Institute and Zane's office. You can borrow some clothes, if you want to go unnoticed by others."

"Unnoticed?"

Alyssa nodded. "The enchanted clothes keep ash off, but that does draw some attention."

"No, I can't impose on you like that."

Alyssa stood up and offered her hand. "Yes, I must insist. Come now. Let's go pack your bags. And bring your research—I told you I could help with your thesis. This is a perfect time."

Frame smiled, a small tear dripping from her face. "Thank you."

S hadow watched from his world as Zane left the warm, well-lit pub for the filthy streets of the city. Shadow liked the atmosphere of Laze Pot, but was glad to get away from that space the agents used. It was a magic that they barely understood, and it made him nervous for Zane to be inside.

The detective limped down the street toward The Body Shop, each step painful and strained. The prosthetic leg under his arm bounced at the joints as he walked. Some of the people stared at Zane as he passed.

Shadow dipped down farther into the Sea of Stars, feeling the currents of its ethereal waters. From beneath the surface, he could feel each person who had one of those prosthetic limbs—just like with Vine's bodyguard. Shadow bobbed up and down between the sea and the above world. When the detective passed in front of the window, he cast himself into the reflection.

What do you think of those limbs?

The detective glanced over. "What's there to say? They're well-made."

Shadow laughed. *Yeah, but what type of resources does it take to make something like that?*

The detective narrowed his eyes and halted. "That all depends, I guess, on how they work. You wouldn't know something more about that, would you?"

There was pure hatred in Zane's face, but Shadow remained silent until the detective turned away. He knew Zane would keep thinking about it.

"What do you think of this limb?"

Someone is backing him. Someone with a lot of influence, or at least someone connected with a lot of power and a vast amount of knowledge. I doubt the doctor could have made these all on his own.

Zane looked around, trying to find Shadow, but he refused to be seen this time. "Are these backers something you can't talk about? Do they have some connection to your curse?"

Shadow hesitated for a moment. *If I say yes, would you step away from this case?*

Before Zane could process the question, Laure appeared with her basket of handmade flowers. Her face was cold this time, and her voice harsh. "You're back. Are you going to see the doctor?"

The detective nodded. "Yes, I had promised to return this, and I would like to get my cane back."

Laure looked at the prosthetic in his arm. "Cane? Are you not satisfied with what the doctor can give you? What about your friend?"

Zane noticed her change. "My friend is still looking over his notes and . . . and cross-referencing with some friends."

Laure narrowed her eyes. "Why all this work? Are we not enough proof of his ability?"

"Yes, but this procedure does away with what I have. What I'm familiar with for what I am not, just for the hope of something better. It's a little much. If I'm wrong, then what? I'm still stuck with less."

She nodded. "Yes, it's an easier decision if you are already missing something."

A silence hung in the air between the two. Shadow followed the currents to the local source, Laure's foot. He gripped it with invisible tendrils, trying his hardest to keep her from moving, like he did with Vine's guard.

Laure smiled at Zane with pity. She tried to turn away, but she tripped. The detective dropped the leg and grabbed her, keeping her from falling into the street. She blushed and scrambled to steady herself. Shadow let go of her foot and gave the woman freedom again. Laure started to apologize, but stopped and went on her way.

Shadow snickered at what he had done, then decided to torment Zane. *You two look cute.*

Zane scoffed.

The big men standing guard outside The Body Shop eyed the detective as he approached, sending a chill down his back. The men whispered to each other. Zane sensed something was wrong, but kept his face as calm as possible as he neared the door.

The detective lifted the leg. "Just here to return the leg and get my cane. I need it back."

One man stepped in his way, his hat blocking one of his eyes. "Sorry, but the good doctor is out. We will take care of it for you."

One of the men extended a hand for the leg as the others surrounded him. His hand itched for his wand, but he didn't want to start a fight that he could avoid. "Here, but can I get my cane?"

The man gave a wicked smile and pointed to the nearest alley. "Sure, it's right over there."

Zane shook his head, trying to look apologetic. "That's all right. I can come back for it later."

He tried to move out of the circle, but one of the men grabbed him by the collar. Another grabbed his left arm and forced him into the alley. Zane wanted to reach for his wand, but decided to wait. As soon as they were out of sight, they slammed him into the wall and beat him.

The men looked as if they had lived lives of hard labor, and Zane could feel it in each punch and kick. The detective balled up his body to absorb the blows. When the hits ceased, a hand pulled Zane away from the wall. "We know ya been sniffing around here."

Zane tried to deflect. "No, I've just been slow to purchase a limb."

A man with a bronze-covered fist spat on him. "No, we been watching ya. We know you've been talking with them agents from the Institute."

The detective didn't react. The doctor's guards knew about the agents—that was information he didn't have before. "I don't know what you—"

The bronze fist slammed into his gut, forcing the air from Zane's lungs. He coughed as a man with porcelain feet kicked at his chest. Zane fanned his arms, pushing the leg off to the side. Surprising his assailants with a burst of strength, he slammed his shoulder into the bronze-fisted man.

The man stumbled back, but didn't fall. From out of view, a hand grabbed Zane and tossed him into the opposing wall.

Shadow pleaded with his host. *You should use your wand* now, *detective! These men will kill you!*

Zane gritted his teeth and went for his wand. A prosthetic foot slammed into his side. He saw it coming, and clenched his muscles at the last moment.

"We are going to beat your sorry a—"

Zane whipped out his wand and fired it into the nearest prosthetic limb.

Bronze and porcelain exploded into a thousand pieces. There, in the center of the mess, was a black stone with hazy light around it. The man fell back screaming as an inky liquid, darker than oil, spread across him. The other two men moved closer to beat Zane.

"You shouldn't have done that!"

The man with the white feet lifted one to kick Zane as Shadow roared in his ears.

I was right!

Zane felt an unnatural chill flow through his body, and the world around him dimmed as if he was shrouded in a deep shadow. His attacker fell backward with a loud thud. The other two men stepped away.

"What happened?"

"I don't know. My legs aren't moving! Give me a hand."

The man, now with just a single hand, reached down to grip his cohort. He attempted to tug him up. "My hand won't move! What's going—"

His prosthetic arm suddenly lashed out, smashing his friend in the face.

"Damn it! What the hell was that?"

"I don't know! I don't have control over my—"

At that moment, he was kicked by the man on the ground, over and over, as fast as his leg could go. All the while, Shadow laughed in Zane's ear.

"Now leave before you three get really hurt," the detective yelled.

They turned to Zane. "What? How are you doing this?"

As if on command, Shadow brought the limbs to a halt. For a moment, the men looked at each other as if trying to decide what to do. Before they could decide, the one-armed man gripped his friend's prosthetic foot and crushed it. The man screamed as a black, stony jewel fell to the ground. He tried to grab it, but screamed as his skin blackened and let go.

Zane leveled his wand at them and motioned to the end of the alley with his head. "Get out of here, now!"

They scrambled away, the man on the ground scraping against the brick of the alley. Zane watched until they passed into the crowd of people, then stared down at the gem on the ground as the shadows seemed to ripple around it. As Zane reached for it, he noticed Shadow's eyes spiraling toward it.

I knew something wasn't right about those limbs. They dabbled in magic that they should have left alone.

Zane picked it up. The stone was warm in his hand, as if it had sat out in the sun. He slipped it into his pocket and shuffled back to the store. "What is this?" he muttered under his breath.

Shadow's voice was silky, shaky and excited, all of which made Zane nervous. *It's a piece of the Well.*

"The Well?"

I can't say any more, the curse . . .

He adjusted his clothes and stepped out into the street.

In the shop, Aluxen was looking over the limb the guards had taken from Zane. His face showed no sign of surprise. "Mr. Vrexon, I didn't expect to see you again. How can I help you?"

Zane stepped up to the table, standing across from the doctor.

He moved his balled fist over the table and dropped the stone, letting it bounce. The light around it darkened and rippled. Aluxen's face went pale, and he jerked back as if the stone was a deadly snake.

From the corner of Zane's eye, he spotted his cane. The detective slowly went over and picked it up. "I'm just here to pick up my cane."

He turned and walked out, leaving the shocked doctor alone. Once he was two districts away, he pulled free his flask and drank deeply. It felt as if he had damaged every bone in his body. His breathing grew weak.

I'm getting too old for this.

36

lyssa handed Frame a hooded cloak that matched the dress she'd loaned the student. Frame glanced in the mirror. It was a simple dark blue dress with an even darker cloak. She felt the needlework, looking at her enchanted clothes behind her. "Are you sure I need to change?"

Alyssa nodded with a simple smile. "It is obvious to anyone watching that if you're clean of ash, then you're wearing clothes from the Institute. That would drive most people away, but . . ."

Frame nodded. It did set her apart, like a target. She started to breathe harder, and sweat poured down her neck. The walls seemed to grow closer and the room darker.

Alyssa placed a hand on her shoulder, pulling her free from the growing anxiety. "Frame, it's going to be okay. No one will hurt you here."

Frame's eyes started to mist, and Alyssa pulled her close. "It's okay. You don't have to come with me. You're more than welcome to stay here, work on your thesis."

"No, I need out. I have been isolated for two weeks, and I feel like the walls are caving in."

Alyssa couldn't quite understand, but she gave a polite nod. She had lived her life inside, but that was in the endless halls of the Institute. "Tell me about your great-grandmother."

"Well, she's always been kind. It's through her connections—and finances—that I am able to go to the Institute. But . . ."

"But what?"

"For some reason, my great-grandmother never thought highly of me. I kind of believe it's because of Vine. She was always belittling me, making me look stupid or foolish. If Vine had her way, I would have never even left the house or been out from under her thumb."

"That's horrible! And even after all that, you still agreed to be her 'agent' in this investigation?"

Anger flooded Frame's face. "No! She asked me to get the address and then went behind my back to the Institute and asked them for time off from the school. She had no business doing that."

"They allowed it, just like that?"

"Yes," Frame said. "She mentioned the Agwen incident."

Alyssa opened her mouth to comment, but stopped. She looked down, appearing to be reconsidering her words. "What reason would your great-grandmother have to seek out someone like this doctor?"

Frame smiled a little as she remembered her great-grandmother dancing at every ball when Frame was younger. Despite being the oldest person there, she would keep up with people less than half her age.

"She was always what I would call a youthful soul. At least, she always looked young. When I got older, I found out that she kept herself so youthful and healthy with all sorts of brews, elixirs, and other magic treatments . . . But that only goes so far."

Alyssa stroked her chin. "The Elaoine End, where flesh and organs can keep going, but bones and joints can't be refurbished."

"Exactly, so I guess that this doctor must be offering something along the lines of fixing her brittle bones and joints, but I can't imagine how, even with all those prosthetics, she would be able to do all she did in her youth. I mean, there's too much to replace."

The bell tower nearby marked noon. Alyssa stood and adjusted her dress in the mirror. "We are going to meet with Zane after we go take a look at that doctor's community."

"Why are we going again, instead of him?"

"Zane got hurt last time he was there; he needs to lay low for a bit."

"Are we going to be safe?"

Alyssa gave her a grim smile. "Is anything safe?"

Frame sighed and collected the cloak. She breathed deeply, steadying her nerves. "Let's go."

37

Frame followed Alyssa, her eyes darting from shadow to shadow and alley to alley, looking for the attacker. She told herself that she was safe, but she still felt nervous.

"Are you sure you wanted to come with me?" Alyssa asked. "You could have stayed behind at the office."

Frame shook her head. "No, I feel safer being with someone else."

"Zane is there."

Frame shrugged. "I don't really know him, and how can I let you go out by yourself?"

The day was bright, thanks to a rare thinning of clouds. Frame brushed the constantly growing piles of ash from her shoulders. She wondered how everyone else seemed unbothered by it.

They passed the pub Zane had mentioned. It looked nice and respectable, a simple little place.

Alyssa pulled out a pair of glasses and studied the café through them. The glasses looked simple, but Frame could see the faint traces of runes. "What do they do?"

"They allow me to better study the ebb and flow of magic. Usually, I only use it to study magical artifacts. It's helpful if runes aren't being used."

"Are such things common?"

"Usually only in the studying of Fey relics."

Ah, I had almost forgotten. Alyssa taught that subject. "Are you getting anything?"

Alyssa shook her head, allowing her glasses to slide down her nose. "If their setup is how Zane described it, they would've taken steps to cover their trail. Let's continue."

The sound of clacking filled the air; it was subtle at first, but the deeper they traveled, the louder it became. The residents ignored them as they passed. There were a few stores and a butcher shop, but most of the buildings looked to be apartments. The majority of the men looked to be builders and other hardworking professionals.

Alyssa veered toward the butcher shop. For the first time, Frame could see a little worry in her face. "Zane has taught me that some of the best places to ask questions are places where everyone has to go."

"But how do we get them to open up to us?"

The bell above the door rang as they stepped through the door. The man behind the counter had a prosthetic arm that reached up to his bicep. With it, he picked up a slab of meat, rotated it, and slapped it back down.

The butcher looked hesitant for a moment when he saw them. "Ah, hello. Welcome to my shop."

Alyssa smiled and started to point out the cuts of meat to Frame. "Just look at those—it's just like we were told."

The man wiped off his hands as he moved to the front counter. "Told? What was told to you?"

Frame nodded, like they had practiced. "That this is the place to find the best cuts of meat."

The man's look of suspicion turned to pride. He gestured around the shop. "Yes, this is the best place to find meat! What can I get for you?"

Alyssa named a few cuts, and the man got to work. Frame's attention was focused solely on the prosthetic limb. He whipped the arm, and a butcher's knife flipped out, the blade extending from his hand. Frame started to hyperventilate, and her vision narrowed on the blade as it cut into the meat.

Alyssa placed a calming hand on her shoulder. "Are you okay?" she whispered.

Frame nodded and adjusted her clothes. The butcher looked concerned, too. "Missy, are you all right?"

She bowed with an apology. "The blood got to me. I was simply light-headed."

He nodded with a weak laugh. "I have seen people faint at the sight of blood. Hell, it took me a while to stand the sight after I lost my arm."

That gave Alyssa the opening she was waiting for. "That is an amazing limb. I hope it isn't too bold of me to ask, but . . ."

He wiped the blade off and flicked his arm to fold the blade back inside. He flexed to show off his limb. "Well, as you heard, I am an excellent butcher, better than my rivals. One came after me, claiming that I had a—"

He paused, looking for a way to say it. "Had a late-night meeting with his wife. Of course, it was a lie. Nonetheless, the man came at me with a butcher knife. I got my arm up to block, but the local doctor was forced to amputate it due to the damage."

Frame's mouth was dry, and she had no idea what to say.

Alyssa frowned in sympathy. "How did you meet the doctor here?"

"I was in a drunken stupor, 'cause what else am I going to do if I don't have my cutting arm? My wife—who is a saint, bless that woman—heard a rumor about his work. She tossed a cold bucket of water on me and forced me out the door."

Alyssa pointed to the limb. "It's an amazing feat, but it must have cost a fortune. I don't know if even nobles could afford such a luxury."

The butcher nodded his head, and flipped his knife back out to cut again. "Oh, I don't doubt it, but Dr. Aluxen had a simple request. He asked me to move down here and keep doing what I was doing. It took some time, but I got used to it."

"That's it?"

"Well, he also requested that I give him all the bones from the shop. He does pay for them, though I sell them at a discount."

"The bones?" Frame narrowed her eyes. "What would he need the bones for?"

He smiled and held up his appendage. "These are porcelain

bones."

Alyssa shook her head. "No, they can't be. I don't know of any porcelain that tough."

He shrugged and wrapped their meat. "It is what it is. I don't need to understand."

He gave Alyssa the total and she paid. As the women walked back to the office, Frame eyed all the food. "Did we need to buy all this?"

Alyssa nodded, making a note on the receipt. "Zane taught me that people are more open if you buy their goods. A customer is a step above a stranger. Also, we needed meat for dinner tonight."

38

Zane scratched the back of his head as he set his flask down. He had gone through half a bottle, much more than he should have drunk, yet his head still felt hazy. It was like the room was filled with pollen. Of all the blows he took, none should have left such pressure in his head.

Frame and Alyssa came in, slipping off their coats and shaking off the ash by the door. Alyssa lingered, looking at the pile, before following Frame across the room.

"Was there anything of interest in the district?"

They glanced at each other before Alyssa gave him a slight nod. "Yes, but we don't know how it might relate to the case."

Zane raised an eyebrow. "What do you mean?"

"We went to the butcher. He could extend a blade from within his prosthetic arm."

Frame's voice sounded dry. "It was just like when I was attacked. I think he must have had an arm just like the butcher's."

Zane rubbed his chin. *What are the odds that someone related to Franxen attacked her?* Too unlikely to be a coincidence. Something else was at play. "Have you met with anyone connected to Aluxen before?"

"No, I . . ." Frame froze, and a look of realization poured over her. "Well, maybe. When I met up with Vine, when she gave me this job. A lawyer working stepped out of her office as I waited to go in. He had a hand that looked like it came off a skeleton."

Her voice was panicked. "Do you think he did this? But why, or how?"

"Did he overhear your meeting?"

"No. Vine's new guard was standing watch."

Zane leaned back in his chair and crossed his arms. "Do you know the nature of the deal that your great-grandmother is trying to make with the doctor?"

"Nothing specific. Just that it was probably related to her Elaoine condition."

Zane noticed the pile of ash by the door and sighed. It hadn't bothered him until he looked at it directly. Now he felt compelled to clean it. "What is this Elaoine condition?"

"Elaoine End refers to a condition where through alchemical means a person tries to keep themselves young. But only flesh, organs, and muscles can be kept that way. Eventually, all the bones and joints break down. It is believed to be named after a noble from the founding of the empire that wanted to be immortal like the old Fey empire before them."

"So what could the doctor give to help with it?"

Alyssa shrugged her shoulders. "The only thing I can think of is that Lady Lexone is trying to replace key parts of her body to make up for the failing ones. I don't think such a procedure has ever occurred, though. I'm not sure what would even happen . . . I mean, after a certain point, nothing would help."

Medical school was a distant memory, growing even fainter as Zane got older. Nothing in his short experience suggested this would work. "I don't think it's possible either. The person would most likely bleed out before you finished, even with large amounts of Troll's Blood. Not to mention her age, on top of all that."

While Frame and Alyssa worked on the thesis, Zane grabbed the broom. As he brushed the debris from outside into a dustpan, Frame lost her focus. "What do we do now? The district knows your face, and I'm being followed."

Zane tossed the ash out the window before taking his seat. "Figure out what the bigger picture might be. We need more information. I don't think we have a choice: We need to go see your great-grandmother."

Alyssa nodded in silent agreement. The young student sighed.

"I don't think I have seen her since my last holiday off, but I heard her schedule is pretty open now. She lives out in the countryside, a good few miles out."

"That's fine," Zane shrugged. "We can hire a carriage and put it down as an expense related to the case."

A small grin crept along Frame's face. "Can I rent the carriage?"

"Fine with me."

Alyssa set the papers and pen to the side. "Come, Frame. We'll go find that carriage."

After they had gone, Zane looked to Shadow's corner. "So how do those limbs and the black stone relate to you?"

Shadow's eyes came into view like blood seeping through cloth. *Directly, I don't know. But I believe that this doctor has a patron. The patron might be something of an old comrade of mine.*

Fear crept up Zane's spine, along with memories of the darker-than-black tunnels of the Ghoul War. "More ghouls?"

Shadow gave a pained laugh, the first Zane had heard him make. *The ghoul lords are not my allies or my friends. I was there as a diplomat of sorts, but that's not right either.*

"Then what were you?"

Shadow's eyes seemed to search the room before turning back to Zane. *In a sense, I was a hunter. But beyond finding man and beast, I looked for anything that my liege . . . my boss would want. My work was much like yours in many ways.*

Zane scoffed at the idea of Shadow being a detective, his critical voice and piercing red eyes being paid to investigate. Instead, he could see in his mind a dark-haired man painting each victim he met. For a moment, he wondered if it was his imagination or Shadow's memory.

39

Frame stared out the carriage window with glee. The magic lantern inside produced a faint light that could be increased or decreased. The seats had been perfumed before they got in.

The detective seemed to squirm at the comfort, as if he was not sure how he should feel about it. He tapped his fingers on his cane. "Are you sure this was the only carriage available?"

"Oh yes," Frame said. "This was the only one of quality befitting one working for the Lexone family. Pulling up in this will give her the best impression."

Alyssa giggled as Zane rolled his eyes.

The ride was pleasant, and memories of fun times with her great-grandmother played out in Frame's mind. She remembered spring trips to the countryside, where fields overflowed with flowers and the evenings were overflowing with party guests. She had never seen anything like it since her great-grandmother became bedridden.

A knock on the door drew her attention back to reality. The carriage driver opened the door. "Uh, the people at the gate are asking who you are—"

The thin man was shoved away by a heavy-set man with a fur mantle around his shoulders. "What are ya doing—" He looked at Frame and gave a polite grin.

"Oh, young miss! I didn't know it was you. How are ya?" The big man threw open the door fully and Frame stepped out.

"Belard! I thought you retired years ago."

His toothy grin gave him the look of a much younger man. "Ah, that I was, but I didn't do well sitting around. I thought you were off studying at the Institute."

Frame nodded happily and gestured to Zane and Alyssa. "I was, before Vine pulled me away to do a job for the family. I am the liaison for these two, Detective Vrexon and Alyssa Benedictus."

"A detective? I never would have thought that the bit—"

Frame knew where the old man was going. "Belard! You know you can't call her that."

He laughed. "Oh, right. Well, what can she do? Fire me? Ha! But if you're here to meet the old mistress, then you better get moving. I'll open the gate."

"Thank you."

Belard helped Frame back into the carriage and shouted for the gate to be opened.

"It seems you are well-remembered," Alyssa said as they waited.

Frame smiled. "I grew up here, and I was always close with the staff. I think I was closer to them than my family."

Zane coughed as he tried to drink some of his brew. "Your cousin runs things, right? So I guess you're a more distant family member."

Frame had to stop herself from gritting her teeth. The phrase "branch relative" was spouted at her by her cousin over and over when they were young. "Yes, I do believe in a normal situation that would be the case."

Zane lowered his flask. "Normal?"

"All that is left of my family is my great-grandmother, cousin, and me. In theory, I have just as much chance of one day inheriting the property. I really don't wish ill on either of my last two family members, though."

As the carriage started moving again, Zane put the flask away. "So what happened?"

Frame closed her eyes for just a moment, the pain of old emotional scars flaring. "There was an outbreak, some type of disease. I don't know what it was, but I remember black lesions that oozed. In the end, everyone's bodies had to be burned."

The carriage came to a stop, and Belard opened the door. They stepped down onto a stone porch before entering through a set of large wooden doors with flower carvings. Two older servants stood on the main staircase smiling down at them warmly. Descending, they met the guests at the ground level.

Lista, head maid and Belard's wife, enveloped Frame in a great hug. "My lady, we weren't expecting you. Please let us help you inside. Is there any luggage?"

She shook her head. "No, we are here on business. Sorry, it will be a little while longer before I come home."

The head butler, Trexon, was a thin-faced man with an abundance of white hair. He bowed politely. "Lady Lexone, I can only assume you are here to see the mistress?"

"Yes. Is she available?"

He gestured for them to follow. "Yes, her weekly meeting should be—"

The conversation was overtaken by the sound of Lista yelling at Belard as he was about to enter the home. "Oh, no you don't! Your boots are covered in mud. You've been out fishing instead of doing your job, no doubt. If ya step in here, we will be cleaning for days."

Belard looked shocked and hurt, but Frame knew he was okay. "But Frame is back, and I haven't seen her in years. How will we know she is doing all right?"

"At dinner when I tell you about it, or when she is outside. But if you set a foot into the house, then you will be sleeping on the floor."

Belard shrugged his shoulders and backed away with a mischievous smile. "Saints, woman! You would keep me out in the cold over such a thing? All right, fine. Frame, you make sure and say goodbye before taking off."

Frame smiled and nodded.

With the door shut, Lista came over to her. "We have missed you so much. How are you?"

She hesitated for a moment. "I'm good, but we really do need to see my great-grandmother."

Lista seemed to catch the hesitancy, but let it slide, much to Frame's relief. "Aye, she is here. Isn't that so, Trexon?"

"Yes, she is in another meeting with the new lawyer."

Zane leaned forward, looking to the upper floors.

The aged man sighed. "Mr. Tom hasn't been around in over two months to make adjustments to the will. The lawyer here is Chiron Falto."

The name sounded familiar to Frame, but she couldn't place it.

"The man comes so often that we have thought of keeping a bedroom for him," Lista added.

Zane's voice sounded rough. "Is she being taken to court?"

Trexon shook his head. "No. From what I can tell, it's some joint business venture."

They made their way upstairs and down the hall until they reached the master bedroom, which was anchored by a grand window overlooking the drive. Frame knew her great-grandmother had watched their arrival from it. She was always looking for another guest to talk to.

Before Trexon had a chance to knock on the door, it opened. Out stepped a man with round-rimmed glasses and a prosthetic arm. *Oh, I remember now!* That skeletal arm was all Frame could remember of the man.

Trexon bowed to him. "My apologies. I should have known that my mistress would want to see her family right away."

Chiron smiled and gave a dismissive wave. "No reason to apologize to me. This allows her time to gather her thoughts, so it is completely fine. I need a break anyway."

As he turned down the hall, Alyssa whispered in Zane's ear. "I'll talk to the lawyer while you two talk with the great-grandmother."

Trexon turned to Frame. "The mistress will see you now."

40

*Y*ou are on edge, detective. Relax.

Shadow's voice irritated the already-tired Zane. He didn't like to give the creature any satisfaction, even when he was right. The detective tried to relax, but his body refused.

The door closed behind them, with Zane looking back after the loud click. On it was carved a masquerade ball under the glow of a moonlit night.

The room was large, far larger than he first expected. The walls were adorned with paintings and rows of books. A piano and harp added to the posh atmosphere. His eyes drifted to the bed, and he was enthralled with its unique look. It hung from the ceiling like a large basket with a green vine design.

A woman's voice called from the bed, but it was not what Zane expected. She sounded much younger. "Please come over here to the couch."

From the seats of a low-backed couch, they could see out the large window toward the city. Alviun looked like a black stain on the horizon. Zane was still staring at the city when Frame moved past him to give her great-grandmother a soft hug. "I'm sorry that I haven't written to you in such a long time."

"Oh dear, I understand. You are a student in her youth. Now who is this gentleman?"

Zane turned to face Lady Lexone, her hair golden and her skin smooth. If he hadn't known the woman's age, he would never have thought that this was a grandmother, let alone a great-grandmother.

Despite the condition of her skin, a closer look showed Zane that her finger, wrist, and elbow joints were swollen. The detective snapped out of his studying and gave a slight bow. Frame smiled and gestured to him. "This is Zane Vrexon, a detective."

"Oh, a detective? What are you doing here?"

He sighed as he sat back on the couch. It was far too soft, and he felt like he was being pulled down into its folds. The tension it took off the injured leg didn't feel right, and he adjusted again. "I am looking into a man named Franxen Aluxen."

Zane studied her face, but couldn't find a hint of surprise or concern. "We were asked to look into him by Vine."

She nodded her head with a warm smile. "Oh yes, I do know about her little investigation. Didn't know who she had hired, though."

Frame's jaw dropped. "You already know about the case? Did Vine tell you about it?"

The elderly lady laughed haughtily. "Vine may be the one who runs our family's business, but I am still the owner. I have several employees who are loyal. They let me know about such things."

Zane laid his cane across his knees. "Then I can get straight to the point. What is Dr. Aluxen asking you for, and what are you looking to get out of it?"

The old lady smiled and looked at the window longingly. "I have always been blessed abundantly by the saints to have both the fortune and luck to pay for the necessities of life, but I always found it strange how we 'die,' little by little, before our time. So, I decided to find a way to stand against time."

"How so?"

Lady Lexone stroked her hair with one of her bony hands. "Well, you see, there are many old alchemist brews. Very old, dating back to the beginning of the empire and the fall of the Fey nations. The records show that many humans wanted to be like the Fey that they'd just defeated. And who wouldn't? It is said they never aged, always remaining young and beautiful. This caused the ingredients of these potions to be overharvested and the recipes fought over until they were lost and fell into story, then into myth."

She winked. "Almost all of them. I was fortunate in some of my endeavors. Yet . . ."

She rubbed her swollen joints. "Well, I can fix most anything but my joints. It's called the Elaoine End." She looked up to the detective. "Have you heard of this condition?"

"I have, but I can't imagine how this doctor could help. He makes prosthetics. And while they are amazing, I doubt that he could replace your bones and joints."

With closed eyes, she nodded in agreement. "I know, but it could provide me with better mobility than I have now. What he asked me for is a minor thing."

Frame spoke up in a quiet voice. "What is that?"

"Besides a small amount of money, he asked me to host a ball."

Frame jumped to her feet, both excited and scared. "Why? You haven't held one in over a decade! Not since—"

She stopped herself, swallowing whatever words she was about to say. "W-what would he get out of such an event?"

"Connections. My balls are still something to talk about, no? They are more like a fairytale now that I have grown old. If I hold one, people from all over the empire will show up. From this, the doctor would like the opportunity to prove the success of his work."

Zane raised an eyebrow, not sure what to make of the situation. "Do you know that he might be using illegal magic to complete his prosthetics?"

Lady Lexone shrugged. "Does it matter? If he shows results, then all other consequences are minor."

Zane had no doubt that she had previously dabbled in some illegal trade, most likely to get some form of elixir. He still couldn't find any information that would satisfy his client. The detective stood up, resting on his cane, and extended his hand in the proper fashion to someone in a station above him. "Thank you for your time, Lady Lexone. I hope I haven't been too much of a bother."

Her eyes looked not at him, but through him, as if he was not there. Her eyes showed a hint of jealousy as Frame moved with ease across the room.

"Thank you for talking to us."

"Of course, my dear."

41

Alyssa followed the lawyer as he walked in short strides down the hall. "Excuse me. I'm sorry to bother you, but I wanted to ask you about your hand."

He stopped, pulled his sleeve up with a smile, and lifted his normal hand. "Oh, this? I think most everyone is born with one."

She blushed and shook her head, now feeling embarrassed. "No, I meant your, um—"

He laughed and waved his hand in front of his face. "No, it's fine. I know what you're talking about."

He switched his briefcase to his normal hand, then used a free finger to pull up his sleeve. "You're more than welcome to take a look at it."

Alyssa pulled her glasses out of her pocket. "Oh, I should be more polite. My name is Alyssa, and I'm a trained wizard from the Institute. I hope it's all right to study your arm using my glasses?"

He shrugged his shoulders, with a rare, undaunted smile that Alyssa didn't normally see when she mentioned the Institute. "That's fine with me. I'm not sure if this even uses magic."

She searched for any sign of magical particles, but the limb was bare. It reached halfway down the forearm, and merged with the flesh at the base with a cuff. The porcelain looked smooth, almost impossibly so. As the fingers moved, weights could be heard inside rising and falling with a clack.

"May I touch it?"

The lawyer nodded.

Gently, Alyssa touched the surface and found it strangely cold, far colder than it should have been. She thought about using eldritch words to see whether there would be a reaction, but decided against it. She pulled back from him.

"It's brilliantly made. I've never seen anything like this before."

He smiled, letting his sleeve roll back down. "I thought that you said you worked for the Institute."

She blushed again as she removed her glasses. "I was a professor in the Fey department."

The lawyer looked genuinely surprised. "A professor? What would a professor of such a field be doing here?"

"Well, it's a complicated story. I'm taking a break from that job for now."

He smiled and studied her for a moment. "I would love to hear about it sometime, if it would be possible . . ."

"Maybe, but I must ask what *you* are doing here."

"Oh, that's easy. I am here on behalf of my client. You see, I am a lawyer by trade. I'm setting up an opportunity to show my client's work. He will be showing it off at a ball that the lady of the house is setting up."

Hosting a ball as a promotion was a long-held tradition. Alyssa knew the practice was even older than most people believed, going all the way back to the Fey courts. She assumed he worked for the doctor. If so, then it would only make sense he wanted to expand the doctor's reach.

"Actually, I will be attending the ball," the lawyer said. "Would you like to come with me?"

She blinked for a few moments. "As a date?"

"Yes. Do you have an address where I could call on you?"

Alyssa was taken aback. "I-I just met you, so I don't think it would be appropriate to—"

He finished the thought. "Ah, yes, I see. That is probably smart to be cautious and all. But is there any way I could contact you? Perhaps a way for me to send you a letter?"

She fumbled as she reached inside her pocket and pulled out a blank charmed letter. He looked at it, confused. Alyssa gently handed him the envelope. "This is a spell-charmed letter. Once the letter is sealed, it will find its way back to me. A marvelous tool of magic. But it's not something that can be mass-produced. It requires the address to be written in runes and infused with magic, which requires special inks and powders."

He examined it, then slid the envelope into his pocket ever so carefully.

"Will this be all right?" Alyssa asked.

"It's fine. This is a wonderful tool. I wish we all had them. When I find out more, I will send you a message. And if it's all right, I think I will see you again soon."

He bowed and walked away. Alyssa felt a slight thump in her chest in rhythm with his footsteps.

42

Frame stepped from her great-grandmother's room with Zane close behind. Alyssa was waiting at the door. Her cheeks were rosy, and Zane's gaze lingered on her for a moment. Neither of them seemed to notice, but Frame did.

The detective leaned heavily on his cane as they were escorted out by the house servants.

Lista stepped close to Frame. "What did Lady Lexone say?" she whispered.

Framed leaned in, as the words she was about to speak would send her into a frenzy of excitement and nervousness. "That there is going to be a ball."

Lista's mouth was agape in shock, and she seemed to be on the verge of shouting. Frame quickly placed a finger over her own mouth, shushing the maid. She nodded and calmed herself. "Oh, it has been too long since the last one. Did you know I met my Belard at one of those parties? It's been years since we had a ball around here; your cousin would never allow it. Any time someone brought it up, she would scoff at the cost."

"A ball is great for gaining advantage over others, but not at the cost of selling my house," Vine would always say to Frame and the servants. *Deep down, does she not like balls because of the cost or what happened to the family?*

Alyssa and Zane connected as they approached the stairs. "What did the Lady Lexone say?"

"She is working with the doctor in hopes of getting new bones or joints or something that would give her just a little more mobility."

"What does the doctor get out of this arrangement?" Alyssa

asked. "The lawyer had mentioned something about a ball."

"That's their plan: To hold a ball so he can demonstrate his work. I assume he will bring in patients who will show how great the prosthetics are. From what she said, she has a reputation—a rather grand one—regarding the balls she has hosted."

"That makes sense, but then what should we do?"

Zane stopped and turned back to Frame. "How does this affect our investigation?"

Frame shrugged. "Why do you ask me? I'm not my cousin."

Zane smirked. "But you're her representative."

She stopped and thought about it for a moment before giving into a heavy sigh. "I'll send a letter to my cousin to see what she wants. I don't know what to expect."

"Of course."

"Vine can deal with not getting what she wants after dragging me out of school. At the very least, she can deal with a ball." Frame turned to her old servants. "You two will have a lot of work to do soon."

Lista and Trexon smiled and chatted about the work ahead of them. They waited at the front door of the mansion for the carriage to pull around.

As it arrived, a cold breeze blew across Frame's face, causing visions of the attempt on her life to resurface.

How does that fit into all this? Was it random? If it was connected, how?

Belard jumped from the front of the carriage with an umbrella in hand. He ran up and escorted each person through a drizzle of rain.

As Frame waited for her turn, Lista approached her again. Her old face was lined with worry. "I didn't know how I should tell you, and I know it isn't my place, but there has been . . . talk about Vine. She was always here when the lady's personal lawyer, Tom, arrived. We don't know how she always knew, but we heard him complain afterward every time. She always cornered him in conversation, and a few times we overheard parts of their meetings."

Frame had never seen this much tension in Lista before. "What was it about?"

"Well, the last time Lady Vine cornered the poor lawyer was right around the time that Chiron started to come around. One of the girls was sweeping the floor near the door when she heard an outburst . . . a string of very unladylike things. She got closer and looked through the keyhole. She heard them talking about changing something and getting you out of the way."

Frame wondered whether her cousin was diabolical enough to send someone to attack her. *We're family,* she told herself, but the fear only grew stronger. "Was there anything else?"

Alyssa called from the carriage. "Frame, everything okay?"

She wanted to scream that nothing was okay, but held back. "Yes, sorry. I'll be there in just a moment."

Frame turned back to Lista, who shook her head. "That's all I've heard. Please be careful."

She grabbed the old maid and guard in a bear hug. With sad goodbyes, she stepped into the carriage. From its window, she watched the servants wave as the trio made its way back to the Black Heart of the Empire.

Frame had slept hard, too hard for dreams or nightmares to intervene. Whatever was in Alyssa's sleeping aid was strong, and she wondered how her host woke up so early. When she rose from the couch, Alyssa was already hard at work. Again this morning, she was staring at her maps.

Frame didn't understand their use, and Alyssa wouldn't explain, saying only that it was a personal project. They made breakfast together, and while they ate Frame asked what Chiron had said the previous day. With a slight blush, Alyssa explained.

The student set her silverware down. "He asked you to be his date to the ball?"

"Y-yes, I was really surprised. He was direct, and that was even after I told him that I was a member of the Institute."

"Why is that surprising?"

"Most people fear the Institute. After I show my badge, they tend to tense up. Chiron still seemed calm and interested."

Frame felt annoyed. She didn't like Chiron, or at least she didn't like his arm. *Zane should have been the one to ask her.* "Wouldn't it be better to go to the ball with Zane? I mean, isn't it strange that the lawyer of the man you're looking into just asked you out?"

Alyssa looked surprised, but thought about it. "I don't think Chiron knows about us looking into Dr. Aluxen. And Zane? No, I don't think that would be appropriate. I mean, yes, the man is handsome in a rugged sense, and his determination is admirable. But we work together, so that just wouldn't be right."

Alyssa's voice trailed off into a silence, and Frame found herself smiling. They finished breakfast and started for the office. When they arrived, Zane gave a polite smile and returned to his newspaper. The women chatted a little, mostly about improvements Frame could make in her thesis. Frame enjoyed the pleasant morning, until something out the window caught her eye.

Vine's carriage was parked outside. Frame's body tensed, remembering Lista's admission.

Vine and her guard could be heard arguing just outside the office door.

Alyssa placed one hand on her wand before opening the door. Vine pushed her way in, moving with purposeful strides toward Zane.

Vine's bodyguard scared Frame, and she still didn't know his name. He laid a hand on the saber around his waist and looked at her and Alyssa.

"Lady Vine is in the middle of negotiations. The office is closed. Get out."

Zane slapped the desk with his free hand. "This is my office! I get to decide when it's closed and who goes."

The bodyguard gave Zane a hard glare, but the detective didn't back down. "It's fine, Davidson." Vine said in a cold tone.

The guard took his hand off the saber and let his cloak fall in place. He stood rigidly, taking turns watching each of the women and then Zane.

Alyssa kept her hand in the slit of her dress even as she took a seat at her desk.

Frame followed. She could hear each beat of her heart and wondered if the others could too.

Vine turned to her. "What did you think you were doing going behind my back and contacting my great-grandmother? You putting that stress on her and—"

With a harsh voice, Zane stopped her. "Lady Lexone already knew about this investigation, and her health seemed just fine. Fine enough, in fact, to host a ball."

Vine froze at the words and sank into the chair. "A ball, really? Why would she hold one?"

"She struck a deal with Franxen. She holds a ball, and he sees what he can do to help with her mobility."

Vine rubbed her chin, thinking over the prospect. "She needs to stop. This would not only end in a financial error, but also a political one."

Zane moved his cane from his desk to his lap. "What do you want us to do? At this point, you would almost be better off trying to bribe some guards to go knock on the doctor's door."

Vine mumbled something that Frame couldn't hear, but she could only imagine that maybe her cousin had already tried it.

"What about those agents you mentioned? Isn't Dr. Aluxen being investigated by the Institute? Is there anything there?"

The detective was silent, his eyes looking to the corner. He stared hard before breaking into a smirk. "It's possible, but it will cost you extra for us to look into."

Vine was caught off-guard. "You can't be serious. I am already paying you far more than I should."

Zane met her glare. "I know, but I believe that following this path will be dangerous. Very dangerous. As such, I think it's fair to ask for compensation for the danger."

They haggled back and forth over the course of a few minutes before coming to terms.

"Obviously, I want you to chase any lead into the ground and stop the ball."

Zane shook his head. "I can't control that. Your great-grandmother seems sure it is happening. If you want to stop this ball, you'll have to go talk to her."

Vine stood up and snapped her fingers at Davidson. The two marched to the door, which the bodyguard opened for her. She turned back. "Find out what that man is up to, detective."

As Vine stepped out, the door slammed shut with a loud thud. Zane pulled his flask out and took a deep gulp before staring out the dirty window to make sure she left.

44

Alyssa glanced over her shoulder, her hand twitching for her wand. She was nervous, but only because Zane was nervous. He was dressed more casually than usual, and he'd even left his cane behind. The former professor had donned a cloak with a hood in hopes of hiding her face on their trek to the Laze Pot.

Stepping in from the dark smog of the city, many of the patrons gave them a careful look. The tension was thick, but it faded as Zane limped to the counter. The bartender's face was bruised, and half his mustache had been pulled out at the roots. "Hmm, I haven't seen you for a while. I thought you'd been knocked off."

Zane shrugged. "I think they were considering it. Are those two still in that room?"

The man nodded and pulled out the key. He escorted them to the door and opened it for them. Alyssa watched the familiar sight as two physical spaces matched up for just a few moments so the door could be opened. She wondered how many places outside of the Institute could hold such a room, and how much effort it had taken the Institute to set this up.

As they stepped inside the odd space, Alyssa felt what Zane had described. The folding of space in the room was rough, and not to the quality that she was accustomed. The hairs on her neck stood up as she made her way across the room.

Both agents reached for their wands. When they saw Zane, Will put his away; Crome kept his ready.

"Detective, I will be honest. I didn't expect to see you again. We heard that the guards around The Body Shop had pulled you aside for 'advice.' "

"Advice? What a strange way to describe trying to kick my teeth in. They tried to kill me, but I was able to crack one of their arms open."

Crome's eyes went wide as the wand slipped in his grasp. "Did anything happen?"

"Crome! We have another guest here. You are, ma'am?"

Alyssa pulled down her hood as she gave a polite bow. "Alyssa Benedictus. We met at my student's apartment."

Agent Will gave a curt nod. "Yes, now I remember. But why are you here?"

Zane pulled out a chair and eased himself down. His breathing was rough as he stretched his bad leg out to massage it. "I needed an extra hand getting around. My cane makes me too noticeable, but a person with a limp could be taken as someone looking for the doctor. Also, I've always come down here by myself, so this way I don't seem familiar."

Crome scoffed. "Is that really enough to disguise yourself?"

Zane shrugged. "I find most people really don't pay as close attention as they like to believe they do. But that's not why I came down here. I wanted to describe what happened after I was attacked."

The two agents looked at each other, then leaned in.

"So after the arm cracked, a black stone fell out. It was about two knuckles wide and smooth."

Crome's face went pale.

"One of the guards tried to grab it, but jerked his hand back like it burned him. I had only a moment to look, but his skin blackened where he touched the stone. He rolled across the ground in pain before his friends carried him off. But then . . ."

Crome was about to say something, but Will stopped him.

Zane waited for the older agent to motion for him to go on. "The weird part was the shadows surrounding the stone seemed to pull toward it, as if a tub of water was being drained."

Crome stood up, knocking his chair to the floor, creating an echo that wasn't right for the room. "I knew it! Jake was onto something. We've got the doctor now."

Will just sat quietly, looking up at Alyssa. The former professor had not taken a seat yet. She stared down at the agents, nervous but remembering a line from the book *Appearance of Strength*: "Height is, without fault, a tool in looking strong. While hard to use in violent situations, it is easily applied by standing over a sitting person, such as in social situations."

Will squinted at her. "You didn't just bring her as part of your disguise, did you?"

Zane's brow furrowed. "I told her about the stone and what happened. She has explained the problem that puts us in."

Alyssa pulled two folded notes from her pocket, handing one to each agent. "As you both should know, shadows are classified as part of the physical world, or *True World*. Even with all our knowledge, we can't augment, charm, or change an existing shadow in any way, except by changing the light source."

Will shook his head. "I have seen an illusion specialist make one, several in fact."

Alyssa countered. "Yes, but only after careful study of how a shadow naturally looks. The specialist can't make something cast a new shadow or move existing ones."

Will looked frustrated and crumpled the note. Alyssa assumed he knew where this conversation was going. "Please get to the point."

"If it lacks runes or signs of magic being used, then this stone may be classified as something from the natural world and not a matter of magic."

"You can't be serious," Crome protested. "With this account and what we saw happen to Jake, you can't think that was *natural!*"

Zane stared at them, rubbing his temple. Alyssa could feel the mounting pressure, but it was like this in academia when debates broke out.

"Something has happened to make this case personal to you two," the detective concluded. "What happened?"

Crome was about to talk, but was cut off by Will. "Do you know how much trouble we could get into if you say anything?"

"Yes, but catching this doctor is more important!" Zane coughed. "I've already signed a contract with you. I think the least you can do is share your information."

The two agents stared at each other before Will gave in with a nod. Crome turned to Zane. "Jake . . . was a far more dedicated agent than me. He was committed to getting to the bottom of things as fast as possible, so he cut off his own arm at the elbow."

Alyssa let out a gasp of shock and disgust. Zane shook his head. "Why would he do that?"

"He figured that if we could recover this magic, then he could keep one of the limbs for himself. So, after his surgery, he came back to the apartment we had rented for the case. We thought it would be safe to open it there, just take a look inside."

Crome's face paled as he recounted the event. "He found the space that Alyssa also pointed out to us, the one that looks to be filled with water. We did see a black stone, just as you described. At the time, we thought it was submerged in oil, not water. He reached in and grabbed it."

Crome's voice went weak, but Will carried on. "He screamed like it burnt him and then dropped the stone. We tried to help, but he was gone in a few minutes."

Alyssa felt for the agents. Zane was intrigued. "What was determined to be the cause of death?"

Will gave him a strange look. "He didn't— no, you misunderstand. He was gone."

Crome nodded. "Jake sank down into the ground."

Will pulled out a stained paper. "We tried to find the stone, but this is all that was left of it. We tested it every which way, but nothing came up. After that, we decided to drop the apartment as our base and set up here. We got permission to even connect it to the Institute to access better equipment."

The younger agent glared at Alyssa. "Now try to explain how this is natural."

She was about to answer, but couldn't find her voice. She didn't have an answer.

Will rubbed his bald head. "No, she still has a point. We need to focus on these stones. We didn't have much to go on before, and we still don't. We thought the limb held some type of charm to protect against accidents or had some type of fail-safe, but we couldn't find anything looking over that prosthetic limb you got us. So, unless we can get one of those stones, we can't prove anything either way. Even then, we have to find out whether they're naturally occurring or magically processed."

Zane forced himself up from his chair. "So we're still at the beginning?"

Alyssa spoke up. "No, we have some idea that this stone is related to shadows."

Will looked both curious and critical. "What do you suggest? You already said they are naturally occurring and unaffected by magic."

"By *modern* magic. It's possible there may be some old Fey stories that mention such things. It is also possible that they may have encountered this substance before. I could look into it."

Zane looked grateful. "Yeah, that's a good idea. Any information is better than none."

Alyssa felt the building pressure fade away as they left the room, but she could tell it still lingered on Zane. As they made their way back to the office, he had to take breaks and drink from his flask.

The third time he reached for it, she spoke up. "Please let me help you the rest of the way back."

Zane looked at her, embarrassed and confused. He grumbled at a nearby window before leaning over. "Okay."

45

Frame strolled through the doors of the Institute. The tension eased off her, like she was home. She felt safe in its ever-changing halls. Out of practice from her time off, she reached into her pocket and pulled out a small compass. The runes along the needle's edge glowed.

Alyssa pointed the way to the grand library before Frame had a chance to register the needle's direction. Frame was a bit jealous of the former professor's natural sense of navigation. Up stairs, through windows, and out doors they traveled before finally arriving at the floor dedicated to myths and legends.

A single student stood behind a large desk marked with the sigil of the library. He looked them over, pausing on Frame's non-Institute clothing. "How can I help you two?"

Alyssa pointed to the books beyond him. "We are looking for any myths relating to shadows. Don't worry, I know my way to the Fey section. If we need anything, we'll let you know. Thank you."

The young man nodded hesitantly and turned back to his work.

The Fey section was odd when compared to the others. The book covers were a blend of beautiful colors, like the feathers of birds trying to impress a mate.

Alyssa handed Frame a book with a large velvet cover. "Arcodus is well-known for his collection of stories and is well-regarded for his meticulous use of references. However, he is also infamous for adding in details not found anywhere else. We don't know if he made those up, or if he had other undocumented sources. Use it as guide. I'll be over there, doing the same with another author."

Frame nodded and got to work. A clock somewhere off in the distance rang once, then twice as the hours passed. She dug through the book, then picked up another. She read the stories of the boy who chased his shadow, the woman whose shadow whispered, and the sailor's shadow voyage. Frame marked each as she tracked down their sources. Each made reference to a specific book.

Again she dove into the books, searching, looking up and down the shelves. She couldn't find the book that was mentioned. Both she and Alyssa found several mentions of a Sea of Stars and water of shadows.

Alyssa pointed at some commentary written in another work. "It's believed to be poetic in nature, the way that Fey described the nature of shadows."

"Okay, but where is this book that's always referred to, *The Fey King's Descent*? I don't see it anywhere."

"I've heard of it," Alyssa said. "It's extremely rare, and only a few copies have ever been found. During the temple's Great Purge, many copies were lost. I am not sure if there's even a copy here."

"Is there anyone who might know more?"

Alyssa looked slowly up from her book. Her face pale, her jaw clenched. "Yes, but I dearly don't wish to see the man again."

"Who?"

"Agwen."

Frame felt her blood chill at the mention of his name. Memories of his eyes and how they'd controlled her washed over her like a flood. "H-how would we even find him?"

"We don't have to find him. He had a large collection in his study."

"But what happened to those books?"

Alyssa shrugged and turned toward the exit. "Let's go to my grandfather. He might have an idea."

They journeyed back into the halls that changed with each

door or junction until they came to a stop in front of a faded red door. Alyssa knocked and waited for a tired voice to call back. Alyssa pushed the door open into the small office. The sides of the small office were covered in large shelves, packed to the brim with books, scrolls, and more esoteric objects.

Behind the desk sat an old man with thinning hair and a beaming smile. He rushed over to his granddaughter, hugging her. "Alyssa! I haven't seen you in weeks. To what do I owe this surprise? Are you taking your job back?"

She shook her head. Frame noticed Alyssa looked comfortable, more comfortable than she had ever seen the former professor. "I'm helping with a case, but it has taken a strange turn. I am hoping to have a look at Agwen's book collection, the one he kept in his study. I had seen it a couple of times, and I'm hoping to find a rare book."

Disappointment flowed across the old archmage's face. "I have the key to the office. Let's go and take a look."

Benedictus-Lasome grabbed his iron staff and made his way out the door. He locked his office with an iron key, sending the door and walls rippling as the tumbler turned. Frame hoped that one day she would earn a set of keys like that, but doubted it would happen.

He switched to another key and placed it into the lock. He tapped the door with his iron staff while reciting eldritch words.

The door shimmered and opened to reveal a second office. The room was covered in dust, and the walls were bare. It lacked a desk and chair, but the back of the room contained large bookshelves that looked well-kept.

Alyssa looked over the room with a wash of emotion. "It's different. The Institute has emptied it."

Benedictus-Lasome nodded his head. "Agwen had stolen a lot from the Institute, so it makes sense that we would sell off the things he bought with those funds. I had them leave the books. . . . I thought that one day you might come back to take over the Fey Department and would want to go through them yourself."

"Thank you, but . . ." She stopped as she pulled a book from the shelf. Frame and the archmage followed suit. "What are you looking for?"

"It's a saga about a fey prince. We believe it might contain some information about our case."

"What is this saga about?"

Frame shrugged. "Besides containing some information on shadows, we don't know."

"How does this help with a case? I can't see myths of a bygone time being of any help."

"Well, you see—"

Frame coughed and stopped. Alyssa was shaking her head, her face showcasing her anxiety. "Sorry, but we can't tell you. It's confidential."

The archmage narrowed his eyes in suspicion. "Fine, but I hope you'll let me know when everything is said and done."

Alyssa smiled with a nod. "I will."

The book wasn't hard to find. Its pages were aged and the ink faded, but it was still readable. Alyssa started reading aloud.

"There once was a prince who lived an easy life. All that he could want was his, and nothing was beyond his grasp. Then one day, the tides of shadows broke free and the sea started to flood the world. Brave warriors went out to find an answer, but none ever returned. The tides climbed higher, and the ancient creatures of the abyss rose up to ravage the land. On a single small ship, the prince left. He spoke to those who swam the waters of the deep and, with their guidance, he found a spring.

"With potions brewed by his many wizards and a prayer, he steeled himself and drank deeply from the spring. From his blood came a stone born of fire and light. He fastened it to the hole at the spring's origin, sealing the waters. As he did, the spring became like that of the abyss, but yet wasn't. He told his father what he had accomplished and how to seal the other springs, yet happiness was not to be. For though he had sealed it away, he had been touched by the waters of the abyss. He vanished into their depths, never to be seen again. No funeral was held until the day the last of the springs was sealed and their locations lost."

Frame stared, confused, at Alyssa. "What does this have to do with shadows? This speaks of waters and the abyss."

Alyssa turned back a few pages and looked over notes in the margins. "The combination of waters and abyss is an old way the Fey described shadows. For them, shadows were seen as a world of black waters."

Her grandfather coughed. "Maybe I don't want to know what this case is about. Please, just stay safe."

S hadow listened intently as the women detailed their trip to the Institute. As the detective and his little group moved one step closer to the truth, Shadow grew nervous they'd uncover the revelation he feared would bring far more attention than he desired.

Shadow took up his roost in the corner as the women collected themselves.

"I think we found something."

The detective carefully folded his newspaper and set it to the side. "I'm all ears."

The old book looked familiar to Shadow, but he couldn't make it out from his angle.

"Is—is Shadow here?" Alyssa asked.

Zane raised an eyebrow and looked at him before nodding.

Frame looked around the room, confused. "I don't see anyone."

The detective eyed him as if daring him to say something, but Shadow was more interested in their words. The detective soaked in that silence for a moment before turning to Alyssa and Frame. "Is this somehow related to him?"

"Maybe, but I'm not sure." Alyssa waved a hand over the book.

The detective moved from his seat to the chair across from her desk. He frowned at the foreign symbols. "What makes you think he's related?"

Alyssa flipped to the inside cover. He cursed under his breath. "From the library of Debroven."

If Shadow had ears, they would have perked up at his name. *Ah, that's why it looks familiar.*

"It can't be a coincidence, can it?"

Alyssa shook her head. "I don't think so, especially going by how you describe him."

"Who are you two talking about?" Frame asked.

Zane glanced again in Shadow's direction. "I have a . . . connection with someone by the name of Shadow. We believe he went by the name Debroven once. Besides that, he's mostly a mystery."

Frame followed his sight to the wall and then looked around the room. "And he's here now?"

Zane scratched his head and gave a shrug. "Let's say for the moment that he's a wizard of sorts who likes to keep an eye on me, and that I can never be sure if he is listening."

The young student looked disgusted. "That sounds highly illegal. Any mage knows there's a high penalty for such actions."

"It's fine, for now," he said. "But what else did you two find?"

Alyssa opened to a bookmarked page and read off the short story.

Shadow listened, too. *Ah, how much more I understand now! What will they take away from it?*

47

Zane moved through the ashen streets of the city, his arm and leg aching from the incoming cold. Where he was going, he wasn't sure, but he had felt cooped up with Shadow in the small apartment. He needed, at the very least, the illusion of having space and time to think.

If only I could get my hands on another one of those black stones. He was so deep in thought that he didn't notice his name being called once, then twice. It was only when the small, feminine hand grabbed him by the sleeve that he finally noticed.

He turned back to see Laure. She stood there in a dirty shawl, her face just barely protected from the ash. She looked tired, with deep bags under her eyes. "Zane! We've been looking everywhere for you."

"Laure, what? What are you doing here?"

"We have all been looking for you, Dr. Aluxen wants to see you again."

"Why?"

She pulled harder on his sleeve, trying to convince him to follow her. At first, he resisted, but finally let her guide him. It might be a trap, but he needed something—anything—to get back into the workshop.

They traveled carefully through the city to the district where The Body Shop was located. Zane tried to regain his composure and his breath as he leaned heavily on his cane. The people stared at him, talking in hushed whispers.

"What's going on?" Zane whispered to Laure.

She smiled in admiration. "The doctor said you could help advance his technique to the next stage, that you were a key." Her tone was one of reverence, like that of a fanatic, when she spoke the word.

They're closer to a cult than I first suspected. The crowd made a path for them as they drew closer to The Body Shop. Even the guards that had fought Zane looked at him with pride. The guard who'd touched the stone was missing.

He stepped into the shop and found Dr. Aluxen standing at one of the tables, working on a prosthetic. The doctor turned his head, but only a little, motioning for Zane to come over.

On the table were parts of a prosthetic arm. The build and components were essentially the same as the leg. The doctor was polishing the pieces as he spoke. "I think we had a misunderstanding, one that has soured our relationship."

"You mean when your men were trying to 'persuade' me into not returning?"

Aluxen chuckled. "Aye, that is one way to describe them dealing with a spy."

He gave Zane a cold look, one that contradicted the smile that shined through his beard. "Let's cut to the chase. I know you're working for the Institute. They have been sniffing around here for some time now. You don't strike me as a mage, so you're an outside contact. That is unusual, from what I understand. I am guessing that gives you some flexibility."

Zane raised an eyebrow and gave a slow nod. "Something like that. But what are you getting at?"

The doctor set his tools down. "I need help. The next stage of my experimentation is complicated. I have read through the instructions multiple times, but the material is . . . well, hazardous, to say the least."

Franxen produced a box from his worn leather apron. He opened it to reveal another box, which he set in front of Zane with careful movements. "I want you to work for me, or at least work *with* me."

"Why me? Wouldn't one of those people out there be better suited?"

"Yes, but no one, and I mean no one, has ever been able to pick up a stone without these special gloves. Somehow, you can."

Zane looked down and opened the box. Sitting there, looking like a matte black pearl, was a stone like the one he'd seen before. The detective scanned the room as all of the shadows were pulled toward it.

Shadow spoke in his ear, louder and more substantial than ever before. *We should take his deal for now, so long as he can provide us with more of these.*

He brushed away the voice. The doctor seemed nervous with the stone exposed, but gestured for Zane to touch it.

It looked cold to the touch, but was warm. It felt pleasant in his hand, and the pains of his body seemed to fade as the world, for a moment, held more depth.

Aluxen chuckled. "I believe that we can work something out."

Zane hadn't realized that he'd been smiling, but shook himself out of it. He set the stone back in the box and took a step back. "What do you want in exchange?"

"I need your help, and I will give you that stone."

His heart perked up just a little, triggering a familiar need, like the one for his flask. "What's keeping me from taking the stone? Maybe I'll give it to the Institute that you claim I work for."

Dr. Aluxen shrugged. "I saw how you looked when you held it. We both know that if you tell them about it, they'll take it away and you will never see it again."

Zane wondered if that wouldn't be such a bad thing. Addiction was a strong force, and it already controlled part of his life. But he needed the stone; it was the missing piece in the investigation.

"I can accept that. Where do we go from here?"

Aluxen smiled deeply, his eyes like two pits. "We start your training now. Your medical experience will help in principle. Now, the first thing you need to know about that stone is that water spreads its effects. These limbs have holes to place the stone in, and its effects are carried through the limb. Think of it like a circulatory system, except there's no going or returning."

The doctor went on, going over the intricacies of the limb. Zane watched carefully and committed each word to memory. When he left that day, he felt a little stronger than normal, thanks to the stone in his palm.

48

Frame hung clothes from the line by the small bed Alyssa had found for her. She slept in the same room with Alyssa, and they even shared clothes. Her diminished sense of pride had allowed her to do this out of desperation, but she now felt guilty relying so much on her mentor. "Can we go by my apartment today?"

Alyssa stuck her head through the doorway to talk directly to her. "Of course, but are you sure you want to?"

"Yes, I think it's fine. I've overextended your hospitality."

Alyssa looked concerned as she entered the bedroom. "Are you sure? We would have to pass through the district where you were—"

"I'm fine. It'll be fine, but I *am* a little nervous about going back alone."

There was a gleam in Alyssa's eyes that said she understood. "I would be happy to take you. Let's head out after breakfast."

The two ate a simple meal, over which Alyssa gave Frame recommendations on how she should write her paper and who she should send it to next.

Frame felt happy in the small apartment. It had that deep sense of belonging that she so desired but that was so hard to grasp. Like the morning mist, it seemed always within reach, yet evasive. She had friends at the Institute, but they all were busy, none wanting to fall behind in their studies.

After the plates had been cleaned and set to dry, they grabbed their cloaks. With each passing day, the weather got colder, the wind sharper. They strolled out into the streets, hoods pulled up and gloves on their hands. Their breath hung visibly in the air.

The ash again fell in clumps that stuck to everything it touched like mud. Workers who swept the storefronts had already exchanged their brooms for shovels.

The closer they got to the Institute, the cleaner the streets became. It was a slight change at first, but rapidly improved thanks to the weather module tower that stood in the front of the Institute.

The shops also became more exotic as the district unfolded. Rare and expensive ingredients were hawked on each corner, along with every snake-oil salesman's newest enchantment. Nobles and common people often traveled here to buy all types of magical trinkets.

Frame's chest tightened and her breathing became strained as they approached the alley where she'd been attacked. She stared down at the spot where Felix had died. His words flooded back into her mind—not just his last ones, but their final few conversations. She wondered whether he would have been safe if she'd let him back into her life, even just a little.

All signs of blood were gone now, covered by the muck. Frame's heart was crushed; it was as if the world had erased all traces of him. She moved to step into the alley, but was stopped by Alyssa's steady hand.

"You don't need to do this to yourself. It wasn't your fault. I don't believe there was anything you could have done."

Frame sniffled, noticing for the first time that she had tears coming down her face. They walked the remainder of the distance to her apartment silently.

Frame looked over to Alyssa. "Does this remind you of your time at the Institute as a student?"

Alyssa looked as though she'd been hit with a pang of regret. "No. In fact, I spent most of my life living in the Institute itself. I never thought about living in the apartments. Sometimes I wish I had, though. I think it would have been good for me."

Alyssa stood silently, her eyes showing deeper thoughts bubbling below the surface. Even after living with her for a couple of weeks, Frame still knew little about the former professor.

As they neared Frame's apartment, they ran into the curly-haired Diana just as she stepped out of her room.

She ran to Frame and gave her a tight hug. "Frame! Where have you been? I haven't seen you since before Felix—"

Diana stopped herself with a hard swallow.

Frame smiled meekly. "I am okay . . . just needed time away. How are you?"

"That makes sense, but is the rumor true?"

"What rumor?"

"That your family hired a man to guard you?"

Frame's forehead wrinkled. "I'm not aware of any guard or anything like that. Where did you hear it from?"

Diana looked confused. "From the man that comes by and checks on your apartment every day."

"What?!"

She nodded her head quickly. "Yeah, the man is so creepy, asking where you are all the time."

Frame's nerves tingled. "I . . . what?"

"Oh, and don't get me started on his face. Those bandages make him look like he had been in a fight recently. I can only imagine what he looked like before missing an eye."

The blood drained from Frame's face.

Diana tilted her head. "Are you okay?" She turned to Frame's apartment. "I guess I should mention that he's probably here. I saw him come up earlier."

Frame was frozen, unsure of what to do.

Alyssa put a hand on her shoulder. "It'll be okay."

The former professor looked to Diana and pointed down the hall. "Go get help now, just in case he's still in there and attacks." The words seemed forced, as if she was telling herself, too.

Diana, who could see the tension and fear on their faces, nodded and took off. The other two moved slowly toward the apartment. Frame reached for the doorknob with shaky hands. It turned easily, unlocked.

All she could do was look to the professor. Alyssa nodded, pulling a thin wand from the folds of her clothes. She took a deep breath and brought a finger to her lips.

Frame watched as Alyssa eased the door open slowly. Alyssa stepped softly inside, but Frame remained frozen in the doorway.

Alyssa looked down the hall before motioning for Frame to follow. The room looked normal, and they couldn't see anything out of place.

Alyssa held the wand tightly in her hand. "Maybe 'the guard' isn't here anymore."

"I-I think you're right. Let's get my stuff and go."

Frame opened the door to her bedroom. Before she took a full step inside, she was struck by something sweeping through the darkness. Frame flew back across the room toward Alyssa, knocking them both to the floor.

In the doorway stood the one-eyed man. With a jerk of his arm, a blade ripped through his glove. Frame was reminded of the butcher.

He sneered as he approached. "Sure took you long enough to come back!"

Wand fire flew past her, missing the man and striking the far wall. He leapt forward, his dagger hand coming down at Alyssa.

Alyssa closed her eyes, her tongue trying to utter any sort of magic. Hot blood dripped into her mouth as she accidentally bit her tongue. For a moment, Frame thought they were going to die. Instead, she heard the man scream.

Alyssa's eldritch words slammed the man into and through a table. He cursed as he rolled to his side, narrowly avoiding more wand fire.

Frame rolled to her mentor as Alyssa tried to get her wand up.

The man retracted the blade and ran for the door, ignoring the trailing wand fire.

Alyssa laid there, her wand still outstretched.

Frame could feel her body shaking, her breath coming in harder and harder gulps. Once she started to cry, she couldn't stop.

49

Alyssa had left her wand sitting on the kitchen table, the burnt-out spell wicks emptied out next to it. Three guards shuffled around the room, surveying the damage from the struggle. The lieutenant stood in front of the women with a notebook and pen. "So you're telling me that the murderer from a few weeks ago was here?"

"Yes, he busted out of my bedroom and charged us."

"With a 'knife hand'?" he motioned with disbelief.

Frame narrowed her eyes in frustration. "I am telling you what I saw! The knife came out of his fist."

The man turned to Alyssa. "Is this what you saw too?"

She had missed the moment the knife had appeared, but the angle didn't look right. "It didn't look like he was holding it in his hand."

The man's face was twisted in thought until he wrote something down in his notes. "So he might be using an unusual knife, something that wouldn't normally be found."

Frame's face was red. "No, that is not what I said—"

The guard nearest to the door cursed. "The Institute rep is here."

The look of disgust was contagious. Lucos strolled into the room wearing a suit and a black cloak draped around his arms. His nose and eyes made him look like a hawk. "I see you have started without me, again."

The lieutenant rolled his eyes. "We don't need to wait for you. I know how to run an investigation."

Lucos smirked and joined him at the center of the room. "Of that I have no doubt, old friend, but it is a matter of principle.

This is related to Institute property and students."

The guard looked offended at being called *friend*, but he gave the thin man space to work.

Lucos smiled at Alyssa. "Ah, professor, it is nice to see you again."

His eyes were always piercing, but now they held an edge, something she hadn't noticed before. "I don't know if you remember, but I'm not a professor."

The man's eyes showed that he knew.

Alyssa directed his attention to Frame. "Frame Lexone has been attacked twice now. I think it goes without saying that she is being targeted."

Lucos pulled a notebook from his jacket. With the click of a pen, he started writing. "Yes, I recall the last time we met. The man described is basically the same, right? Except for your description of 'a knife coming out of his hand,' if I overheard correctly in the hall."

Frame cocked her head in confusion. "But how did you know?"

Lucos smiled and pointed toward the hall. "Your neighbor—nice woman—mentioned a man skulking around your place. She was kind enough to give me the description."

He pivoted to the lieutenant. "What actions are you and your men taking?"

"The standard ones, of course. The description from the last attack has been passed around to all the shifts, and all the shops are being notified. If he sticks his head into this district, we will find him. Now we'll go and start passing around the information."

Lucos sounded disappointed as he turned his back to them. "I guess that will do. Young woman, do you have a place to stay other than this apartment?"

Frame gave a slow nod. "Yes, I've actually been staying with Alyssa since the first attack."

"Good. I suspect that is what saved your life. Would you give me the address so I can find you later?"

Alyssa reached into her coat and pulled out a charmed letter.

He stopped her. "No charmed letters. I need to know your physical address."

One of the guards scoffed. "What's the point of magic if you don't use it?"

Lucos ignored the guard and ripped a page from his notebook, handing it to Alyssa. "A physical address will make it easier for me to speak to you both if I find anything."

"So you're looking into this?"

He nodded. "Someone targeting students is the same as an animal targeting another animal's young; a threat to the next generation cannot stand."

Alyssa nodded and wrote down the address to her apartment. With that, Lucos said his goodbyes and left.

The guards lingered a few moments more before one of them commented. "That man's got this under control. Let's get out of here before we get cursed or something." They left the apartment promptly.

The door clicked shut, leaving them alone. "Let's get your things and leave," Alyssa said.

Frame started sorting through her belongings immediately. With clothes and a few books in hand, they traveled back across town. At every shadow and corner, the two watched with anticipation of another attack. It never came.

"Let's make some tea. My nerves are shot," Frame suggested as they approached Alyssa's apartment, exhaustion dulling her tone.

"That's the best idea I've heard all day." Alyssa opened the door and headed straight for the kettle.

50

Zane stared down at the black stone sitting in the center of the desk. The room's shadows twisted and turned toward it. Shadow's red eyes moved freely across the darkness. For a moment, he reminded Zane of a large fish just below the surface.

The detective reached out and touched the stone. As its warmth moved up his arm and into his body, a feeling of relaxation overtook him. Something about the world seemed more . . . complete.

Shadow's silky voice interrupted his peace. *How does it feel?*

Zane pulled his hand back, but Shadow just laughed.

"Is this related to the mission, the one that ended with you getting cursed?"

Shadow was silent, and for a minute Zane thought he wasn't going to answer.

Yes, this is a small piece of the Well that I was sent to find.

"Why were you sent to find it? . . . No, let me guess: You can't say."

Correct.

The detective reached out and touched the stone again, slowly moving it back and forth in his palm. "How did the doctor get ahold of this thing? It sounds like something that would be hard to find."

Shadow's voice was harsh. *Don't worry about that! Just finish this case and leave it behind.*

Zane paused. The harsh tone felt more like a mask to hide fear. *Fear of what, though? What could Shadow fear?*

"That will come to light no matter what. The Institute won't let something like this go."

It doesn't matter what the agents do after, but don't go following them.

The detective was about to dive deeper when Alyssa opened the door. She looked around the room before waving Frame in. Something wasn't right.

Frame jumped at the sound of the kettle whistling, then shook her head in shame. *You're falling apart. It's safe here.*

Alyssa went to the kitchen and poured her a cup while Frame returned to her thesis.

The student passed a page to Alyssa when she returned. It was stained and smeared with ink. Alyssa looked over the disaster of a page. She sighed and set it down. "Frame, you don't need to keep pushing yourself."

"I need this! I need something. If I just sit around, I'll go mad with every single sound."

Rogue thoughts of when and where another attack might come haunted Frame, like a pack of hounds snapping at the feet of their prey.

Alyssa took a seat across from her to clean the wands she had used. The student found this daily ritual unnerving, something she never would have expected from the professor.

After a minute, Frame set down her pen. "Why do you do that?"

"Do what?"

She gestured to the wands. "Why do you clean those wands every day, even when you have only used it—"

She didn't want to think about the attack, the violation of privacy and security.

Alyssa looked over the wands, the books, and then to the maps. "I never want to feel vulnerable again, and I wanted to find a way to . . . combat my fear."

Combat my fear. The words rang out in Frame's mind. A part of her rallied at the thought, wanting to *do* something, rather than just wait for a third encounter with the knife-handed man. What could she do, though?

Alyssa looked her over. "Frame, is everything okay?"

Frame watched as a pool of ink spreading from her pen. The page of notes was ruined. "I don't know, but I need to borrow a charmed letter. I have something I need to look into."

51

Zane stared at the dark stain of dried blood that covered the table and chair.

"If you are going to be assisting me in this special project, you need to know how I work. First, the procedure often requires that we cut open the wound and attach the limb down to the bone," the doctor noted, as if reading the detective's mind.

Zane shook his head in disbelief. He wondered how the people survived losing so much blood.

The doctor went on. "It takes too much time to tailor the prosthetic for each person. It's better to make the injury match what we have."

Zane nodded and moved to the next thing that bothered him. "Why the clacking sound? I've seen the weights, but they don't seem to serve a purpose."

Dr. Aluxen gave a halfhearted laugh. "Well, they serve no functional purpose. They're only there to cover the noise."

"Noise? What noise?"

"When placed in fluid, the stone can create a sound similar to moving water. The clacking is there to distract people from it."

The answer didn't sit right with the detective. "Fine, but how do you make them move? I've seen several soldiers use prosthetics. They too used levers and springs, but they couldn't do what you're doing here."

The doctor pulled a leather-wrapped stone out and set it down on the table by the limb. Shadows started to move and swirl toward it. Light in the room seemed dull.

Shadow called out from the corner, his voice more solid and real. *Pay attention: This man uses powers beyond his understanding.*

"Do you know what this is?"

Zane was about to give an answer, but stopped himself. "Some piece of magic rock?"

The doctor chuckled, revealing his teeth. In the dull light, they looked too white to be real. A slight chill ran down his spine as he wondered if this man had ever practiced on himself.

"Yes and no. As far as I can tell, this doesn't give off the normal markers that magic produces. In that sense, it could be argued that this produces a scientific effect, though if I were to describe it, I would say that it is closer to being like a curse."

"What do you mean?"

"Anyone that touches this is . . . is, perhaps, left to a fate worse than death."

Zane's eyes dashed from the doctor to Shadow.

The doctor followed Zane's eyes to the dark corner, before returning to him. "Perhaps you're already touched, or cursed. Maybe that's why you touched it so easily."

Shadow answered him. *Yes.*

The doctor's smile was gentle with a trace of cunning. "You mentioned some training with the Surgeon Guild?"

"At the College of Surgeons, but yes. I had been training to be a doctor before the war—"

"The war that left your leg in that state?"

Zane nodded and leaned against the cold, brick wall. "Yes, that one. What of it?"

"You have skills that could be useful to me, and I could be useful to you."

"How so?"

"My trade has inherent limits that are hard to overcome, due to the dangerous nature of the work. Your immunity means you can help me. If we work together, then perhaps we can even find ways to remove this struggle from humanity for good."

Humanity—the way he said it sounded strange. The detective thought about every person he had seen in the district and suddenly realized that every one of them had been human.

The doctor noticed Zane lost in thought. He raised a finger. "Rule one: These stones can never be used on those that have strong Fey ancestry. Goblins, gnomes, even people with sharp ears."

"Are you against them getting help?"

Aluxen shook his head. "No! Like any other person, they would easily find a home and purpose here. But there are . . . side effects when it comes to their use of the stone. Trust me that the time is coming soon when that will change. For now, just know that I believe it would be dangerous, not only for them, but for us."

What am I getting into? Zane pulled out the flask and took a swig.

Shadow whispered in his ear.

The detective waited for the doctor to turn away before glaring at his companion. There in the dark basement with its swirling shadows, Zane swore he could feel a hand on his shoulder.

Trust me, detective. I know much about these things, and I won't let anything happen to us.

52

Alyssa rubbed her tired eyes, trying to get comfortable again. Images of gore had leaked into her dreams. Red Hood had emerged from a sea of blood that pooled behind her eyes before swallowing her whole. Her scream had awakened Frame, and Alyssa felt dreadfully sorry about it. The nightmare clung to the back of her mind even as the day dragged on.

Alyssa and Frame followed a trail of ash into the office, which had to be from Zane. It led all the way to his bedroom. Two thinner paths followed them to their desk.

Frame looked exhausted. The last few nights, she had been working as if possessed. Frame would switch her focus from adjusting the thesis to sending charmed letters.

Zane entered the room looking like some half-crazed captain at the head of his ship when he emerged and walked to stare out the window. It was as if he was trying to absorb as much light as possible. Sitting on his desk was a small bundle of cloth that held the stone.

Alyssa stepped close to the desk and started to reach for it.

"Don't!" Zane's voice was rougher than normal, with a sharp edge to it. His face was pale, and his eyes were heavy with sleep. At his side was his flask, held lazily in one hand. He set it on his desk, then limped over to Alyssa.

She looked from Zane to the cloth. "I haven't seen it yet."

He stared down at it. "I am not sure it was ever meant for light."

Alyssa pulled out her glasses. "Let me see it, please."

Zane gave her a tired nod and removed the cloth. The room

seemed to dim, and then the shadows began to move. She watched in shock as the stone acted just as Zane had described. Even now, seeing for herself, she couldn't believe it. With an eldritch word, she focused her glasses. Alyssa studied the stone and the moving shadows, finding no signs of magic.

She put the glasses back in her pocket. The room felt like it was filling with water. "I can't find anything."

Frame gave a confused look. "But how? The imperial method is the most advanced form of magic, making use of logic through science. I don't see how this could be natural."

Alyssa shrugged. "The imperial method isn't the only way to approach magic. It's the only method taught in the empire, but it is possible that the principle behind this follows some method we don't understand yet."

"And where does this leave the case?" the student asked.

Zane scowled at the corner before tossing a pen toward it. "We should stay the course. There is something much bigger going on, I think."

Alyssa worried about how weak he looked, both physically and mentally, as he crossed the room. Her eyes lingered for just a moment before he closed the bedroom door. "Frame, let's go back to my apartment. We can work there."

At Alyssa's apartment, they got to work on Frame's paper. Between reviewing pages and giving advice, Alyssa read. Her mind couldn't focus. She felt useless, wishing for a way to help with the case.

A knock at the window drew their attention. Through the glass, they saw a charmed letter, tapping with its metal corner.

Alyssa opened the window and caught the letter. It was addressed to her. She gracefully opened the letter and read it. Frame moved closer, excitedly trying to get a look at the letter. "What did he say?"

Her cheeks blushed. "Chiron is asking me out to dinner tonight."

Frame frowned. "Should you go? He works for the doctor."

Frame had a point, but Alyssa needed this. This was also a way to get information for the case. "I might be able to learn what he's doing for the doctor, or at least get a better idea of who he is, maybe."

Frame nodded. "Okay, but we need to get you dressed appropriately for a date."

As Frame went about trying to decide which dress would be best, Alyssa worked on her reply. "What about you? Will you be all right by yourself?"

Frame smiled. "I will. Now let's get you ready for this dinner."

The evening was still early, the sunlight fighting against the blanket of clouds. Frame watched through the window as Alyssa left the building. Alyssa's apartment was bigger than hers, with more amenities and books. Although she was from a rich family, Frame had never really lived that life. There was glamour in how her relatives carried on, but they'd always seemed so removed from their servants and other normal people.

She looked over at the stack of charmed envelopes on the desk and quickly wrote a short message. *We do it today.* She sent it out the window with a few eldritch words, the runes glowing as it left.

Frame latched the window and rushed to apply what little makeup she owned. She studied herself in a mirror, trying to decide the best way to look empowered.

It was a couple of hours later when a familiar face appeared on the street. Belard was a welcome sight. She unlocked the door and waited patiently for him to arrive. When the knock came, she threw open the door and hugged the old man.

"Thank you! Thank you for helping me."

He laughed gruffly and pushed into her arms a bundle of clothes. "I brought just what you asked for. It took Lista a little bit to sneak them out without the other maids noticing."

She hugged the bundle tightly for a moment before looking over the contents. It was a white blouse and black pants that belonged to Vine. Frame smiled and hugged Belard again. "Thank you both so very much. Were you able to find the lawyer's address?"

He nodded and pointed through the window, down to the carriage. "The driver has the route mapped out."

"I hope I'm not going to get you and Lista into trouble."

Belard laughed again and shook his head. "There are enough servants to cover for us, and any one of us would do what we could to help ya. You're like a daughter to all of us."

"Thank you." Frame smiled gently. "I need to get dressed and then we'll head straight out. I need to know what my cousin is planning."

53

Zane felt the heat from the blood through his gloves. Reopening the old wound caused the patient to shudder and jerk. He was strapped down, with a stick in his mouth to keep him from biting his tongue. Grunts of pain continued from the patient.

Zane pushed all distractions out of his mind and worked swiftly with the scalpel. He cut through the old scar tissue down to the bone.

Blood poured out rapidly, but Zane had the knowledge and experience to keep it controlled. He dabbed at the cut with a rag drenched in healing potion. At the touch of the rag, the new injury tried to knit itself back together. Zane knew it wouldn't be enough, but it would help stem the flow of blood.

Aluxen looked over his shoulder, but didn't say much until the bone was showing. "Good. Clean the edges, then we will get the limb attached."

Zane finished up around the bone, and the doctor leaned down beside him. "Here's the tricky part. I have had the rod soaking in healing potion, which will help everything around it. This end of the rod needs to be attached to the bone with this clamp."

The detective wondered how this procedure didn't drive the patient insane from the pain of both the prosthetic and the incisions.

Dr. Aluxen and Zane worked together on the clamp. The patient jerked, then went still as he passed out, his shallow breath the only sign of life. Dr. Aluxen filled a small cup from a bucket of water and splashed it on the patient's face. "Hey, stay awake!"

"Do we need him awake?" Zane asked. "Wouldn't this be easier with him asleep?"

Dr. Aluxen nodded as he opened a box that held the patient's new prosthetic arm and started to make adjustments. "Yes, but the stone won't work how we want it to if he is unconscious. Don't know why, but that's just how it is. Now then, are you ready?"

Zane nodded and grabbed the stone from a pouch in his apron. The detective hesitated for a moment, feeling the warmth of the stone before setting it inside the limb.

Dr. Aluxen shut the compartment and filled it with water, which quickly turned an oily black. He lifted the limb and rocked it back and forth to make sure everything was saturated before passing it to Zane. "When I turn off the light, I need you to slip the arm on and fix the clamp. Once in place, you're done. Get away from him, and I will turn the lamp back on."

The patient had a combination of pain and fear in his eyes, but Zane tried hard not to look at his face. He worked the best he could while fumbling in the dark. Once the limb was secured, he moved away from the patient and called to Dr. Aluxen.

The doctor flooded half the room in light.

The light cast the patient's shadow on the wall, and his breathing calmed down. The pain on his face faded quickly. The doctor pulled the gag from his mouth and freed him from the restraints. "Now give your new arm a try."

The patient stood up and tentatively flexed his fingers before squeezing them into a fist. The man fell to his knees, gripping his arm. With tears in his eyes, he cried out his thanks to the doctor over and over.

Dr. Aluxen helped him up and guided him to the door. A woman on the other side helped the man up the stairs. When the patient was gone, the two men went to work cleaning their tools.

Zane was leaning heavily on his good leg, exhausted. The basement's dim lighting played with his mind, reminding him of darker times. As he was finishing up the equipment, Zane noticed the doctor also looking tired. The detective saw an opportunity.

"Who supplies you with these stones?"

The doctor raised an eyebrow, then tilted his head. "What makes you think I get these from somewhere?"

Zane pulled the stone from his pouch. "It's too smooth not to have been polished, but the way you act toward them suggests to me that you don't seem that accustomed to handling them. They make you nervous."

The doctor flashed a fake smile. "I have a healthy fear of them, and you should, too. But how do you know that they aren't naturally like that?"

"I don't, but somehow I doubt it."

Dr. Aluxen gave him a stern look. "Now, look. We may be working together, but we aren't that close. I can't tell you anything about this."

Zane moved to his next question. "Why porcelain? Why not use something stronger?"

The doctor nodded his head with approval. "That one I can answer. You see, the stone works best when there is something compatible between the limb and the patient."

The detective felt a slight shiver at where this conversation was going. "Then why porcelain?"

"It's bone porcelain. All humans have bone, so that's why it's used in the limbs."

Zane didn't need to push the line of questioning, but he knew. Dr. Aluxen used both human and animal bone in the limbs. From what the agents had described, if this was magical, then it was most definitely black magic. He didn't know whether he could prove it, but he doubted these stones worked based on any type of science.

Dr. Aluxen patted Zane on the shoulder and drew his attention to a box under the table. "I might be able to tell you more, but first you need to help me with this job."

The box was heavy, and the detective grunted as he lifted it. The doctor unlocked it with a silver key and opened the lid. Inside were snow-white prosthetic legs with green highlights. They were elegant compared to the other limbs he had seen.

Dr. Aluxen pointed to the compartment. "Open it up."

The detective picked up one of the limbs, shocked at how light it was. Under it were several well-worn sheets of paper. Zane tried to read them, but the script was rough. He turned his attention back to the limb, running his fingers over the thigh until he noticed a miniscule gap in the surface. After a minute, he managed to open it. Inside was a small metal net he guessed would hold the stone. Coming down from the bars that held it were runes that Zane didn't recognize.

"Are these arcane runes?"

Dr. Aluxen scratched his head. "I don't know, and it doesn't matter."

"Doesn't matter? If we're using magic, then that's a crime, isn't it?"

He laughed. "Look. You and me, we are replaceable . . . just like those people walking around. But by the saints and the first knights, we have a chance."

"A chance to what?"

"To make history, to create the perfect procedure, and to be irreplaceable. All we have to do is get these legs to work."

Zane shrugged his shoulders, expecting something more serious. "That doesn't seem too hard; it's a bit different from the normal limbs, but it should still be doable."

Dr. Aluxen laughed. "Well, wait until you see the instructions. I was starting to wonder how I could do this. With you here, it shouldn't be any problem to perform the operation on-site."

Silence hung in the air for a moment. "They're elegant," Zane said. "Who are they for?"

"They are for a dancer," Aluxen said. "She was very well-known, with a full schedule, until an accident stripped her of her ability to perform."

The doctor touched the leg again. "There is going to be a ball soon, where this dancer is going to make a glorious return. This event will be hosted by Lady Lexone, with whom I have set up a contract. She is allowing us to market these prosthetics at the ball and will even back us financially in the future. In return, I will attempt to fix all that is wrong with her physically."

Zane leveled his breath and relaxed his face, trying his hardest not to reveal anything. "What's wrong with her, this Lady Lexone?"

"Her joints have eroded with time, but for a long time now, I have been working toward a solution for such things."

"Sounds like it will be complicated. If her joints are failing, how will you replace all of them? She could die in the surgery."

The doctor smiled and shook his head. "The answer is simpler than you think."

Zane hoped that the doctor had momentarily forgotten the detective's connection with the Institute. "Does it have something to do with the stones?"

Dr. Aluxen raised one hand, rocking it back and forth. "Yes and no. It would be more accurate to say the stones and the prosthetics are a byproduct of my research into a much more perfect procedure."

"How is that?"

The doctor pulled out a medical journal and a picture of a marionette. "Have you heard of the studies on blood transfusion?"

Zane had heard a little while he was in college, but that was a long time ago. "Please enlighten me."

"Studies show that blood is accepted by those that are alike. They have roughly grouped the types, as they call them, into two categories: Type A and Type B. Some argue there are more. A blood can be given to people with A blood, and B blood can be given to people with B blood. There is some research finding that some can take both types. Similarly, the limbs I make must be made to be 'like.' "

Zane nodded trying to follow the logic. "What about the marionette?"

Dr. Aluxen scratched his beard. "That is how the stone works in connection to the limb. The best way I can describe it is that the person puppeteers the limb."

"How did you come up with all this?"

"Once again, we are *not* that close." He put the limb back in the case and locked it.

Shadow whispered in Zane's ear. *I think I know how he got started on this.*

Zane didn't want to risk speaking to Shadow, even in his mind, so he motioned for Shadow to get on with it.

The papers in there . . . that's my handwriting. I think they're my notes from when I worked with the Ghoul Lords. When you were my "guest."

54

Chiron's voice was warm as he pulled Alyssa's chair out for her. "Thank you for meeting me. I am sorry for the last-minute invitation."

Alyssa smiled, a slight blush warming her cheeks. "It is completely all right. You have invited me to the ball, so it is not beyond expectation that you would call on me earlier."

Chiron smiled as he fidgeted with his prosthetic hand. He kept rubbing the design etched into the porcelain.

A waitress came by with two cups. Alyssa blew on the steaming tea as she looked around the café. It was a marvelous little place, not far from the Institute, yet she had never heard of it. *Then again, I never left the Institute until meeting Zane.* "How did you hear about this place?"

Chiron smiled and pointed to a group of young men studying in the back and arguing over the vague wording of some law. "It is a favorite for those studying law, especially with the younger students. I haven't been here in years."

She raised an eyebrow after taking a sip. "Then why did you pick it for this—"

The word date was caught in her throat like a boulder that dammed a stream. Chiron motioned to an opened door near the students. "This place is a library of sorts. That is the real reason many come here—to study."

It made sense to her now. "Ah, wonderful resource materials, easily accessed. That would make this an excellent place for study groups. If only I had known of this place when I was younger!"

"If you don't mind me asking, what was your field of study? I could tell when we met that you are well-educated."

"Fey studies." From her pocket, she pulled her state mage badge out and set it down on the table.

Chiron gasped, and his prosthetic hand inched forward. "That's right. You mentioned being a state mage before. May I look at it?"

She nodded.

"I didn't expect you to be so accomplished. You didn't seem to be working for the Institute when I met you."

"I wasn't, and haven't been for a few months. But if they called on me, I would have to answer them."

He looked hesitant for a moment, as if he was holding his breath. "What did you do for them?"

It touched her more than she had expected, the memories of the Institute, her grandfather, and the coworkers she had lost. "I was . . . I was a professor."

He sighed what appeared to be a breath of relief and began to smile. "What made you leave?"

"It's complicated, and I would rather not dwell on it."

"I can understand that. I have had my share of workplace . . . drama," he said, lifting his porcelain hand. "Let's go take a look in the back. There is much more to see there than out here."

She took his outstretched hand as he led her through the back door. The room they entered was lined with books, each case labeled with a wooden sign. In one corner was a chalkboard, in use by two young Institute students arguing over the structure of a spell broken down into its phonic sounds. At a long table, a group of students were arguing over the meaning of several legal statutes and precedents.

Alyssa sighed, relieved. The place felt familiar to her, like the Institute had before she was attacked.

Chiron pointed to the table and explained to her what the students were arguing about. Alyssa, in turn, explained what the students at the chalkboard were talking about. They laughed, sharing stories of their education. Going from shelf to shelf, they pulled out books they had enjoyed or would recommend.

The sound of the city bells went off, announcing the time. Alyssa looked down at Chiron's prosthetic. *I need to know.*

"How does that hand work?"

He pulled his sleeve up. "I don't know, but it is far better than anything I had ever seen before or since."

"How did you get it, if you don't mind me asking?"

"Well, I was a young lawyer and had been working my way up the ladder. Some of my coworkers were jealous of the progress I had made, so they decided to stop me. One day, as I was standing near an intersection, they ran up behind me and shoved me out in front of a carriage as it was pulling away.

"There was a loud crunch as it rolled over me, demolishing my hand and arm. My friends—well, my former friends—and coworkers laughed. My boss, who happened to be at his window as it happened, looked down and just shook his head. As far as I know, he never saw the push."

"He told me that I should have paid better attention and that it was a shame. But it wasn't enough for my coworkers who worked to drive me away. The next thing I knew, I was out of a job. I didn't know what to do, thinking my career was over, until I was directed to the doctor. His work was extraordinary, and the people who rallied around him warmed my heart. He offered to give me back my hand for free, so I happily joined his growing family and told him that I would do all I could to help. Since then, I have acted on his behalf through legal dealings and contracts with nobles and businesses."

She touched his hand. "That's horrible. I am so—"

Chiron shook his head. "It is in the past, and I am thankful to leave it there."

Alyssa nodded and ran her fingers through her hair. "How long, then, have you worked for this doctor?"

"About four years now. I was one of the first, back when he was just starting to do his miracle work."

I should ask him more. What else? Alyssa could've kicked herself for getting distracted by Chiron's story. Alyssa tried hard to think of questions. "How is it I haven't heard of this doctor before? His work seems miraculous."

Chiron's face became harder to read. "I can't actually say. He prefers a low profile, as per his contract with another individual."

She smiled softly, now with a new question. *Who is this private partner?* They finished their dinner and headed out, each looking forward to the ball.

55

Frame and Belard opened the door to Tom Witmark's law office. She addressed the receptionist, informing her that they were from the Lexone family and needed to see Mr. Witmark right away. They were led straight to his office.

Tom, who had worked for her great-grandmother as far back as she could remember, sat behind his desk. He looked up from the documents he was reading. "How can I help—"

His glasses had slipped down for a moment, so he adjusted them. "Do I know you? May I know your business here today?"

She hoped her voice sounded confident. "Yes, but not directly. You do know the family I represent."

"I know many families, and I represent several."

"Lady Lexone?"

Tom raised an eyebrow, and nodded his head. He leaned back in his chair. "Are you here speaking for the older one or for the younger one?"

Frame tried to look in control. "Does it matter? They both are Ladies Lexone."

"Ah, yes, but only *one* of them is called *Lady* Lexone."

She nodded and took a seat in the chair across from him. Belard stood behind her, like a personal guard. The old man was not as intimidating as Vine's guard, but Frame trusted him—much more than Vine could her guard. "I am here to read the will."

Tom shook his head. "Like I told your employer, Vine Lexone, she cannot see it just because she wants to."

Tom pulled out a cigarette and tapped it against the back of his pack. "Now you two can get out of here. I don't care what you want or do, but you can't see it. Leave."

The fat lawyer tried to light a match, but try as he might, he couldn't get it lit. He cursed, and threw away the match. The cigarette hung loosely from his mouth. Frame mouthed the arcane words for a simple spell. She was nervous, and her lips twitched at the effort to keep her confident facade. The lawyer gave her a nasty look. "Why are you still—"

The cigarette ignited. The lawyer jerked back at the sudden flash. With a shaky hand, he took the cigarette out of his mouth and looked it over. Frame smiled. "Now, may I see the will?"

His face was slightly pale. "I wasn't aware that Vine had employed a wizard, but that doesn't matter. And if you think you can strong-arm me with magic, then I will report you! It's, it's a legal thing, you know, about the proper use of magic."

Frame smiled, trying hard to be subtle. "I don't believe that I ever said that I worked for her."

He took a drag of his cigarette. "Oh?"

"I work for Lady Lexone, Vine's great-grandmother, and she has asked me to check on her will."

Tom narrowed his eyes and ran his fingers through his thinning hair. "She would have hired a wizard. That makes more sense, but do you have any proof?"

She froze for a moment, but was saved by Belard. "Lady Lexone, our employer, has sent us to ensure that her will hadn't been tampered with by Lady Vine."

"What?"

"You stated that Vine has been trying to see it, yes? Then how do we know she hasn't already seen it and made changes?"

His cheeks were almost red as he tried to find words, but Frame stopped him. "Please just let us take a look and put Lady Lexone's unease to rest."

Tom sighed and put the cigarette in his ashtray. Stepping away from the desk, he went to a nearby drawer, pulled out a file, and handed it across to them.

Frame tried not to look eager as she opened it. It was short, far too short for all that her grandmother owned. There should have been a list of business deals, contacts, properties, titles, and more. Her face paled as she got past all the legal jargon to the one, single, important line.

Written in her grandmother's hand, she read: *All possessions, titles, and properties shall go to Frame Lexone.*

She felt like she was on a ship that was rocking on a violent sea. Frame's stomach dropped, and she wanted to throw up. "Ma'am, are you okay?"

Frame's mouth felt dry as she tried to calm herself. "Yes, I—" She coughed and adjusted her collar. "Yes, it is just as she had requested. I will let Lady Lexone know that you have stayed the course."

Tom smiled wearily. "I would hope so, especially with how much the lady pays to keep me from accepting bribes. Now, is there anything else I can do for you?"

Frame's body shivered, and her knees shook. "No, thank you. Everything is in order."

Frame lifted her arm and let Belard help her up. With a gentle hand, he guided her up to her feet. "Thank you again for your time."

"Of course. I hope that you will instill faith in our practice in Lady Lexone."

Frame bowed. "Of course." Her body felt stiff, and she was afraid that one moment of weakness would drive her to the ground like a large raindrop.

Belard opened the door and escorted her out.

As soon as the lawyer was out of sight, Frame dropped to her knees, breathing hard.

Belard bent down and whispered to her as he glanced back to the door. "Are you okay? What did you see? The will looked small to me."

She looked up wide-eyed at him. "I-I am set to inherit everything!"

56

The wet ash caked his shoulders like epaulets. Zane swished his flask around and took a large gulp. He tried to look out through the mist, but the street lamps still seemed so far away.

Shadow's red eyes reflected off the mist as Zane walked, creating the illusion of walking next to him. The detective slipped the flask back into his coat and reached for the stone. Its comfort and warmth ran up his crippled arm. "Were you aware the stone could be used like this?"

No, but I was never really a scholar, sage, or wizard.

That was more information than Zane had received in a while. *Is the parasite in a talkative mood?* "What were you then? I remember you saying that you were an artist for a time."

Shadow's red eyes looked tired for a moment, as if remembering something heavy. *Being an artist was something I had chosen for myself. It was nice.*

Zane felt a pang of sympathy, and he hated himself for it. Shadow was a monster that had scarred him. "What were you before then?"

I was a knight. If my liege needed something, I would be sent out. There was nothing that I couldn't find. Shadow faded away in the mist, and Zane was left alone.

As he passed the coffee shop at the edge of the district, Will stopped him. "Fine night for a walk, isn't it?"

Zane gave a gruff answer. "Only if you're trying to hide."

Will nodded and offered him a cigarette. The detective shook his head, and Will lit his own up. Under the edge of the Laze Pot's roof, the agent was sheltered from the filth of the world. "So how has life been treating you? It's been a bit since I last saw you."

Zane looked around, but the mist was too thick to see whether anyone was coming. "What can I say? Saints open doors for you when you need them, right?"

Will smirked. "So the temple priest tells us. I heard you're the doctor's new apprentice."

"I don't know about being an apprentice, but we are working together. It has given me some insight."

Will took a long drag from his cigarette. With his free hand, he pointed to the door. "It's late and, like you said, it's thief's weather. Why don't you get off the street for a bit, come in and talk about your 'insights'?"

Zane started to move toward the door, but a voice cut through the darkness. "Mr. Vrexon, could I speak with you?"

From the wrapping tendrils of mist stepped Laure. Her shawl was pulled tight around her, and her hat was covered in a thickening layer of ash. "Laure, this is no weather for a young lady."

She smiled warmly. "Then would you escort me back?"

Zane sighed and nodded. Before leaving the light of the doorway, he turned back to the agent. "Perhaps some other time."

Will smiled and tossed his cigarette down. "I will hold you to that. Have a good night."

He stepped back into the bar as the door slammed shut. Laure took up a slow walk beside him. Zane didn't know where Laure lived, but he allowed her to guide him through the mist. The night was quiet, and the lights seemed gentler than before.

The young woman tugged on his sleeve. "That man is dangerous."

Zane played dumb. "What man? The one from the coffee shop?"

She nodded and glanced back through the mist. "That man doesn't believe in our doctor. No, I think he even means him ill."

"How do you know?"

She narrowed her eyes and stared hard at the ground as she stepped across the cobblestones. "I know he has been spying on us. He sends people to see what we do."

Laure stepped through the dark without difficulty, as if she had light. *Maybe the stone affects some of the patients in different ways.* He nodded to Laure. "I see. Then I will be careful. Thank you for telling me. It's always better to know who is a danger."

She stopped and turned around at the door of her apartment. "Will you take me to the doctor's ball as your date?"

Zane was stunned, his cane nearly slipping on the stones. "What—"

"I wish to be your date."

Laure stared into his eyes. There was conviction and determination in them. Zane closed his eyes and started to shake his head. "Sorry, ma'am, but I am—"

"A respected man of this community who works for our doctor. Now, yes or no?"

He sighed in resignation. "Yes, I will take you."

She smiled triumphantly and turned to leave. The door was half-open as she turned around. "Thank you, Mr. Vrexon."

The light from the hallway was cut off as she shut the door tight against the cold of the night. Zane stood there in confusion before Shadow spoke. *Well, she seems nice.*

"Shut up."

Shadow might have yawned if he still had lungs. The group sat around, going about their business. Frame worked on her thesis while Alyssa looked over her pages with a pen and a critical eye. With large bags under his eyes, the detective read the newspaper, smoothing out the page's wrinkles every few minutes.

Frame set her pen down. "I know we're still waiting for the others to arrive, but what's the plan for the ball?"

"We have a small window—very small—to put this case away," Zane said. "It looks like the doctor is using magic. Well, he *will be* at this event."

Alyssa looked up. "Will be?"

"Yes, he will be attempting to use a new set of limbs given to him by his sponsor."

Frame looked perplexed. "How do you know there is magic involved? I thought we couldn't define the stone as magic."

"I saw some type of runes written inside, but I didn't recognize them at all."

Alyssa's eyes flashed with realization. "Chiron mentioned a nondisclosure agreement of some sort. One for Dr. Aluxen and Lady Lexone's business."

A knock at the door interrupted their conversation. Zane picked up his cane from the side of the desk. "There they are. I was worried they wouldn't come."

He was about to step around the desk when the door opened with a bang and Vine strode through. The scarred guard was only a few feet behind. She slammed a hand on Zane's desk.

"Why is the ball going on? I thought I was paying you to stop it!"

The guard laid a lazy hand on his sword's hilt.

As Zane took his seat again, he gripped his cane, ready to unsheathe the hidden sword if necessary. "No, actually you aren't. You hired us to look into Dr. Aluxen—"

"Yes, but what do you have?" Vine turned to Frame. "Where are my updates on this investigation? I haven't seen any in much too long."

Frame tried to say something, but her cousin stopped her. "Don't try to justify it to me, you lazy sack of—"

Alyssa stood up and spoke in a tone that Shadow didn't know she had. It silenced Vine in an instant. "Frame has nearly *died*—not once, but *twice*—because of this job!"

The guard now had a full grip on his sword, and Zane had unlocked his blade.

Vine looked from the professor to Frame again before taking a seat across from Zane.

"Attacked twice? Why are you taking my cousin out in the field? She is only supposed to be relaying your findings."

Zane kept his eye on the guard. "She was attacked in her apartment. We think it was someone working for Aluxen, but we aren't certain."

Before Vine could speak again, the door opened. Agents Will and Crome stepped into the office, shaking the ash from their coats. The older agent gave Zane a grim smile. "I wasn't expecting others. Who are these two?"

"This is my client, Vine Lexone, and her personal bodyguard . . ."

"Davidson."

"Davidson," Zane repeated dryly. Will bowed politely.

"And who are you two?" Vine demanded.

Frame stood. "These are Agents Will and Crome. They work for the Institute. Agents Will and Crome. I believe I have mentioned them in some of the updates."

Vine nodded. "What are you two doing here?"

"We are here finishing up our plan to arrest the doctor," Crome said.

Vine jerked her head back to Zane. "What? Why didn't you lead with that? I could be already preparing the paperwork to shut the ball down."

Will spoke before Zane did. "Because we need the ball to make the arrest."

Vine's face turned a dark shade of crimson. Shadow laughed to himself at seeing the woman lose all control.

Crome looked serious, if not frustrated. "Do you have something we can arrest the doctor on? Something about the stones?"

Zane tried to explain what he had seen.

Will and Crome looked at each other with a nod. The older agent turned back with a smile. "*That* we can work with. Using the ball will be our best chance, because the illegal goods will be out in the open. There is no guarantee that we would find them if we forced our way into his store."

Vine scowled as she motioned to her guard for a cigarette and lighter. "I can see what you mean, but where does that leave our family? Looking embarrassed for hosting illegal magic at a ball."

Frame showed a spark of insight and smiled. "We're not hosting, but assisting the Institute in an arrest."

Vine took a deep drag, then stood, dropping the spent cigarette on Zane's floor. The detective glared as she did it, and Shadow laughed. "That might be for the best."

She left without another word, her guard stomping behind her. With each step, he sent out small ripples along the Sea of Stars. Shadow wondered how the guard was connected to everything, and whether he worked for the doctor. Shadow suspected he did, and their plan had just been leaked. Shadow started to speak, but stopped.

What if capturing him leads them closer to his backer? That backer is probably connected to people I hope believe me dead and gone. Hmm, no . . . let their net rip. He dove down into the dark abyss, away from their conversation. Away from the world.

58

Lights reflected off the mist in an ethereal display. Alyssa's dress pinched her in places she was unaccustomed to, but the carriage seats were soft, and the light of the candle inside was bright.

Chiron smiled and handed her a simple, yet elegantly crafted, flower. "Thank you for allowing me the honor of being your date."

She smiled, feeling the blush again on her cheeks. "You're being silly. You invited me, so I am the one who should be thanking you."

"Still, you could have said no. It's hard to meet people as smart as you."

Alyssa looked out the window. The road leading to the mansion seemed to go on forever as they waited for their turn to reach the entrance. She noticed the way her date fidgeted with his prosthetic hand; something seemed to be eating at him.

He's very nice, but he's working for a criminal. She went over the plan they'd devised in Zane's office the night before.

After the dance had concluded, she would stop the guests from leaving, using magic if necessary. Zane would keep the doctor from escaping as the agents moved in for the arrest. The plan was simple, but she couldn't think of anything else they needed.

While she was still deep in thought, their turn came to exit. A servant dressed all in black met them with an umbrella. "Your invitation, sir?"

Chiron pulled the invitation from his coat. The servant inspected it and handed it back. "Please follow me."

Chiron stepped out and offered his hand to Alyssa. Despite

her soft gloves, the cold of the prosthetic chilled her skin. Part of her wanted to pull away, but she resisted.

Standing on each side of the mansion's door were pairs of servants. "May we take your cloak or jacket?"

Chiron took the cloak from Alyssa's shoulders gently and handed it to one of the servants. He then did the same for his coat. Another pair of servants swept the floor, collecting any ash and muck the guests might bring in.

Yet another servant rushed up, catching his breath as he gestured for them to follow.

The servant walked with a slight skip in every step. "This way, please."

They entered the central hall, its walls lined with gossiping servants. The colors of their coats revealed allegiance to their various families, orders, and companies.

The guide led them to the next set of halls before turning with a click of his heels. "Welcome to Lady Lexone's ball. Please enjoy your evening. If you need a priest in the morning for confession, we recommend the Chapel of Saint Revolas."

The servant pointed down the hall leading north. "You will find the chapel down that way. The priest is already at work for your convenience."

The guide then pointed in the opposite direction. "We ask that you please avoid the servants' room down that way."

With a bow, he left and made his way back down to the entrance. Alyssa smiled and motioned to the ballroom. "Shall we?"

Chiron led the way as the sound of instruments filled the air. He leaned over. "My employer has told me that no expense has been spared. Lady Lexone rented this building and filled it with servants. The doctor has brought dancers and musicians to show the quality of our work, plus one major surprise. It's a long-term project he has been working on."

Alyssa looked over the band. Several of the musicians were missing sleeves, revealing their elegantly designed limbs. They almost looked to be carved from ivory, with musical notes and little instruments decorating each of them. Their arms were thin, and their joints were enclosed in spheres.

Chiron pulled her closer to whisper in her ear. "These are the doctor's best work, masterpieces. They lack all the little sounds that the older ones made. They're even smaller, lighter, and more durable. Sometimes I am shocked that he made them."

Alyssa knew what Zane had said about how this set had come from a sponsor. The quality of the work was extraordinary, and she wondered how it was done. From a distance, each looked perfect. "Do you know how he made them?"

Chiron froze for a moment before shaking his head. "Not these, no. But aren't they marvelous?"

Lady Lexone sat at the front of the room, overlooking the dance floor. She watched with a smile, moving her body to the rhythm of the music. Standing next to her on the platform were Frame and Vine.

Frame smiled softly as she watched the happy couples come and go from the floor. The men wore suits, bearing coats of arms or company sigils. The women's dresses stopped at the ankle, their hair adorned with flowers. Most were artificial, but those of higher status had real blossoms tucked into their elaborate hairstyles.

Frame noticed the crown of fake flowers on Vine's head. She found it a strange choice for her cousin.

Vine did nothing to hide her frustration as she twirled her glass. "You were supposed to prevent this from happening," she whispered to Frame.

Frame shrugged. "Even the Institute had nothing but suspicion about how Dr. Aluxen works. It was this or let him go free. What could we do?"

Vine rubbed her eyes and looked toward the band and their prosthetics. "Damn it, I can't even call them cheap either. I guess Grandmother does have an eye for quality . . . but are these people real?"

"I think I mentioned in an earlier letter that the 'stones' are undocumented. Because of that, we don't have clear evidence of whether Aluxen is using magic or some unknown scientific process. The new limbs that Zane mentioned look to be using magic, without a doubt."

Vine sneered at the band. She sipped her drink and relaxed her shoulders. "You have outplayed me. I don't know how you did it, but you did."

Frame turned to Vine, confused and annoyed. "What are you talking about?"

Her cousin spun to face her. "Don't act like you don't know. You have charmed our grandmother, and now you are the sole heir." Vine jabbed at her cousin with her finger. "The sole heir!"

Vine's face was red-hot, her voice just a bit too loud. Frame could already see people looking over at them, but she didn't care. She gritted her teeth.

"You think that justifies you trying to kill me?"

Vine's mouth dropped in shock. She stepped back, hand pulled to her chest. "K-kill you? Wait, you think I sent a man to kill you? I thought you said he worked for the doctor."

"We don't know for sure, but there's no reason for him to send someone after me. Only you would benefit from me being gone."

Vine was silent for a few moments. "I would never do anything of that sort. You're my cousin, my family."

Now Frame's face was red-hot. "Why not? You were trying to get the will changed, trying to write me out. So why not just get rid of me?"

"Now hold on a min—"

Frame snapped, her voice carrying over the music of the band. The nearest dancing couples turned to face them as they tried to not block the dance floor. "I didn't even know about the will until a couple of weeks ago, but you have obviously known for a while. I know that you've been looking to 'get rid of me.'"

"I-I . . ."

Memories of the attack bubbled to the surface, including Felix's cold face. Frame's body started to shudder as sobs rolled over her, and with one large intake of air, she steeled herself and left. The crowd parted for her.

Vine started to follow, but was stopped by her great-grandmother.

Frame retreated to a corner, away from the curious eyes of guest and servant alike. As she wiped her eyes, a rough, slurring voice asked whether she was okay. She sniffled, accepting a napkin from a gloved hand. "Yeah, I'm just tired. It has been an exhausting few weeks."

"Sometimes life can be like that."

With her eyes cleared, she handed the napkin back.

Her blood froze in her veins as she looked up to see the scarred face that haunted her nightmares and stalked her through the streets. The stitches were gone. Before she could scream, a hand covered her mouth and a knife pressed against her stomach.

Her attacker's voice shifted and changed as if he lacked control, but his eyes were strong. "You make a sound, and I will gut you here."

59

Zane felt out of place at the ball. Despite *technically* being a landed noble, he had never been to a ball. He had attended village and community festivals, but nothing as opulent as this.

Shadow's eyes stared out of Zane's shadow, watching. His voice sounded almost happy. *How long it has been since I have had the pleasure of attending a ball!*

Then his voice sobered. *It's just too much like the old times, though.*

Zane looked over his shoulder. The detective's thoughts drifted around the creature's strange comments as he kneeled in front of a lady cloaked in a thick robe with her prosthetic legs revealed.

"What are you thinking about?" Laure's soft voice from behind him drew him away from thoughts about Shadow. She smiled as she adjusted her stance, favoring her leg with the prosthetic.

"Sorry, I was distracted . . ."

As his voice drifted, Laure placed her hand on his shoulder. "Then we should dance soon."

He didn't look back to her, instead focusing on the pair of legs in front of him, with golden rings around the ankles. Both were the new design the doctor wanted to show off. All they were missing were the stones.

Dr. Aluxen entered the room with a box. "Are you ready for these?"

Zane nodded and the doctor handed it to him. From inside, he pulled out two black stones. He carefully placed a stone into its slot, then repeated the process on the other leg. When both were sealed back up, the room's shadows returned to normal. The lady in the robe jerked, and Zane could hear her suck in a breath as she clenched her teeth.

"Are you all right?" Dr. Aluxen asked.

The dancer nodded her head, and the doctor patted Zane on the shoulder. "Good job. Now everything is ready."

Zane stood up, grabbing his cane for support. Once on his feet, he checked the holster under his coat to make sure his wand was still there. Frame had provided the formal attire through a charge to Vine. He hadn't worn anything like it since before he went to war.

Zane kept his cane under his arm, trying to look casual and still be ready to act. Tension spread across his shoulders and back muscles as he waited nervously for the performance to start. It should be near the end of the ball.

Laure came up to him with a smile. "Shall we dance now?"

The detective wanted to do nothing but get lost in drinking from his flask. He looked toward the back door and then back to her. "I don't know, I think I should wait—"

Dr. Aluxen cut him off. "Go ahead, Zane. Go dance. It's still early."

Zane judged their faces before nodding. "Okay."

Laure guided him into the ballroom. He didn't want to leave his post, but he didn't need to make Dr. Aluxen suspicious. *One dance won't hurt anything.*

Zane reached into his suit and pulled out his flask. Bringing it to his lips, he drank heartily of the potion. It relaxed the tightness in his throat, but did little for his pain.

Laure watched him with great interest. "Why do you keep drinking that stuff? You could have your leg replaced and be free of that pain."

"Maybe, but it's mine."

"You still don't trust the doctor, do you?"

Zane stared out at the people dancing. He didn't have the right words for a response. Laure walked to the nearest waiter and grabbed a glass of wine, then stood facing away from Zane.

The detective wondered if he'd hurt her feelings, but before he had a chance to act, she turned back to him with a pained smile.

Laure offered him the drink. "Please, you must need a real drink. I cannot imagine that whatever is in that flask tastes good."

He took the glass and drank it quickly. Zane had barely passed the empty glass off to a roving servant before Laure dragged him onto the dance floor. The band's music was smooth and soft. His date pulled him closer, helping support his bad leg.

As they completed a second trip around the dance floor, Zane began to feel light-headed and his legs went weak. "I-I need to sit down."

Laure nodded, putting her arm under his shoulder and guiding him to the nearest table.

His hands and feet felt heavy and numb. Zane dropped his cane, and Laure picked it up, setting it on the table. His breath came in weak gasps.

Laure leaned close with a frown, her eyes sad. "I am sorry."

"Sorry? What are—"

The wine. He tried to reach for his flask, hoping that the potion could give him strength to overcome the poison, but Laure kept his weakened hand from reaching it.

"It's okay. You won't die. The doctor was worried that you would prevent his progress."

Before he could plead with her, a well-dressed servant stepped into the center of the room, bringing the band to a halt. He bowed formally to the audience before straightening, arms behind his back. "The Lady Lexone welcomes you to this ball We are happy to have Dr. Aluxen here tonight to demonstrate the use of his creations."

He motioned to the stage where the musicians sat. The violinist stood up, waving his prosthetic arm. He demonstrated the motion of his fingers before picking up the instrument and playing a complicated theme.

His last note brought an explosion of applause. The musician bowed, taking a seat, and the servant motioned for silence.

"We have another surprise. Now, for the first time, we have a famed dancer whose career was cut short due to a horrific tragedy. She lost her legs in a carriage accident."

Zane's heart raced. *This shouldn't be happening for another two hours!*

The servant bowed his head and pointed to the side of the room. With a rising voice, he called out, "Now with our greatest honor, back from the grave like a saint of old, I present Shelina the Lily!"

He clapped his hands and backed away from the center of the floor. From out of the crowd stepped a woman draped in a heavy cloak that swirled around her shoulders. With catlike grace, she stepped lightly into position and let the cloak drop to the floor. She wore a dress that barely reached her knees but had a long train. The white porcelain of her prosthetic legs shone brilliantly in the light.

60

Alyssa watched as the dancer made her way to the center of the room. She had to admit that the woman had the type of beauty that no accident could take away.

The music started slowly, the lights in the room dimming. The dancer's elegant moves pulled the focus straight to her legs as she began.

Alyssa looked for Will and Crome, but couldn't find them. *This is too early.* She looked to the stage where Lady Lexone and Frame had been standing, but Frame was gone. Alyssa turned back and scanned the room with dread. On her second pass, she spotted Frame moving toward a door with a man holding her arm tight. The hair on Alyssa's arms stood on end, and her body stiffened.

The man looked behind him, and the faint light of the doorway revealed he was missing an eye. Alyssa grabbed Chiron's good arm. "I need to go check on my friend."

Chiron studied her face for a moment before giving a forced smile. "Do you need me to go with you? Is she all right?"

Alyssa discreetly patted the wands hidden under her dress. "I don't know, I need to go find out."

With the crowd enamored with the dance floor, she had to work hard to part the sea of guests. Stepping out of the room, all she could see in the hall was a servant at the door. "Did you see a man and woman come through here?"

The man nodded and pointed down the hall. Alyssa gave her thanks and rushed around the corner toward the servants' quarters. She could already hear yelling from inside.

"What are you doing with—"

"Get out of the way, or I'll kill her! Move it, *now!*"

There was a scream and then a clashing of dishes. Alyssa slid into the doorway. With her right hand, she pulled her steel wand free from its leather holster.

Belard laid on the floor holding his arm, blood soaking through his fingers. His wife kneeled next to him. The one-eyed man held a knife in one hand, while the other held a fistful of Frame's hair. Blood dripped from the corner of her mouth.

He snarled at Alyssa and whipped Frame around, pressing the knife against her throat.

"Don't move, or I'll slit her throat!"

Alyssa's wand hand was clammy, her stomach churning.

The man's eye dropped down to her hand. "I remember you! This time, you won't be able to get that wand off. Drop the wand and kick it here." He motioned with his knife.

Alyssa's mind raced, stopping on words from *Arcanum Combatom*: "Let ignorance of magic be your blade." She tossed her wand to the floor.

Frame's assailant navigated the helpless student through the broken dishes toward the back door. With a rush of eldritch words, Frame tried to push the knife away, but the charm was too weak. The man struck Frame with the back of his hand.

Alyssa's eyes felt like they were bulging as she shouted the eldritch words, focusing all her concentration into them. Of all the charms she could do, she kept it simple. She used the same one that Frame had attempted, a push. However, this one was far stronger, much more focused, and it slammed into him like a sledgehammer.

The hapless kidnapper's feet left the floor as his body crumpled in half. His grip on Frame's hair didn't loosen, so he took a chunk of it with him, but his knife skittered across the floor. He slammed into the wall next to the back door and slumped to the floor.

Alyssa rushed forward as the two elderly servants lunged to cover Frame's body with theirs. Alyssa rushed past them, worried the attacker would get up again.

The man didn't move. If he made any noise, she couldn't hear it over the blood pounding in her ears.

"Is it over?" a tired voice asked from behind her.

With a deep breath, Alyssa worked up the nerve to check the kidnapper, preparing a charm to shroud herself in electricity. As she reached down tentatively, his left hand lashed out and pulled her close. A blade erupted from his fist, but the words left her mouth in a heartbeat, sending electricity pouring from her. His hair stood up, and his knife arm went wide. The knife jerked past her and across her side.

Adrenaline coursed through her veins, masking the pain. Muscle memory kicked in, and she leveraged his prosthetic limb across her shoulder. She kicked his feet out from under him, sending his body back into the floor. As she was gasping for air, another eldritch word crossed her lips, binding his limb to his side. She took his other arm and twisted it, rolling him over.

Alyssa turned to the servants. "Get me rope, now!"

The one-eyed man turned his head and spat blood onto the floor. "Damn it, woman! You're as bad as that goblin!"

"What? What goblin?"

"That damn Red Hood. Just go ahead and kill me."

She shook her head. "No, I'm no killer. You're coming with me."

Lista rushed back with other servants. Some wore formal dress, while others were dressed as servers. One of them had a rope, and they worked together to bind the man.

Alyssa wiped her forehead with her sleeve. Frame sat there crying, a bald spot bleeding in her hair, but otherwise okay. She looked up. "Is it over now?"

Alyssa was shaking. "I-I don't know."

61

The music began with a slow and steady rhythm, the dancer matching the pace with gliding movements across the floor. The sound of the band and the brilliance of the dancer combined for an awe-inspiring show. As the tempo increased, the dancer moved faster and faster, to the enjoyment of the audience.

Zane's senses were dulled, and he fought to stay awake. Yet, he felt something. He couldn't tell what it was, but it felt as if he was floating in a massive river that threatened to drag him away.

Zane sat nearly limp in his chair, his eyes helplessly following the white prosthetic limbs of the dancer. The runes on the legs began to glow, faint at first, but blazing like flames within seconds.

Laure's eyes were wide, matching her fanatical smile. "The doctor is a living saint. I don't see how you couldn't see that. I-I almost faltered in the task that the doctor had given me—"

She went on, but her voice was soon lost in the intensifying music. The light of the room dimmed, and he worried that he was about to pass out.

They need to stop! You need to stop them! Shadow's voice was filled with fear.

Zane's eyes dropped to the floor, where he could see all the shadows of the room pointed toward the dancer. When he found Shadow, his two red eyes were shaking. "What?"

Shadow screamed at him. *Stop them!*

The undercurrent he felt grew, and Zane's stomach flipped. The dancer gave an exaggerated stomp at the height of the composition. The prosthetics cracked, shattered, and then exploded with a loud boom. Shards of leg flew in all directions.

The sound that followed the explosion was strange and alien, like running water draining into a deep void. All the shadows of the room plunged toward the center. When one fell over Zane, it plunged him into darkness. Its depth was something Zane had never seen. The detective and his chair lifted off the floor.

In the ribbons of remaining light, Zane could see that everyone else was flying through the air, too. The people and objects in the room started to spin, as if toward a great drain. He tumbled limply through the air, his body slamming into others trapped in the same fate.

Zane blacked out, only to be awakened by Shadow screaming in his ear. His diaphragm contracted in a fit of coughing, as if his body was trying to clear something from his lungs. Before he could stand, he threw up. His head spun, but he felt a little stronger. He pulled his flask from his jacket and downed all of it.

The room looked like a shipwreck cove, with broken tables, chairs, couches, and chandeliers strewn across the floor. Among the wreckage, people moaned in pain and cried for help. One of the surviving musicians lay next to him. His prosthetic limb was broken at the elbow. Large black splotches grew out of the busted prosthetic.

Two other survivors pulled themselves close to the musician. They spoke in panicked voices as they tried to help. Zane watched as the black splotch spread to their fingers.

The rat-faced man casually walked in with his team, sporting heavy leather-and-cloth suits that left almost no skin bare. They moved carefully around the floor, as if someone might jump out at them. With heavy iron tongs, they picked up the broken pieces that had once been the dancer's legs.

At the edge of the room stood Dr. Aluxen, watching over the destruction and the team. He sighed, but forced a smile when he noticed Zane.

"What did you do?" he screamed at the doctor. "What was that?"

The doctor shrugged as if nothing here mattered. His voice

was level. "Fulfilling my part of another contract with my patron, but it is as I told them . . . we don't give Fey bloods prosthetics. Never worked before—always some type of mess like this—but they thought they had it figured out with their enchantments."

Laure's weak voice gave an injured cry. "Please help me, doctor. It hurts."

Zane searched for her as the doctor just smiled and shook his head. "The saints and the first knights be with you. There is nothing I can do."

Dr. Aluxen turned and stepped into another room, followed by the rat-faced man and his team.

Laure pulled, trying to drag herself over to Zane. He watched in horror as one of her legs slipped into black smog on the solid floor. The detective half-crawled, half-walked through the debris to her.

Laure's lower half was covered by a torn tablecloth. Zane ripped it away and gasped. Her prosthetic was disappearing below the surface.

Zane grabbed for her leg, but his hands slipped through. He moved his hands up the leg until he could get a hold. He pulled with all his strength, but it wouldn't budge. Laure cried in pain, her body slipping further with no way to stop it. Zane held her hand. "I-I am sorry. I don't know what—"

He jerked his head around in desperation. "Shadow, you damn parasite! I need you. What can I do?"

A sympathetic and oddly merciful voice rang in his head. *Nothing but cut her pain short.*

Everything below her waist was gone. She looked up to him, pleading. "It's so bad, Zane. It burns. Please do what your friend said and make it stop."

Zane stared down at her in shock. "You could hear him?"

Shadow whispered. *She is halfway to my side of reality, but it's not a pleasant place for living people.*

"Please—"

Laure's body slipped further. Zane closed his eyes and unsheathed his sword cane. "I'm sorry."

He gripped her shoulder and pressed the tip of the sword into her heart. Laure gave a sigh of relief.

Zane pulled the sword free and let her body sink below until nothing was left, not even the blood on his sword.

Zane screamed and scratched at the floor, but there was nothing. Another person called out, and he recognized the voice as Alyssa's date. He was suddenly wracked with guilt; he'd forgotten Alyssa was there, too. He couldn't see her and prayed she wasn't in the room.

The detective found Chiron, his head bobbing up and down in his own dark sludge. His face was pale, and sweat dripped down it. "I-I never thought I would go like this."

Zane could feel his eyes getting puffy and red from tears he didn't realize he was crying. "It's all right. We'll get justice—"

He laughed weakly. "Justice? For what? Our lives were already over. The doctor simply gave us a new lease, but . . . No, I wish that I could have met her earlier."

His face sunk below the surface and disappeared before the detective could say anything.

Zane's heart was bursting with rage and regret. Looking over the room and hearing the cries for help, his instincts took over. He forced his tired body up again and moved to the nearest person still breathing.

"It's going to be all right. Hold still. Let me see what I can do."

Shadow dipped his form into the Sea of Stars. He watched as people sunk from pockets of light into the swirls and streams of the darkness. Something larger moved in the depths, like a giant sea creature. Shadow recalled the words written on a parchment, from an age before even he was born, that warned of the bottom of this sea before light and dark were divided. "How man exists on land, and things beyond his imagination exist in the sea, the same can be said about light and dark. We exist in light, while things beyond our mind exist in darkness."

He was torn between fear and astonishment. The thing moved sluggishly, but would then quickly propel itself through the sea to devour the sinking bodies.

Shadow saw one large eye, white like the full moon, penetrating the darkness. It locked on Shadow and stared at him with an alien sentience. Shadow dove for the light closest to Zane.

He could feel the thing approaching him, but he dared not look back. Fear coursed through him, even after he emerged on the other side. He watched as Zane played doctor, trying to help those who'd been injured. The detective ripped dresses and suits to make bandages and used broken furniture to make splints.

Shadow wondered who would risk such public destruction and only one name came to mind: Loudwick.

62

Frame had a cloak draped over her shoulders. Belard's shirt had been pulled back and his arm bandaged. Despite the red stain, he refused to leave Frame's side, just as Lista never left her husband's side.

Her attacker's sleeve was wadded up on the floor next to them. It had been ripped away during the melee, uncovering a prosthetic that could only have been made by Dr. Aluxen.

Even more questions surfaced in Frame's mind. *If the attacker worked for the doctor, and the doctor was working with my great-grandmother, then he wouldn't have been sent by Vine, right? Why would Grandmother want to get rid of me?* She felt faint, but she carried on. The guards would be here soon, and she wanted to stay out of sight until then.

Noise drew her attention from outside the room. She sighed as they cautiously exited the servants' quarters and turned back to the ballroom.

Alyssa and Frame watched in silent horror as people rushed wildly from the room. They screamed and yelled as they pushed past each other, some getting trampled in the surge. The screams brought Lista up behind them.

"What the—"

Alyssa's face was a mixture of panic and concern. It took Frame a moment to process the scene before she knew they needed to act.

"Is Zane still in there?" the professor finally asked.

Without waiting for a response, Alyssa rushed toward the stampede. She tried to push her way in, to no avail. Frame could see Alyssa starting a charm, but Frame stopped her.

"Don't do it! These people are scared."

Frame took a deep breath and pointed to the people lying on the floor, injured. "Lista, bring all the servants here. We need to get these people help! Tell Belard we need to move them out of the path."

Lista nodded her head and ran to get help while her injured husband arrived and started pulling people to safety. Frame joined him, forgetting her own pains, and called for Alyssa to do the same. After the crowd thinned, Frame sent Belard to find her family and the Imperial Guard.

A third servant was sent for doctors, any and all that could reach them. The doors to the ballroom hung loosely on their battered hinges. The people still in the room recounted exploding limbs, devouring darkness, and a hellish storm.

From the doorway, the women saw Zane checking on those left inside. His clothes were torn around the sleeves, his hands covered in blood. His face was pale, and he looked to be in pain. Alyssa crossed the room to him.

Frame followed behind, taking in the destruction.

"What should we do here?" one servant asked.

"Where are Lady Lexone and Vine?"

The servants looked at each other. "Sorry, my lady, but we don't know."

Frame gave a tired sigh, fear and regret sapping her strength. "Then do what we were doing out in the hall or what that man is doing. These people need help."

She turned back just as Alyssa asked about Chiron.

63

Zane sat in a dim room, with what little light there was coming from gas lamps. They were painful to look at, and he wondered if they were enchanted to be intentionally uncomfortable. Around his hands were cuffs engraved with glowing runes. From the only door in the room, agent Will stepped in. The detective looked up at him. "Why am I here? I thought we had a contract."

The agent rubbed his head before pulling out a cigarette. He offered Zane one. "Yeah, we did, but the Institute is breathing down my neck. A lot of people died, and that is not something that a contract can just make go away."

Zane was tired, exhausted even, and he wished they would let him clean the blood from his clothes. "That still doesn't explain why I am here. I thought we were working together."

Will shrugged, lit up his cigarette, and took a long drag. "My bosses are hoping to have this mess cleaned up quietly, and you are an easy sacrifice. Of course, that is all dependent on what you tell me."

The detective wiped at his clothes, but the stains were dry. "Things just didn't go as planned."

"That is a massive understatement. Why weren't you at your post?"

"The doctor knew our plan. He had one of his people poison me, and then he moved his event up. That's when everything went so very wrong."

Will nodded. "So what caused this . . . shadow storm?"

Zane looked for Shadow, but his red eyes were nowhere to be found. "I don't have a definitive answer, but I have a guess. The dancer was of Fey descent."

"How would that make any difference?" Will looked doubtful. "It doesn't seem possible."

"Not my job to know that. That's the Institute's problem; mine is to be a detective."

"Fine, but where is the doctor now?"

"I don't know."

Will's face turned harsh. "You know that isn't good enough. Nobles are dead—many nobles—and their families are chomping at the bit for answers."

Realization pulsed through Zane as he looked up at Will. "Do you think I was in on it?"

The agent shrugged. "It doesn't matter what I think; someone has to pay for this."

64

Alyssa sat in a soft chair in her grandfather's office, surrounded by familiar rows of books, scrolls, and glass jars. Her grandfather's iron staff clanged against the floor as he made his way around the desk. With a sigh, he sat down. Two cups of steaming tea sat between them.

Her grandfather moved the books in front of him to the side, clearing a space for his arms. The old eyes of archmage Benedictus-Lasome were downcast. "I knew I should have tried to stop you from going with the detective."

Alyssa brought the cup to her mouth. "It was my choice."

"But what has it brought you?"

The fear in his eyes felt familiar, as if she was looking into a mirror. "I don't know, but I think it is a better place for me to be than here."

"I don't understand. You have spent your entire life here at the Institute. Even now, they would welcome you back as a professor."

Her left hand reached for where Red Hood had stabbed her. Then, looking into the mug, she could see Chiron's expression right before she left to find Frame. Chiron had been so nice, and his death seemed disrespectful, given the reverence he'd held for the doctor. "There are some things you can't learn from the Institute."

Benedictus-Lasome raised an eyebrow. "What could that be?"

"How can I just sit here when there are monsters out there that will sacrifice others like that?"

"What happened?"

She took a deep breath and started to explain more about the case, Dr. Aluxen, and the power source they'd found. The only thing she left out was Zane's connection to the black stones.

Her grandfather looked stunned, unsure what to make of it. "This is all very concerning. How could we have missed this? Generations of wizards, and yet . . ." He furrowed his brow. "Our detection charms should have picked something up."

He mumbled something to himself. An anger rose up in her, one she had not felt before. "Where is Zane?"

"With the agents. Why?"

Alyssa sat her cup on the desk and stood up. She patted her pockets, making sure that her wands were still holstered securely as she reached for the door.

"Where are you going?" her grandfather called out to her. "What are you planning to do?"

"I don't know, but that doctor is still out there. I can't tolerate that. I don't imagine Zane can either, so I'm going to go collect him."

Alyssa slipped into the shifting halls. She let her instincts guide her to the room that she needed to find. She passed students and staff making their way by compass, her damaged ball gown seeming to make them feel even more lost.

Finally, she came to a clerk's window next to a metal door covered in large runes. Even the most novice of students would be able to tell these runes reinforced the door.

The clerk raised a cynical eyebrow. "What business do you have with the agents of the Institute?"

Alyssa pulled out her state mage badge and laid it on the counter. "I am here to pick up Zane Vrexon. He is here with agents Will and Crome."

The clerk took some notes and then pointed to the chairs lining the far wall of the hall. "Please take a seat."

She sat there waiting for the heavy door to open. It was not long before Will appeared.

"Ms. Benedictus, what can I do for you?"

Alyssa's hands gripped her dress. "Where is Zane? Is he still in your custody?"

The agent looked away. "Maybe, but what has that got to do with you?"

"I would like you to release him, immediately."

Will gave a grim smile. "I can't do that. A head must roll for this."

She bit her lip. "We can be more help working with you rather than with him being arrested."

"Really? How?"

She nodded. "What is it that you want?"

Agent Will was slow to raise his voice. "I want justice for Jake."

"Then, please, let's work together."

He sighed. "The higher-ups have spoken on it . . . but I guess they can wait." He pointed to her. "But first, you and the detective must help us deactivate the limb of the other guy in custody, the one who tried to kidnap Frame. From there, we will decide how this will play out."

After the carnage had been removed, the ballroom floor was still covered in spilled drinks and dishes. The spot where the dancer had last been seen was now scorched black, and no matter how hard they scrubbed, the floor would not come clean. After many attempts, the spots were abandoned and the servants' focus shifted to things they could control.

From the window, Frame could see a hint of morning behind the clouds. The embers of carriages smoldered in the courtyard. The servants and guards had put out the flames overnight. Her eyes drifted from there to the lines of bodies draped in white cloth. The weight of the night had only grown heavier with the coming of the light.

Belard came up next to her. "We've looked everywhere. We can't find either of them."

She squinted, trying hard not to cry. "Even among the dead?"

Belard hesitated for a moment before nodding. "We're pretty sure, but a few of the bodies are disfigured. I don't believe they are among them, though."

Frame turned to him, noting his face was downcast. "Then why are you so hesitant?"

"Because we can't find them. I-I have had all the men looking."

Where did they go? Was someone targeting them, too? Then an even darker question came to mind. *Is this a ploy by Vine? She claimed she didn't know about the attacks, even after several letters. Could this all be her design?*

They stood in silence. From the doorway, the guard captain waved for her to come over. He was a gruff man, and didn't wear a breastplate like the others. Frame wondered whether he even could, with how far his stomach stuck out. His face was ruddy with rage.

"Saints, woman! Are you the one in charge?"

Frame looked around. "I believe so, at least—"

He cut her off with a harsh gesture, stepping even closer. "Do you have any damn idea of what you have done? There are fifteen dead, and nobles, no less. Their families are already slamming us with demands. My bosses are getting charmed letters . . . charmed letters!" His breath was hot, and it smelled like he had been kissing a bottle of alcohol.

Belard stepped between them, staring the captain down. "You are in the House of Lexone, and you will respect a lady of the house!"

The captain's eyes were wild, his hand gripping the wand in his holster. The hair on the back of Frame's neck stood on end at the escalating tension.

A younger, more cheerful voice interrupted them. "You are making things worse, captain. Do I need to report this?"

They all turned to see a sharply dressed officer approaching. On his hip were both a wand and sword. The captain's eyes seemed about to bulge out of his head, and his hands went white on his wand. A few tense breaths came from the man before he marched off.

The young officer stepped forward and gave a formal bow. "I am Lieutenant Kellim, and I overheard that you are a lady of the house. However, if I remember correctly, it is Clelia Lexone, or even Vine Lexone, who is normally addressed as the lady of the House of Lexone."

Belard stepped to the side, allowing the young guard to speak comfortably.

Frame nodded. "Yes, they are my great-grandmother and my cousin, but they have been missing since . . . the ball."

Kellim's smile faded as he rubbed his chin with a gloved hand. "I'm sorry to hear that. I can't imagine that this is just merely happenstance. I don't mean to be rude, but have any clues been found?"

Frame turned to Belard, and the old guard shook his head. "No, we were just going over it. We have fears that something has happened, but we are still looking."

Belard turned to face a family guard, who was standing awkwardly to the side, waiting to be acknowledged before speaking. "Here is one of our household guards looking into it."

Kellim nodded and pointed at the man. "What is your name, and what news do you bring?"

The guard spoke anxiously. "One of the injured household servants says he saw Lady Vine being taken away by force. The servant would like to speak to all of you."

The four of them walked into a room that was being used for medical treatment.

"May I question him first?" Kellim glanced away from the servant to Belard, and the old guard nodded his approval.

He kneeled down next to a young man with a bandaged head. "What did you see?"

"I-I was outside watching the carriages when I started to hear screaming from inside. That's when a carriage exploded. A piece of wood slammed into me. I don't know how, but I didn't pass out. I was laying there when the young lady's bodyguard came out of the building, dragging her."

Belard spoke in panic. "Was it Davidson—"

Frame interrupted. "Could he have been trying to get her to safety?"

The servant shook his head, wincing when he moved. "Not unless it was appropriate for her to be dragged by her hair. They were moving really fast, then another carriage came out of the smoke. Davidson loaded Lady Vine and himself into it."

Frame stepped forward, scared for her cousin. Despite everything, they were still family. "Did you recognize the carriage?"

The servant nodded. "Yes, because it had strange shapes on it. It was the one used by that doctor."

Kellim turned to Frame, confused. "Do you know what he is talking about?"

She felt her face pale, as her world rocked. "I know exactly what he is talking about," Frame said weakly. "We need to find Zane and Alyssa."

66

Standing on his injured leg was taking more strength than Zane had thought he possessed. His hands were still cuffed together in front of him, but Alyssa's quiet voice gave him strength in spite of it all.

"You okay?"

He nodded, fighting the tightness in his throat. "I think I will be. Thank you for getting me out of that room." He wanted to ask whether they would remove his cuffs, but somehow he doubted that was on the table right now.

Crome and inspector Lucos led them to a strange room. The walls were lined with runes in overlapping circles. In the center of the room was a large stand as thick as a log. Sitting on top was a glass orb twice the size of a human head. Several small stones with similar runes sat in small grooves around the edge of the stand.

On each wall of the room were two sets of doors. Zane knew that the doors could lead anywhere or nowhere inside the Institute.

Agent Will stepped forward and rested a hand on the glass orb. "We have the criminal known as Lash here in custody. His arm is one of the special prosthetic limbs made by Dr. Aluxen. Now, we have tried several maneuvers to cancel out any functioning spells, but nothing has seemed to work. That much we had anticipated."

He traced shapes on the glass orb, and an image appeared inside.

Zane could see a small room, much like the one he was being held in. At the table sat the one-eyed attempted kidnapper, his wrists bound in handcuffs attached to the table. There were two other men in the room, wearing suits with wands in black holsters on their hips.

Will turned to Zane. "Now, how do we go about shutting that limb off? I know you mentioned it earlier, but walk us through it."

Zane gestured with his cuffed hand to the man in the orb. "The black stone is located around the bicep area. You will need to open it in the dark, and be sure the person doing this is wearing gloves—thick ones—with sleeves tucked in."

"Why?"

"Even the water that engulfs the stone can be dangerous for people. I guess the stone poisons it, in a way. The ball showed me just how dangerous it can be."

Will nodded and reached down to the rune-covered stones. While tapping on them, he leaned down and spoke into a metal rod with a metal web attached. "I need you to grab a night helm and kill the lights. The power source is in the bicep. Make sure you're wearing gloves with sleeves tucked in. Don't let the stone touch you in the light, and wrap it once out."

From the device came a voice. "Understood."

The device was quite different from any other form of magical communication Zane had seen. After a few minutes, on the orb, a man stepped into the room wearing a rounded helmet with glass lenses over the eyes. The detective recognized the helmet from the Ghoul War; it was an enchanted item that allowed its wearer to see in the dark.

The lamps in the room were extinguished, plunging the room in total darkness. Zane couldn't see anything that was going on, but the sound still carried over. "What are you doing? Hey, let go of me! You can't be doing this to me."

Rustling and movement could be heard, followed by the sound of scissors cutting through cloth. Zane imagined the man was fighting to get control of the limb. He could almost taste the tension.

An irritated voice called out over the globe. "The arm is free.

We see the panel, and we are opening it now." The faint sound of water could be heard slipping out, followed by a curse. "Damn! I missed the stone! It slipped out with the water."

There was the sound of movement before the voice came back. "We can't find it. We are going to turn the light on real quick."

Shadow spoke for the first time in a while. *You have to stop them now!*

Zane turned to look at the red eyes, swearing he could detect fear in them. "Tell them not to—"

The light flicked on, and the screaming began. The criminal had turned black, and the room started to swirl with shadows, as if they had all become tendrils of smoke. The tainted water stained everything it touched. The agent with the helmet was slammed into the wall as he gripped his arm. Another agent worked to help him out of the gloves.

Crome turned to Zane. "Can you help them?!"

"I-I don't know—"

"Can you or not?!"

Zane glanced at the red eyes, seeking a response.

Get us out of this room, and I will help.

Zane nodded. "Get me in the room."

Will pulled a key free and opened the door to the interrogation room. The moment it was open, the room's shadows started to lap and seep toward the larger space. Everyone's shadows jerked toward it, except Zane's.

With quick strides, he made his way through the door. Already, the table and the one-eyed man had started to sink. Zane didn't fully understand what was going on, but it was like watching the tides of a river or ocean going mad.

This will be hard. The nature of the building amplifies the effects of this stone, but we can use that to our advantage.

"Then what should we do?" Zane whispered.

Grab the stone, and we will have you absorb the essence.

"Is that safe?"

I don't know, but I don't think we have a choice. If we do nothing, this could spiral out. Everyone in this stupid building is in danger.

Zane moved quickly to the criminal and pried the stone free from his grip, despite his handcuffs. "Now what?"

Swallow it.

Zane hesitated, but only for a moment. He put the stone in his mouth. He was sure this was going to choke him, but knew that Shadow needed him alive. The stone that felt so solid in his hand easily molded to his throat. His body felt cool, as if he dove into a cold lake in the winter. The room spun, and his head pounded.

He could hear Shadow's voice, but he couldn't make out the words. Strange symbols and images passed through his mind, but he had no time to deal with that. The shadows of the room stopped moving, leaving black marks on all they had touched.

The prisoner's body looked like it was covered in one large bruise. Red streaked across his face. Shadow spoke quickly. *He has been stained by that stone. He is going to disappear soon.*

Zane's head still spun, but he knew he didn't have time to wait. He yanked the man from the ground and slammed him into the wall. "What the hell is your name?"

The man coughed, and his one good eye wouldn't focus. "I-I am Lash. I was a gang member."

"What are you doing for Dr. Aluxen?"

Lash's breathing slowed. Zane slammed him again. "Speak!"

His eye focused on Zane. "All I had to do was kidnap one stupid girl. And when that failed, he offered me the perfect operation. New everything. New eye, new arm."

Lash started laughing. Zane could already feel a difference in Lash's weight, as if he was fading away. "It was perfect: He gave me someone else's body! B-but it wasn't my body. It never felt right. My voice was never right, and I had to make changes to feel like me. The doctor understood and helped me remove things that made me not me."

Zane flinched at this, that this man had his eye and arm removed. He shook his head. Already, Lash's body was disappearing faster.

"Where is Dr. Aluxen?"

A whisper passed Lash's lips. "I don't know."

The man faded away, sinking into the same place as the victims at the ball. Zane's vision was blurry, and he felt like he was about to pass out. Alyssa rushed in and helped steady him. "That was stupid! What were you thinking?"

He forced his shoulders into a shrug. "It was the advice that I was given."

"Advice?"

He nodded and pointed to his shadow. Alyssa understood.

Will, Crome, and Lucos arrived just after her. "Damn it," Will said, looking around the room. "This is why magic outside of the Institute is illegal!"

Alyssa looked over at the three. "Can we get Zane out of these cuffs?"

Crome looked to Will. "He did just risk his life to save two agents."

Will shook his head. "We just lost our lead."

Lucos pulled his own cuffs out. "I am sorry, but my boss wants someone for the murder of the student. Your boss can take it up with mine, but mine might want to talk to the detective."

Will sighed. "Look, I got people breathing down my neck, too. We still need someone. A real lead."

"Let's all work together," Alyssa pleaded.

Will looked at each of them. "Fine. I didn't like the order anyway. The whole situation feels wrong."

Lucos put his cuffs away.

Zane extended his arms out. "Good. Get me out of these cuffs, and let's head to my office."

"Why?"

"So we can put an end to this case."

Frame leaned against Alyssa's desk. Belard refused to leave her side. She knew where Zane kept his stash of healing brew and gave some to Belard.

Within a bell period, the knife wound was gone. The old guard sat in a chair across from the detective's desk. It was two more rings of the city's clocks before Frame started to feel ready to leave.

The door swung open, and a tired Zane marched in with a line of people behind him.

Frame was happy to see Alyssa. The former professor came over and hugged her, offering her the chair behind her desk. Frame smiled and let the professor take a seat instead.

Zane laid his cane over his desk and fished the partially empty healing potion out.

Imperial guards followed them in and found a place near the detective's desk. Will took the free seat next to Belard.

As they got comfortable, Frame spoke up. "I am glad you're both back. I was worried that I had missed you."

Alyssa's hands shook just a little, but she put them out of sight under her desk. "We were taken to the Institute for questioning. The statements about black magic are a bit understated."

The student turned to Lieutenant Kellim, surprised to see him. "What brings you here?"

Kellim bowed to the agents first, then to Zane and Alyssa. "The deaths among the nobles have caused a significant number of complaints, not to mention the kidnapping of Vine Lexone."

Zane's jaw fell. "Kidnapped? Did someone take advantage of the situation?"

"We have an eyewitness that saw Lady Vine being dragged by her bodyguard into a carriage belonging to Dr. Aluxen. We are here in hopes that we can find him quickly. Frame explained that the doctor is the subject of your investigation."

Will turned to the detective, looking frustrated at the growing complications. "Could he have gone back to his shop? Should we do a raid on the place?"

Kellim shook his head. "The Imperial Guard's men already went down to take a look. He wasn't there, but now we also have a riot. The people of the district were not happy that the Imperial Guard marched down there. It should be cleared up before long."

"Zane, you worked with the doctor for a time," Crome added. "Do you know where he might have gone? Does he have some house out there? A mistress maybe?"

Zane rubbed the bridge of his nose. "None that I know of. He didn't really trust me that much, but I suspect he has support from someone in the upper class."

"Really? Why do you say that?"

"The stones, those shadow stones, were being sent to him. He didn't make them."

Kellim stopped the agent from asking more questions. "That line of questioning can be continued after we first find the man."

"But how? What else do we know?"

Zane looked deep in thought before answering. "He did have a business partner."

"What's the name?"

Zane shrugged as he tapped his desk. "I don't know, but it should be written down at the shop. The doctor was obsessive about keeping records."

Kellim sighed. "Then I will be back when a path to the shop is made. We will rip it apart board by board, if necessary."

In less than an hour, the lieutenant had returned. Alyssa and Frame had served up tea, and food was on the way.

Kellim strode in with his smile gone, his once-calm eyes seeming distant. "The district is under control."

"What happened?"

He looked down in shame. "That damn old fool. The captain marched down to the shop and something went wrong . . . the same type of wrong as the ball. Five are dead, and ten are missing."

Kellim locked eyes with Will and Crome. "I understand now why the Institute is involved. The reports I heard were disturbing. The description of 'drowning in shadows' at the ball sounded foolish. I thought about dismissing it, but now it's happened twice."

He straightened, trying to regain his composure. "There is a carriage outside that will take us to the shop. Though it is under control, it will be better for all of you to ride with the guard."

Zane stood slowly. "Lieutenant, what exactly happened?"

"They were throwing bricks and one of the guards took a shot. It blasted through a prosthetic limb, and then came a wave of darkness."

They loaded into the carriage in silence and rode off. When they arrived at the district, it looked like a war zone—or at least what Frame thought one would look like. The Body Shop's window was broken, with glass littering the interior.

Zane stepped inside, leading the way. The weary guards by the doors didn't bother to stop him. The limbs that had once lined the walls were scattered, their hooks swinging freely from the ceiling.

With the end of his cane, Zane opened the back door and motioned for everyone to follow him. The next room was an office with a desk. A door to the side was locked with a large padlock.

Zane sank into the desk chair and laid his cane on top. He went through the drawers until he found an accounting ledger. He laid it out and flipped through the pages until he came to the name. "Here it is. His partner is a man named Rufus."

Alyssa looked shocked as she moved to read the name for herself. Kellim also looked stunned.

"Does it say what he does?"

Zane shook his head. "Nothing specific, just that he brought a shipment. It does list the business name as 'corpse collector.'"

Alyssa and Kellim shared a look. "I can't believe those two are working together," the lieutenant said. "And to what end would the doctor need a corpse collector?"

Alyssa turned to Zane. "Didn't you mention a large man-sized oven in the basement?"

"Yeah, in the basement of the porcelain shop." He jabbed one of the limbs on the floor with his cane. "That's what these are really made from."

The room was dead silent until Alyssa spoke up meekly. "I know how to find Rufus."

68

Alyssa stormed into her apartment, leaving the door open for her entourage. Kellim, Will, and Zane followed. She dumped books out of chairs and swept them off the table holding the map. With their help, she moved the table to the wall so the map on the wall and the map on the table again reflected each other.

Of the three matching compasses laid out on the map, two were spinning in circles. The other pointed toward the docks.

Zane sat down to massage the muscles in his bad leg. "How will this show us where the body collector went? I thought you said you knew where he was."

"I know how to find him," she corrected, making notes and cross-referencing.

The agents studied the runes on the compass needles. "Are these runes designed to track?" Will asked. "We have used them to track suspects through the streets of the city. But why so many, and why this arrangement?"

She pointed to where the compasses laid. "A compass is secured in each of these locations. Those compasses follow Rufus, and these here reflect what those show. The ones spinning have been damaged somehow."

Kellim looked at the map, his eyes following the lines that she drew pointing from each needle, showing where they overlapped. "Brilliant."

Alyssa stopped and looked up at him. Kellim's face showed a thousand thoughts running through his head. He looked up at her. "Why did you make this?"

Alyssa's cheeks reddened in embarrassment, the words to explain suddenly lost. After an awkward silence, she found them. "I wanted to track down Red Hood, and the body collector kept going to these goblin attack sites. Using the information I learned from these, I collected the data and was hoping to figure out the next place he would be."

Zane shot up in surprise, his eyes wide. "Alyssa, I am so sorry. I didn't realize you were trying so hard to feel safe. I should have been a better friend."

Alyssa gave him a polite smile. "No. How would you have ever known unless I told you?"

"I should have known."

Crome clicked his tongue. "You know, it is illegal to place tracking charms on people without permission. This map needs to be destroyed."

She knew that rule, just as any state mage did, but Kellim placed himself in front of the maps before she could respond. "This could change so many things in the Imperial Guard. With this method, we could make proper moves against the growing crime within the city. I can see it now: Rooms filled with teams following criminals back to their lairs like rats given poison."

Will looked to the guard, then to the map again. "This is well thought-out. If I remember correctly, you were a professor of Fey studies. So, how did this idea come to you?"

Alyssa picked up a book off the shelf: *Fey History, A Story Told in Maps*. She flipped through the pages to her bookmark. "This is a map that was recovered from an old enclave to the south. From what I understand, this was etched into the ceiling and then modified with illusion magic. The records show it was how they tracked their ships, mages, and other important people through the Fey empire."

Kellim looked to Will. "Why hasn't the Institute figured out something like this before?"

Will shrugged. "The Institute was originally a center of learning. Only later did we take on more responsibility from the crown. So, you could say it's because of our foundational creed."

Will looked less harsh than Crome as he studied the map. The two agents exchanged looks, then Will spoke again. "For Jake."

Crome nodded. "For Jake."

Will turned back to Alyssa. "I believe that I can convince my bosses to ignore this, but I want you to provide a paper explaining, in detail, exactly what you did to create this."

Alyssa let out a breath she didn't know she had been holding in. She hadn't realized how uneasy she'd felt about the idea of this getting out.

Kellim stepped forward. "I, too, would like a copy of that paper."

Agent Will shook his head. "This would be the Institute's property, not something the guards would want part of."

The lieutenant smiled. "They want many things, but many things are not what they once were. The world changes, and we caretakers must change too."

"I shall send a request to our bosses about this, but don't expect much."

"Thank you. Now I must get my men together so we can prepare to head that way."

He stopped and turned back to Zane and Alyssa. "Once this case is put away, I would like to hire both of you again to help with the goblin gang war still going on."

Zane's rough voice sounded surprised. "I thought you said that you didn't have the budget to hire us again."

"After seeing this case, I think I can make use of both of your unique insights . . . innovation is needed."

Agent Will pulled a pen from his coat. "Do you have any charmed letters? I need to let my bosses know where we are looking. They will want a team on-site to help handle this strange magic—or at least try to handle it."

Zane cracked a smile. "So should we wait here until the operation is over?"

Crome looked grim. "Won't you be at the docks?"

The detective looked like he was going to laugh it off for a moment. "Why would you want me there? You already have all the hands you need."

"Because the doctor has unknown magic that you, and only you, seem to be immune to. Do I need any other reason?"

"No, you're right."

Zane looked exhausted and pale. Alyssa doubted he was truly immune to whatever the magic was, instead suspecting some form of resistance. The difference in Zane's face was clear as night and day.

Their efforts were a blur of motion from the apartment, to the carriage, and to a dark alley at the dock. Will and Crome left to join the rest of their team.

Alyssa and Zane sat in silent darkness until they could see wand and staff fire through the ash-filled air. The sound of screams carried through the darkness to them.

Zane looked up. "It looks like the mission has started."

69

Zane whispered under his breath. "Shadow, is the doctor out there?" Shadow's silky voice responded right away. *How would I know?*

"I think he might have one of his followers with him."

His red eyes slipped away, then returned a couple of moments later. *The ship is too far away, but I think his followers are there.*

Zane stepped out into the darkness of the street, where the shadows cast by the street lamps felt deeper. As he trudged along, he felt like he was moving through knee-high mud.

His perception of the world threatened to spin out of control, and his stomach could barely keep up. Zane's cane hit a broken cobblestone, and he slipped into the cold muck. A hand grabbed him as he felt for a foothold.

"Where are you going?" a kind voice whispered in darkness.

Alyssa's face was masked in deep shadows, but remained a beacon of light, like a lighthouse for a lost sailor. "You whispered something to yourself and then jumped out of the carriage."

"I-I was going to go look for the doctor."

She looked confused. "Doctor? Isn't he at the ship?"

"Your tracer showed the corpse collector was there, but that doesn't mean the doctor is. I had Shadow check it out, but he couldn't see anyone but the doctor's followers. Shadow thinks he's still nearby, though."

In the light of the street lamps, he could tell she was concerned. "So you're following Shadow out into the night alone? You should have said something."

He started to nod, but stopped. *Shadow never said anything, so how do I know which direction to go?* The world felt like it was filled with underlying currents, as if there was constant movement even when there was none.

Zane looked in the direction he had been going, and something ahead caught his eye. Some of the currents were breaking away and creating a new stream.

Shadow's voice interrupted his thoughts.

So you can feel it now. Good. You are heading the right way, but be careful. The first time experiencing this can be confusing. The voice carried notes of sadness and fear. The depth Zane could now sense in the voice felt unsettling.

"I think that we will find the doctor if we go this way. You don't have to follow me. Go back to the carriage with Frame."

"No, I'm not going to hide while you rush off to your death."

"It will be dangerous, and we have no time to argue. Go back or go for help."

"I made the choice to join you on this case. We are partners in this. I am with you. Now lead."

They crossed streets connecting to the alley, staying parallel to the dock. The ripples Zane followed became stronger and stronger. Through the fog and ash, he could see a man standing watch outside a door. The man's cloak was dark as night. A hat and high leather collar hid his face, but Zane knew it was Davidson.

As they closed in, Davidson opened his cloak to show a thin saber and extended a wand that was strapped to his left arm. Over his chest was a breastplate that had been darkened to rid it of its shine.

Zane cursed under his breath at the prepared fighter. He reached for his wand, and noticed Alyssa had already pulled a metal wand from a slit in her cloak.

With smooth movements from years of training, Davidson moved to separate them. Zane switched the grip on his cane, preparing to use it as a weapon.

Davidson charged, firing at Zane while going after Alyssa. The detective dove to the side as wand fire slammed into the building behind him.

The shattering window was a distant thought as he rolled onto his knee, laying his wand hand over his other arm to get a steadier shot.

Davidson had closed in on Alyssa, who was backpedaling with her own wand raised. Wand fire exploded in front of Alyssa as her eldritch words blocked it. He turned to fire on Zane, but Alyssa stepped to create an invisible wall of protection.

Davidson was obviously an accomplished duelist, but Zane was no beginner. The situation was not ideal, but having a trained mage heavily weighted things in their favor.

Zane moved up behind Alyssa, his limp slowing him down. She repeated a train of words like a mantra, protecting them. He didn't know how many spell wicks the man had, but they couldn't last forever.

The very air in front of them seemed to burn. Zane couldn't see anything, but he could feel a disturbance, like waves moving toward him.

Shadow called out in his ear. *Right in front of you! He's swinging!*

Zane shoved Alyssa to the side, blocking the blade with the wooden sheath of his cane. The blade caught in the sheath and uncovered the sword inside. Zane whipped his weapon around, but found only empty space. He could feel the air woosh past him as Alyssa threw a spell at Davidson.

She let loose a spray of fire, not stopping until her wand was empty. Davidson moved fast, light on his feet.

The pair tried to catch their breath as the man prepared to charge again. Zane's head pounded like a drum, but in a moment of clarity he saw an invisible tendril reach out from his body and grip the man's arm.

Zane dropped his sword and reached out toward the tendril. Davidson fought to pull his wand up, and Alyssa dove for cover. Zane didn't move. Davidson lined up his shot as Zane finally jerked his hand back. Davidson's prosthetic arm suddenly pulled him to the ground, and his wand went off. Alyssa rebounded quickly and slammed an invisible wall into the man on the ground.

He screamed and dropped his weapon. Zane limped over to the man, reaching for a pair of iron cuffs on his belt. Davidson twitched on the ground. Zane checked for a pulse, then breathed a sigh of relief. He was happy that Alyssa hadn't killed someone.

Alyssa brought Zane his sword and scarred sheath. When Zane turned for it, she gasped while pointing to his eyes. "What happened?"

"What do you mean? What's wrong?"

"Your right eye is pitch black. You don't have any white, and your pupil is red."

Red eyes? The detective looked around him, trying to find Shadow.

A weak voice called out to him. *Behind you.*

Zane looked back to his own shadow, where he saw a single red eye staring back. Zane reached up to touch his eye, but stumbled back. He breathed heavily, trying to gain control of his shuddering body.

Shadow's warnings that they would eventually merge shook him to his core. The foreign memories felt so much like his own.

The detective watched as the second red eye slowly appeared back in his shadow.

Alyssa pulled on his arm and helped him off the ground. She smiled, but was clearly concerned. "It's back to normal. I don't know what happened, but it's good now."

Zane nodded and took his sheath, gripping it so tightly that his knuckles turned white. "Thank you. I think I'm okay now. Shall we try to finish this?"

With grim resolve, the two made their way to the door that Davidson had been guarding. Alyssa reached for the handle while Zane stood to the side with sword at the ready.

70

Alyssa focused on her breathing, trying to bring it under control. Her body knew what to do. The spells she cast were not complicated, but she spoke them with more force than she usually did.

The former professor twisted her wand's cap and let the spent wicks spill onto the ground. She pulled a quick reloader from her clothing, placed fresh wicks inside, and twisted the cap back on.

Zane's face was pale, and in the dim light she could almost swear his sweat was dark, like the ink of a pen. She wondered what had happened with his eye, then banished it from her mind. She pushed open the door with a loud creak.

Zane rushed in with his wand and sword at the ready. Alyssa charged in after him, finding a dark, empty room. The two looked around, confused, before moving into the next rooms. Alyssa stepped into an empty kitchen that was home to mice and spiders.

From a couple of rooms over, Alyssa could hear Zane call her. "I found it!"

She rushed into a makeshift bedroom, where Zane stood next to an overturned mattress. There in the floor was a poorly made trap door. "How did you know it was there?"

Zane wiped the sweat from his brow with his jacket sleeve. "I figured that if he used smuggler holds at his shop, why wouldn't he do it here too? Are you ready?"

"Yes."

They opened the trap door and descended the stairs to find a thin hallway of dirt and stone walls held in place with wooden planks. At the end was a shoddy door with light streaming through. Alyssa was about to ask a question, but Zane stopped her. He gestured at the door and started walking slowly toward it.

The doctor spoke as they touched the door. "Davidson, are you back already?"

They stood there paralyzed over what to do next.

"You can come in now, anyway," Aluxen shouted. "I just finished up the procedure—"

Zane rushed in, with Alyssa close behind him.

The doctor was wearing a thick leather coat, his face hidden behind a large leather mask with two glass eye holes. Next to him was a blackened post covered in red markings. On either side of it lay Vine and Lady Lexone wearing hefty helmets.

Dr. Aluxen snatched a knife from his belt and brought it to Vine's throat. He pulled his mask down with his free hand, revealing an absurd smile. "Ah, detective. I should have expected you. I knew who you were all along, but I couldn't let you just walk away—at least, not until I had a chance to see your special immunities. Now I know our relationship has been based on lies, so shall we start fresh?"

Zane shook his head. "You're a monster, an old one, that will never change his ways."

The old man laughed. "A monster? Would a monster have given life back to so many people?"

Zane pointed his sword at the doctor, and Alyssa could tell he was ready to charge. "You gave people limbs, that is true, but you didn't give them life. You're not God or a saint. You're a man who used those people as disposable pawns in your plans."

The doctor looked away. His smile was now just a slight smirk. Alyssa readied her eldritch words. She didn't have a lot of strength left after the last fight, but she would pour everything into it.

"Perhaps you have a—"

Zane leapt, and Alyssa shouted an eldritch word to push. The wave of force slammed into the detective's back and threw him forward, his range becoming something superhuman. The doctor was caught off-guard as Zane slammed into him with the sword.

The two went flying over the table and into the wall with a loud crack.

Alyssa tried to call out, but she couldn't form the words. Before she could run to his side, the detective called back. "I'm fine! Make sure the Lexones are okay."

She nodded and rushed to the women. Vine's chest raised and lowered weakly. Alyssa touched her face, finding it clammy. "Vine's alive, but weak!"

Alyssa put away her wand. She moved next to Lady Lexone, touching her cold skin. With a sigh, she knew she didn't need to check further.

The detective stood over the doctor, breathing hard and staring down at Vine.

Alyssa yelled for him again. "Zane, we need to get out of here."

He nodded and turned back to her. From his jacket he pulled out his flask and drank all of it in one gulp. "Right, let's give you a hand."

71

rame cried, the stress and exhaustion overcoming her. Her cousin was laid across the carriage seat, with a guard's coat over her to combat the cold. Frame watched as Vine's chest slowly rose and fell.

Belard knocked on the door before opening. "We are ready to head out. Be ready for any shaking along the way."

Frame shook her head. "No, I'm still needed here. I need you to watch over her."

"But I can't—"

She stopped him. "Please go with Vine. Make sure she's safe, as if she was me."

Belard looked from her to her cousin before nodding. "I can do that, but what will you be doing?"

Frame stood up and pulled her cloak tight around her. "I still need to see my grandmother. I-I know she's connected to this somehow. Maybe a victim, maybe more."

Belard nodded and traded places with her. She pushed the door shut and joined the circle where Zane, Alyssa, Kellim, and Will stood. They looked at her with surprise as the carriage rode off.

"Aren't you going with them?"

"No, there are still things to do here. Now, Zane, where did you find my cousin?"

Zane looked around the circle, leaning heavily on his damaged cane. "Is everyone ready?"

With solemn nods, they made their way through the streets back to the building. Along the way, Zane stopped them to point out where they fought Davidson to get inside.

For a moment, Frame wondered if Davidson had been hired by her great-grandmother. The guards dragged him away into the fog of night.

The detective led them down into the building and to the makeshift room. He stopped abruptly at the door, as the rest of the group stuck behind him. Alyssa looked over Zane's shoulder and gasped. "The doctor's body is gone."

They stepped into the room one at a time. It was filthy and poorly made, with some of the walls properly constructed, while others were held together with planks. Kellim looked around, inspecting the scene. "This doesn't strike me as a last-minute safe house. Seems like they had this place ready for a while."

Frame's eyes went straight to her great-grandmother. She lay under a white sheet, like a realistic doll. Frame's hand shook as she reached out to touch her cold, lifeless face. Frame grabbed the sides of the helmet and had started to remove it when Will stopped her.

"Don't do anything yet. Look."

Will pointed to a series of faint glowing lines that traced the side of the helmet. Frame's eyes narrowed. She could barely make out the arcane formula there. It was complicated beyond her understanding. "What's going on?"

"I don't know . . . I have never seen anything like this."

Alyssa slipped on her glasses and spoke an eldritch word. "This . . . this is incredible. I have never seen anything this small, or this complicated. But—"

Frame watched as Alyssa turned to the post, its red sigils still smoldering with an unhealthy light of arcane power. "I think they're connected," the professor said, looking back and forth from the posts to the beds.

Zane called out, but they couldn't see him. Then, from behind a curtain against a wall, Zane stepped out with a packet of papers. "This leads to a room that has an exit into the sewer lines. I think Dr. Aluxen might have crawled away."

"What makes you think that?"

"Blood leads into the sewer line, then his trail gets lost in the water."

"I doubt we can find him," Kellim said. "Those old sewer lines are a maze. But how did he survive?"

"I saw Zane stab him in the chest," Alyssa said.

The detective flipped through some of the notes he found and passed the rest to Alyssa. Zane held one up. "A prosthetic heart . . . I don't know how it could even work or what pain he went through to put it into his chest."

Frame's voice quivered. "What about my great-grandmother?"

Alyssa snapped to attention. "Sorry, yes. Agent Will, Frame, can you please help read these notes?"

Frame couldn't add much to the discussion, but she was trying to understand. She felt hollow.

Alyssa looked at the posts, stopping on a single sigil. "These notes don't make sense. There is no explanation of how or what the helmet does, but it's near the end of the list."

Frame reached forward and touched the magical sigil. The burning sensation left two of her fingers black. She screamed as she pulled her hand back, then heard more screaming behind her as her relative came back to life.

Lady Lexone yelped as she attempted to roll off the table. The others grabbed her to keep her from hurting herself. Will spoke an eldritch word to put her to sleep. Once out, the group raced Frame and her great-grandmother to the room above.

Frame kept close to her great-grandmother as they moved. When a carriage pulled up, Lady Lexone stirred. Her eyes were foggy and uncertain as she looked around. "Where am I? Why does my body hurt?"

Frame settled in close, holding her hand. "It's okay, Grandmother. You're safe. We saved you from that horrible doctor."

Confusion and dread bled across Lady Lexone's face. "What? No. I'm Vine."

Icy-cold dread flooded Frame's face. "What?"

72

Zane sat in his office, his cane laid across his lap. On his desk was a single paper, which bore the crest he had recovered from Dr. Aluxen's operating room. It was all that he had left; the Institute had taken everything else. Alyssa set a steaming cup of tea on his desk.

"How are you doing?"

"How do you think?"

She put her hand on his. "It's not your fault."

"Maybe not, but I feel responsible."

Shadow's red eyes stared out from his corner. They filled Zane with rage and a strange type of shame that belonged not to him, but to Shadow.

Alyssa brought her chair around to his side. "There was no way you could have known."

His voice leaked out, like pressure releasing. "They were Shadow's notes. These notes are from when I was his prisoner; the things he did to me are the things Aluxen did to them."

Alyssa's voice was gentle. "You're a victim, just like them."

Zane felt the heat of embarrassment. "Thank you for all you've done with this case and with lining up our work with the guard on the goblin mobs. And, of course, all you have done for me. . . . I know a good restaurant. It's nothing fancy, but it's nice. Would you like to go there sometime?"

She raised an eyebrow. "Business or—"

He shook his head, feeling the color change in his cheeks. "No, not business."

"I-"

A knock at the door drew them from their conversation. Zane

thought about ignoring it until Shadow spoke. *It's Frame.*

Shadow's voice remained stronger and more real to Zane. He sighed. "Please come in, Frame."

The door opened, and Belard stepped in. Frame stood there in black funeral garments. Her eyes were still red as she stepped across the room followed by a woman her age dressed in Institute clothing.

Alyssa jumped from her seat and embraced Frame. "I am so sorry for your loss."

There was a sniffle. "It hurts . . . it hurts knowing that I've lost both of them."

So they never caught her, the real Lady Lexone. Zane stood up and limped around to pull out a chair for Frame. "Here, take a seat. Tell us what has happened."

He looked to the young Institute woman and Belard. "Sorry, but I don't know if I have enough chairs for everyone."

Belard waved his hand. "It's fine. I am accustomed to standing."

Frame gestured to the woman. "This is Diana, a friend from the Institute. Alyssa, you met her at my apartment."

Diana gave a simple bow and a modest smile. "Frame has offered me a part-time job with her family, and has even been nice enough to help pay for my classes."

"It's the least I could do, especially since I can't continue."

Alyssa looked devastated. "What about your thesis?"

"I'll publish it, and maybe in the future I will have a chance to do more research. However, I am the last Lexone, and I have other responsibilities now."

Zane hung his head in shame as he took his seat. "I'm sorry to hear about Vine."

Frame shrugged. "I suppose it makes sense. My great-grandmother's body was old and fragile. When she traded bodies, I guess the strain was too much."

Alyssa moved her chair around to Frame. "I am sorry to bring it up, but what about the former Lady Lexone?"

Belard gave a sigh. "That is my fault. After I got her back to the mansion, she was already up and moving. I was exhausted and went to sleep, never thinking she would pack up and leave."

"And she hasn't been seen?" Zane asked.

Belard shook his head. "No sight of her. She has gone underground. We believe Dr. Aluxen knew of Lady Lexone's plan to disappear, so he sent someone to kill our Frame. With her gone, there would be no one to reveal what he did."

Frame looked up at Zane, her eyes angry. "What of the doctor? Any leads?"

He slid the paper across to her. "It's all I could get. The Institute took all the other papers."

Diana stepped up to the desk, pulling out a quill and a piece of paper with several runes. She laid the paper on top of the crest. "This enchanted quill and paper can copy it."

She spoke an eldritch word and the quill sprung to life.

"What did the Dr. Aluxen want out of all of this?" Frame asked.

Zane shrugged. "I don't know, but I believe he really wanted to help people at one point. He was onto something either amazing or horrific. I'm sorry."

Frame looked confused. "No, you did everything you could to help. We were in over our heads. I never thought that something like this was happening."

That's not what I meant. Frame gestured to Belard, who reached into his coat and pulled out a stack of banknotes. He passed them to Frame, who laid them on Zane's desk.

The detective's frown deepened as he counted them. "This is double the amount that I agreed to with your sister. Not to mention, I wouldn't call this a successful case."

"You did your part, even going as far as risking your life to try to arrest him. You both have earned it."

Frame stood up. "I am tired and ready to be home. I hope to see you both again soon."

Alyssa stood up with her. "If you need anything, please let us know."

Frame nodded, and hesitated before speaking. "Of course, and if either of you see or hear from Lady Lexone, please let me know."

She and Belard walked out, with Alyssa following them to the door. Zane picked up the paper and stared at it. Alyssa gave Frame another hug and closed the door behind them.

She turned back to Zane. "Where did you have in mind for dinner?"

He set the paper down and smiled at her. "Is that a yes?"

Alyssa smiled. "Yes, you silly fool."

Jordan Reed graduated from West Texas A&M University. He lives with his wife, kids, and dogs out adjacent to the middle of nowhere, where he works at keeping a small school up to date on all things tech.

His first novel, *The Wizard's Brew*, was a finalist for the 2023 Killer Nashville Falchion Award.

Jordan Reed